TOTAL CONTROL

Books by Jackie Ashenden

The 11th Hour Series

Raw Power

Total Control

The Motor City Royals Series

Dirty for Me

Wrong for Me

Sin for Me

Published by Kensington Publishing Corporation

TOTAL CONTROL

JACKIE ASHENDEN

KENSINGTON BOOKS
www.kensingtonbooks.com

KENSINGTON BOOKS are published by

Kensington Publishing Corp.
119 West 40th Street
New York, NY 10018

All Kensington titles, imprints, and distributed lines are available at special quantity discounts for bulk purchases for sales promotion, premiums, fund-raising, educational, or institutional use.

Special book excerpts or customized printings can also be created to fit specific needs. For details, write or phone the office of the Kensington Sales Manager: Kensington Publishing Corp., 119 West 40th Street, New York, NY 10018. Attn. Sales Department. Phone: 1-800-221-2647.

eISBN-13: 978-1-4967-1635-4
eISBN-10: 1-4967-1635-3
First Kensington Electronic Edition: July 2018

ISBN-13: 978-1-4967-1634-7
ISBN-10: 1-4967-1634-5
First Kensington Trade Paperback Printing: July 2018

10 9 8 7 6 5 4 3 2 1

Printed in the United States of America

To Serena, Nicki, and Sherilee, my NZ crew.

You guys rock.

PROLOGUE

"I thought you said that you could fly this thing."

Kellan ignored Ian's growl from behind him and tried to keep a tight grip on the joystick, the helo bouncing around in the air like a ball in a pinball machine.

Of course he could fly this thing. He'd been a Night Stalker once, a member of the elite helicopter unit who dealt with the insertion and extraction of military black ops teams. But that had been a couple of years ago and he'd gone from green to blue, leaving the army and joining the Navy, becoming a SEAL instead. And although he'd tried to keep up his flight skills, he hadn't had as much practice as he would like.

Certainly not for a mission like this, where the team's extraction point had been compromised, which meant they had to rely on him, his chops as a pilot, and a helo with a bullet-damaged rotor to get them out of here.

"Fucking hell," Ian muttered, grabbing at his seat as the helicopter lurched again, almost brushing the tops of the heavy fir trees below them.

"Jesus," one of the other guys in the back said, amid

more cursing from the rest of them. "You need more practice, Kel."

Kellan tuned them all out. He had to. If they were going to survive this, his concentration had to be total.

Keeping a helicopter in the air was bad enough at the best of times, but with a damaged rotor? Fucking thing was like a bumblebee with only one wing and those things shouldn't have been able to fly without two.

Impossible in other words.

The helicopter lurched again as something hit it, the joystick in his hand jerking hard. He could feel the machine become even more unstable and then more fire hit, taking another piece of rotor out.

Shit.

His last thought before the helicopter dipped, then began to tip, the skids brushing the tops of the trees, was that his father was going to be *really* pissed with him for fucking this up.

Then the world turned upside down and there was a massive bang, and the darkness and the heat came for him.

CHAPTER 1

"We suspect your father's been associated with an illegal arms ring, Kellan." Faith Beasley's blue eyes were coolly sympathetic. "I'm sorry, but we're going to need to investigate."

Kellan Blake, former Night Stalker helicopter pilot, former SEAL, now member of the "special projects" semilegal 11th Hour team, and still total badass motherfucker, laughed.

He liked Faith. She was the one who gave the team their "jobs" on behalf of Jacob Night, the shadowy figure who'd set up and basically owned the 11th Hour. She was cool, calm, and collected, a complete professional, and he had a lot of respect for her.

But this? This was bullshit.

They were sitting in the gutted building that comprised the 11th Hour's San Diego HQ, a massive wall-less space that had been divided off into various areas with furniture.

The area Kellan was in was the "living area." There was a couch, a couple of armchairs, a coffee table, and a floor lamp with a fringed shade. In his opinion all they needed was a large screen TV so he could watch the Giants play and it would be fucking complete.

Sadly no one else was a football fan. Philistines.

In the recliner near the couch sat Isiah, the grizzled former army ranger who was the ostensible CO of the team. He wasn't laughing.

In fact, no one else was laughing. Not Jack, a former marine who'd joined a few months earlier, not Faith, and not Callie, Jack's fiancée, who'd somehow become part of the team along with Jack, even though she wasn't ex-military.

Then again, Sabrina, his best friend, wasn't ex-military and she was also part of the team. And she wasn't laughing either.

Her wholesome freckled face was pale and her big hazel eyes were full of what looked a hell of a lot like worry.

Kellan stopped laughing. "Jesus Christ," he said to her. "Please don't tell me you believe this arms dealer bullshit?"

She shifted on the couch beside him, glancing at Faith who was sitting in one of the armchairs opposite, then back at him again. "I . . . don't know. Do you think there might be . . . you know . . . something in it?"

Kellan was aware of a deep kind of shock seeping through him.

Sabrina had lived with the Blake family since she'd been ten years old, after her father—the Blakes' gardener—had walked out and left her behind. She knew his parents. Sure, she was closer to his mother than he was, but surely—*surely*—she didn't believe this gun running crap?

The Blakes were an old money New York family and his father had been one of the top brass in the army. He'd had a well-respected career and was still incredibly well thought of even after he'd retired.

Kellan had wanted to be just like him.

Until the helicopter accident had put an end to that.

Best not to dwell on *that* failure. Best to think about what was happening now. Sabrina and her reaction, which was . . . weird.

He laughed again, because that tended to be his general response to shit that didn't make any sense. "You're kidding, right? Come on, Bree. Dad? Five-star general Dad? Running guns?"

But Sabrina didn't laugh along with him the way she normally did. Instead, she glanced down at her hands where they clutched her favorite laptop and said nothing.

Okay, this was getting weirder by the fucking second.

Kellan looked at Faith. "So this is according to who? How? Why?"

"Mr. Night has reason to believe—"

"Mr. Night can go fuck himself."

Faith didn't even blink. "As I said, Mr. Night has information that implicates your father, along with a number of other high-ranking members of the military, in a black ops mission that went wrong two years ago. A mission that was deliberately sabotaged."

Kellan grinned, pushing his shock and anger way down deep the way he did with every emotion he didn't like. "Do you know how fucking crazy that sounds?"

"We think that this mission was sabotaged because it was getting too close to uncovering an illegal arms ring providing guns to various drug cartels in Central America. An arms ring that was being run by these high-ranking military members."

"Including my father, presumably?" He grinned wider. "Because Dad really likes guns and loves selling them to people who shouldn't have them?"

No one smiled.

Isiah's hazel eyes were sharp. "This isn't a joke, Blake."

"Yes, it is." Kellan flicked a glance at him, then back to Faith again, skewering her with it. "It's a massive fucking joke. Dad gave forty years of his life to the military. He was a general, for fuck's sake. He wouldn't throw that all away to sell a bunch of guns."

"The information Mr. Night has is—"

"Wrong," Kellan interrupted. "The information Mr. Night has is wrong."

Faith opened her mouth again then shut it. She let out a breath. "Then consider this a chance to prove your father's innocence."

A bolt of pure fury shot down Kellan's spine and he could feel his smile become edged and sharp. "I don't need to prove Dad's innocence." He had to fight to keep his voice steady. "I *know* it."

And he did. Phillip Blake would *never* turn traitor. The man who'd raised him, who'd taught him how to learn from his mistakes and move on, who'd protected him, shown him what it was to be a good man, to aim high and to never accept anything less than complete success . . . Yeah, the idea of a man like that being associated with a secret and highly illegal arms ring, along with a whole lot of high-ranking friends, was ludicrous.

Beside him, Sabrina shifted and he felt her hand come down on his thigh. She squeezed his leg in reassurance and, he thought, as a warning.

Both of which he ignored.

"Well," Faith said in her usual calm way. "Mr. Night disagrees. Your father is implicated. So your choice is to either accept the job of investigating and discovering the truth yourself, or he'll find someone else to do it."

The job . . . what a goddamned joke.

He and Jack, with the support of the rest of the team, had just finished up a mission dealing with a scumbag drug lord when yet another job had come in from Night. Usually the jobs involved protection or handling threats, and most of them barely legal, though he'd never had a problem with that.

He had a problem with this.

"We need you, Kellan," Faith went on when he didn't say

anything. "Mr. Night wants the contents of a computer file apparently in your father's possession."

"What file?"

"Well, that's it," Sabrina muttered. "We couldn't find it. There was nothing on his computer when I hacked in to take a look."

Kellan gave her an incredulous look. "You hacked into Dad's computer?"

She flushed and opened her mouth, probably to explain, but Faith answered before she could.

"I asked Sabrina to," Faith said. "She's the best hacker in the business and your father had some heavy firewalls."

Jesus. What the fuck did Faith think she was doing getting Sabrina to hack into Phillip Blake's computer?

"Regardless of the fact that Sabrina didn't find anything," Faith went on, "Mr. Night is convinced that the file is there. Either on another computer elsewhere or stored on a portable hard drive. All of which means that we need you to search for it personally." She paused. "You *and* Sabrina."

Well, shit. Bad enough that it involved his family, but Sabrina too? Christ, no. Just . . . No. She never went physically to jobs since that wasn't her strength, and there was no reason for her to go now.

"Why Sabrina?" he asked, making no effort to keep the demand from his tone. "She doesn't need to be part of this."

Beside him Sabrina stiffened, but he ignored her.

"Why?" Faith glanced at her. "If the file is anywhere, it'll be heavily encrypted, plus, if it's on another computer, there's likely to be all kinds of other protections in place to keep it safe. Which means we need her skills."

He hated that it sounded so . . . logical.

"Fine," he said curtly. "But find someone else."

"Easy enough." Faith's blue gaze was steady. "We have others who can be Sabrina's backup."

The fury inside Kellan seemed to solidify at Faith's deliberate misunderstanding. "No, you don't get it. If I'm not going, then she's not going either. We're a package deal."

Sabrina stiffened even further, removing her hand from his thigh as if she'd burned herself. "Hey, wait a second—"

"Sabrina is nonnegotiable," Faith said before Sabrina could finish her protest. "As I said, she's the only one with the necessary skills. Your family connection would make the job easier, but we can do without it if necessary. Sabrina knows your parents. Jack could easily pose as her friend or boyfriend—"

"What?" Jack interrupted from his position near the armchair Isiah was sitting in, at the same time as Kellan let loose a growl, not liking that thought *at all*.

Faith merely looked back at him. "A friend, then. Jack could pose as her friend."

Kellan gritted his teeth, fighting to get a handle on himself and keep that fucking smile on his face. But for the first time in years, it was difficult. Anger—or indeed any extreme emotion—was unproductive and didn't get you what you wanted, or at least, that's what his father had taught him. Charm. A smile. And action. Those were the three keys to success according to Phillip Blake and Kellan had found that to be true.

He'd certainly gotten everything he'd wanted by employing them.

Not quite everything.

Well, no. But the two other things he'd wanted and hadn't gotten didn't matter anymore. Not since he'd decided he didn't want them after all.

"I could," Jack said after a moment. "It wouldn't be that hard."

Kellan only just stopped himself from snarling. The scarred former marine was good, and since he'd joined the 11th Hour team three months earlier, he'd gotten even better. And if there was a guy he needed at his back or to protect those he cared about, Kellan would have chosen Jack King.

But only if Kellan himself were dead. And since he wasn't, the only person who was going to be protecting Sabrina was him.

"No," he said flatly. "Not happening."

There was amusement in Jack's green eyes, which was annoying. Especially seeing as the guy hadn't had a sense of humor at all when he'd first joined the team. That seemed to have changed since he'd hooked up with Callie, the pretty socialite he'd been guarding for an 11th Hour job and had subsequently gotten engaged to.

But it turned out that Kellan didn't have a sense of humor either, at least not when it came to Sabrina's safety.

"Oh, for God's sake." Sabrina's voice was tight.

He turned sharply to meet her green-gold eyes, glowing with anger. "What?" he demanded. "You don't think your safety's important?"

"I like my safety, believe me. What I do not like is you being a territorial asshole about it."

He raised a brow in surprise. "I'm not being territorial. I just don't want—"

Isiah cleared his throat loudly. "Perhaps you two need a moment to discuss this?"

Kellan's attention snapped round to the older man. "No, I don't," he began at the same time as Sabrina said, "Yes, that's a great idea."

There was a silence.

"Seems like Sabrina has a different opinion," Isiah pointed out. Needlessly.

Fuck.

Kellan turned back to her, trying to not to let his anger show. Her familiar freckled face with its small upturned nose was set in lines of determination and there was a mulish slant to her chin.

She almost never disagreed with him. Almost never got angry with him either, at least not like this. It was as if a friendly kitten had suddenly grown razor sharp teeth and bitten him.

"Bree," he said. "What's the problem? You can't possibly—"

Sabrina suddenly pushed herself off the couch, not giving him a chance to finish, presenting him with her long, slender back and the bouncy ponytail of dark curls that ran down the length of it. "Tell Mr. Night I'm in," she said to Faith.

Then before anyone could say another word, she strode to the door and walked through it.

Sabrina headed straight down the corridors that led from the 11th Hour HQ to Mac's, the bar that fronted the place. The bar was kept deliberately seedy to discourage too many patrons: cracked linoleum and vinyl seats, crappy TV above the bar, the scent of cigarette smoke from the decades before the first smoking laws imbued into the very walls.

When she'd left her job at an internet start-up in Silicon Valley in order to join the 11th Hour, she'd taken on some of the Mac's bar work when there was some downtime, and she'd found she'd liked it. Pouring drinks and listening to sob stories from the few patrons that Mac's did have didn't require any brain power and neither did wiping down the bar and messing around with the bottles stacked on shelves behind it. She found both tasks soothing.

But she didn't find it particularly soothing today as she slammed the door that led to HQ behind her and stormed into the empty bar.

Not that she would have found anything particularly soothing if she was honest with herself.

Her hand was shaking as she reached for the least crappy of the bourbons, pulling the bottle off the shelf and grabbing a glass, pouring herself a hefty measure. Then she picked the glass up and downed it.

Drinking was another thing she didn't do very often, but shit, after what had happened in there, needs must and all of that.

She poured herself a second glass, then put her hands flat on the bar and stared down at the bar top, taking a few calming breaths.

Fear and shock sat like small hard stones in her gut, the rush of alcohol doing nothing to dissolve them, along with a flickering anger that didn't help either.

The moment Faith had gotten her to hack into Phillip Blake's computer a day or so earlier, Sabrina had felt that fear touch her, and it had only gotten worse now Faith had made the latest mission clear. And the more Kellan had protested, the angrier and more afraid she'd gotten.

It wasn't fair to get angry at him, not when she knew how much of a shock finding out about this latest job had been to him. He idolized his father—always had—so it was no surprise that he hadn't reacted well to the news.

And that was part of the problem.

His father wasn't the man Kellan thought he was, as Sabrina had good reason to know. And if there was one thing she didn't want, it was Kellan finding that out.

He'd already been through so much after the helicopter crash that had effectively ended the military career that had given him his identity. Physical pain from the burns he'd suffered. Emotional pain from the medics' decision that he wasn't fit to resume military service and wouldn't ever be.

Now this.

She stared down at the amber liquid in the glass, pain twisting inside her. Then there was him getting all territorial on her. It made her think things she shouldn't be thinking, feel things she shouldn't be feeling.

Friends. That's all they were. Just friends.

She'd been telling herself that for years, but it never made any difference to her poor stupid heart. Her poor stupid heart had been in love with him since she was ten years old.

But that was beside the point.

The point was the potential of this mission to uncover a lot of skeletons in Phillip Blake's closet. Skeletons that Sabrina had been trying to keep secret from Kellan for years. She didn't know for certain that Kellan's father was involved in the things that Faith said he was, but she knew he wasn't the fine, upstanding former general that everyone thought so well of either.

She also knew that Kellan couldn't find out, not ever. He was a man who protected people, but someone had to protect him, and she'd decided years ago that someone was going to be her. Because she'd do anything for him.

Anything at all.

Besides, she'd made a promise to Charlotte, Kellan's mother, who'd been a mother to Sabrina too, after she'd lost her own and her father had left. A promise that she wouldn't tell Kellan a thing.

Charlotte had been very clear to Sabrina how important it was that Kellan know nothing about the cracks in Phillip's smooth facade. Family. That's what it was about, and Sabrina, having lost her own, could only agree. Her own father had once been the Blakes' live-in gardener and when he'd simply left one day and never come home, Charlotte had taken her in and made her part of the Blake family.

Well, maybe not quite part of the family. Charlotte was always very careful to make sure that Sabrina knew she wasn't actually a Blake. Her purpose was to be Charlotte's confidant without all the "messy" stuff around being her actual child, which was how Charlotte herself had put it.

Anyway, Sabrina had always been grateful to the Blakes for their kindness to her and to Charlotte in particular for making her feel less like an abandoned stray and more like a valuable family member.

God, Charlotte would be appalled if she knew what was happening now—and she'd certainly be expecting Sabrina to make sure Kellan had no part of it.

Except . . . Sabrina had no idea how to do that, not if this mission was driven by Jacob Night. None of the team had met him or knew anything about him, only that he had the money and connections to somehow run an ex-military team—well, except for her, as she wasn't ex-military—who took on "special projects" that were just on the right side of legal.

Soon after she'd joined the team herself, she'd looked for traces of him online—and she, if anyone, knew where and how to look—but she'd found nothing. Weird. Because everyone left some digital trace, *everyone.*

But not Jacob Night.

A worry.

She reached out for the glass again, picking it up as the door behind her banged open.

"Bree?" Kellan's voice, deep and with that husky edge that never failed to raise a shiver across her skin, came from behind her. "What's up? Why did you walk out?"

So he'd followed her. Well, that wasn't a surprise. She was going to have to get her game face on though, because although she didn't have to explain her own shock, she couldn't show him her fear. Especially given how protective he was and what a terrible liar she was.

Then again, she'd been successfully hiding things from him for years, so there was no reason to think she'd fail now.

She took another steadying sip of the bourbon, then turned around.

Kellan was standing just outside the door that led from the bar to HQ, filling the doorway with six foot three of long, rangy muscle. He was built like a quarterback and looked like a Hollywood movie star, massive shoulders, high cheekbones, and a perfect jawline. Dirty blond hair and stunning ice-blue eyes. He was in faded blue denim that clung to his lean hips and a fitted T-shirt that outlined his broad chest, powerful biceps, and flat stomach to perfection. Today's T-shirt was a dark navy that made his eyes look even bluer.

He made her heart beat way too fast whenever she looked at him, and no matter how many years passed or how many other guys she dated, it had never gotten the message that he wasn't for her and never had been.

They were best friends and nothing more.

Sabrina leaned back against the bar, cradling her bourbon. "Why do you think I walked out? It's a hell of a shock. And I . . . didn't appreciate being told what to do."

He snorted, thrusting his hands into the pockets of his jeans. "I'm not apologizing for that. Not that it matters anyway since the mission isn't happening." The expression on his face was guarded, but she knew him. She could see the shock still resounding in his eyes.

Her chest felt tight and she put her bourbon down, her first instinct to go give him a hug. It was a measure of her own shock that she almost did, but at the last minute held herself back. He wasn't physically demonstrative—none of the Blakes were—so she tried to keep her own need to give physical comfort to a minimum.

"I'm sorry, Kel." She folded her arms instead. "The whole thing is crazy."

"Damn right it's crazy." He glanced away, his jaw hardening, anger written in the tense line of his shoulders. "I don't know where Night got his information from, but it's wrong. Dad's got nothing to do with this."

For a second Sabrina debated about what to say. She wanted Kellan to know she was on his side, but her lying skills were crap and if he picked up on the fact that she was hiding something from him, he'd soon get it out of her; he could be relentless when there was something he wanted to know.

"Maybe he has," she said carefully. "Perhaps you should speak to Night personally?"

Kellan's sharp blue gaze came to hers. "Are you really shocked about this?"

She froze, feeling like a rabbit in the headlights. "Sure I am. What makes you say that?"

"You just seem . . . unsurprised."

Shit. Had he picked up on something in her voice?

Sabrina shifted against the bar, trying not to give herself away any more than she already had. "I guess you could say I'm a little . . . stunned." And she had been, though not quite in the same way as Kellan.

His gaze narrowed at her for a second, then he let out a breath and came over to where she stood, grabbing a glass for himself and reaching for the bottle of bourbon that stood on the bar. "Yeah, Christ. It's a bit un-fucking-believable."

Okay, perhaps she hadn't given herself away too badly. Thank God.

Hoping her relief wasn't too obvious, Sabrina picked her own glass back up again as he poured himself a drink.

"You're right though." Kellan turned around and leaned back against the bar beside her, mirroring her stance, lifting his glass and taking a hefty swallow. "I should talk to Night. Figure out where the hell he got his intel about this file from."

"Good plan." She kept her voice neutral. "He and Faith seem pretty ready to move on it."

"Yeah, but that's not going to happen." The words were hard, certain, and not a little grim.

Kellan was generally laid-back, his good looks and easy smile masking a nature that was pure, sharp-edged steel. It was that steel that had driven him into two different branches of the military, pushing him to become the best of the best. She could hear that steel now. Whoever Jacob Night was, Kellan would give him a hell of a run for his money.

With any luck, Night might even change his mind about the mission and decide to leave well enough alone.

Except she had a horrible feeling that wasn't going to happen, no matter how stubborn or forceful Kellan was. Night was a law unto himself and he was powerful. Then again, when Kellan wanted something, he tended to go out and get it.

Pity that's not you.

Sabrina took another swallow of her bourbon, the rough alcohol sitting in her gut, trying to ignore the thought. God, she hoped this wasn't building up into another one of her moods.

She had them periodically, where all she could think about was how badly she wanted him and how much it hurt that she didn't have him. They didn't last long, but when they did, she usually got out her dating app to find herself a hookup.

Maybe it was time to find a guy again, one who didn't have blond hair or blue eyes. A nice guy who was up for a couple of dates and a few pleasant hours in bed. Though to be honest, she'd never found sex all that fulfilling, no matter who it was with. She could give herself a better orgasm with her own imagination and her vibrator.

"Bree? Are you even listening?"

Feeling him staring at her, heat crept into her cheeks. He was very close and she was very conscious of the warmth of his long, hard body next to hers. Of the familiarity of his aftershave, a fresh scent that reminded her of the sea, or of rain.

Oh hell. She was *definitely* going into another of her I-want-Kellan moods.

"What? Sorry, no, I wasn't." She drained her second glass of bourbon and put it down on the counter. "I still . . . can't believe it, I guess."

Kellan had three smiles: one for charming people generally,

one for charming women he wanted to sleep with, and one for her. The one he kept for her was warm and protective and tender, and she loved it as much as she hated it. And she hated it because it was very like the one he kept for his mother.

His long, beautiful mouth quirked in that smile now. "Hey, don't worry, okay? I'm sure it's only that Night got some bad intel from somewhere, and it's all a mistake." The smile became a little sharp, though the look in his eyes remained reassuring. "This mission isn't going ahead. I'll make sure of it."

He always thought he was protecting her.

He had no idea it was the other way around.

Sabrina gave him a smile in return, because what else could she do? "Sure," she said, ignoring the cold foreboding that curled its way through the warmth of the alcohol. "Of course you will."

CHAPTER 2

Kellan sat astride his motorcycle in the rough brick alleyway, watching the long black limo that waited at the curb.

It was near midnight and the Gas Lamp District was full of people partying and generally making a huge racket. Normally, he'd be part of that party since life was too short not to indulge in whatever pleasure you could find for yourself—at least that was the conclusion he'd come to after the helicopter accident and he'd been forced to leave the forces—but not tonight.

Tonight he had a man to stalk.

It wasn't the first time he'd tried to find Jacob Night. When Faith had first contacted him about joining the 11th Hour, he and Sabrina had tried to find anything they could on the guy and failed. Turned out he was a digital ghost, though apparently not an actual ghost, since Kellan had spoken to him a number of times on the phone.

Finding him physically though . . . Yeah, that had proved difficult. Kellan had followed Faith a number of times, hoping to at least catch a glimpse of Night, but somehow she always seemed to get away from Kellan, a difficult thing to do since it wasn't as if Kellan didn't have insane tracking skills.

Normally this would have presented him with just the kind of challenge he liked. At least it would have if Night hadn't called him personally to tell him that if he didn't stop following Faith, Kellan could consider himself fired from the team.

The threat wasn't an empty one, and since being part of the team was the only thing that gave Kellan purpose these days, he'd done what he was ordered to do and stopped following Faith.

Things were different now though, and all bets were off.

After a minute or two had passed, Faith appeared, coming out of Mac's bar and heading toward the limo that was waiting for her.

Time to move.

He reached for the bike's ignition.

"If you want to speak to me, Mr. Blake, all you have to do is ask."

Kellan froze.

The voice was deep and even rougher than Jack's slightly hoarse tones, and very, very cold. It had come from behind him, which was an impossibility because he'd sworn he'd checked out the whole of the damn alley before he'd decided to wait there for Faith, and there had been nobody there.

How the hell had whoever it was managed to get past him? Not that there was any doubt who this was.

It could only be one person.

Kellan waited a beat, then without any hurry, swung off his bike and turned around.

Down the back of the alley, in front of a lone streetlight, a massive, hulking figure stood, leaning one shoulder against the rough wall. A man in jeans and a T-shirt, a leather jacket thrown over the top. The way the light fell put his features in shadow but did nothing to disguise his height or the fact that he was built like a brick shithouse.

He was taller than Kellan. Taller even than Jack and broader too.

How a man of his size had gotten here without Kellan seeing, Kellan had no fucking idea.

"Jacob Night, I presume?" he asked, folding his arms and staring at the figure. "'Bout goddamn time."

The figure didn't move. "What do you want, Mr. Blake?"

"Hey, you're the one who followed me."

"Because you're following me. After I told you not to."

Kellan lifted a shoulder. "I don't give a shit what you told me. And you already know why I'm following you otherwise you wouldn't have bothered making like fucking Batman and coming to skulk down the back of this alley."

A soft rough sound escaped Night and it took Kellan a moment to realize it was a laugh. "Batman, huh?"

Kellan ignored him, getting straight to the point. "Your intel is wrong. I don't know where you got it, but my father has got nothing to do with any illegal arms dealing."

Night said nothing.

A couple of tense moments passed, but Kellan made no move to break the silence. He was very conscious of the weight of his Glock sitting at the small of his back—a necessary precaution—and his fingers itched to get it out, point it in the direction of Night's huge figure, because the threat pouring off the man made every one of Kellan's military senses go haywire.

"We've had this discussion, I believe," Night said after a very long moment. "The mission will go ahead whether you like it or not."

Kellan could hear the steel in the asshole's voice, but he didn't give a shit. "The hell it will. Call it off."

Another low, rumbling laugh echoed in the alley. "Or what? You have no leverage, Mr. Blake."

Kellan gritted his teeth. Yeah, he knew that and not for want of trying to find some. But that was the problem with Jacob Night. He didn't exist, which meant there was nothing Kellan could use against him. All he had to change the prick's mind was his own determination and sheer balls.

Good thing he had both in abundance.

"You need a good pilot in the team," he said flatly. "Jack can't fly a helo and Isiah isn't as good as I am."

"So? There are many good pilots out there. I can get another."

"Hiring and vetting takes time. Oh yeah, and there's also the little matter that if I go, I'm taking Sabrina with me." And she'd follow him, no doubt in his mind. If he left, so would she.

"I can replace her too." Night's massive form was still. "No one is indispensable."

Kellan nearly laughed. Sabrina's intelligence was genius level and her coding skills were unparalleled, and the fact that she'd been snapped up by a Silicon Valley firm almost the minute she'd left high school was testament to how valuable she was. There was no one else like her anywhere.

"You won't find another hacker with her skills," he said. "Not one who'll want to work for you."

"I find that many people want to work for me, given the right incentive."

Kellan felt a muscle jump in his jaw, tension crawling through every inch of his body. Normally a charming smile would get him what he wanted, but obviously that wasn't going to happen with Night. Not that he thought it would. Then again, what else did he have?

"What's in this mission for you?" he asked, trying a different tack. "Is it money? What?"

Night shifted against the brick. "And now you're asking the right questions. Though sadly, that's none of your fucking business."

Kellan ignored him. "Are you doing this for yourself? Or for someone else? Where did you even get that intel from anyway?"

Again, there was another silence.

"I understand your issues, Mr. Blake," Night murmured. "But this isn't only about your relationship with your father. The cartels who have the weapons your father and his friends are selling are killing people. Innocent people. Which is why the mission remains the mission. Your approval is not required and neither is your participation."

No, Night was wrong. His father would never allow a civilian to be put in harm's way and the fact that innocent people were dying was simply another reason why this whole thing was bullshit. It also gave him more impetus to change Night's mind.

Though that was looking like an impossibility.

You really thought you could?

He'd hoped. Though if he'd really thought about it, he should have known he wouldn't have a chance in hell.

Fury wound through him, but he pushed it back where it had come from, thrusting his hands in his pockets, rolling his shoulders to get rid of the tension. He even forced out a laugh. "Then why the fuck are you here talking to me?"

"Because I was curious." Night shifted again. "You think a lot of your father, don't you?"

Defensiveness prickled through him, but he wasn't going to give this asshole any more ammunition. He gave another shrug. "What's it to you?"

"It's nothing to me. Merely curiosity."

"Then I guess your curiosity is satisfied."

"I guess it is." Night didn't move. "The mission stands, Mr. Blake. You can either join in and prove your father isn't responsible for the deaths of innocent people. Or you can sit on your hands and pretend that shit isn't real. The choice is yours."

Kellan dearly wanted to laugh in the guy's face, or alternatively pull out his Glock. He didn't want to kill him, but he'd settle for a nice friendly bullet wound to soothe his fury.

But that wouldn't accomplish anything. The mission would still go ahead, like Night said, because if there was one thing he'd learned since joining the 11th Hour team, it was that what Jacob Night said, went. And once Night made up his mind, he didn't change it.

Kellan hated the feeling of powerlessness though and it made him even angrier. Made him feel like he was back in the hospital, listening to the medics telling him his career in the military was over, that despite the burns that had healed, he wasn't of sound mind, or some such shit.

Nothing he'd said—and he'd said quite a bit—had made the slightest bit of difference. It was the one and only time he'd thought about asking his father to step in and use his influence with the top brass. In the end, though, he sucked it up, determined not to let that setback affect him.

His career was the military, but that didn't mean his life was over. It was simply another challenge he had to overcome, and if there was one thing he'd always relished, it was a challenge. Life was a boring piece of shit without challenges, and this setback right here? Yeah, this was just one more. And it sure as hell wasn't going to involve sitting on his hands.

Kellan stared into the shadows where the other man's face should be. "Then I guess I'm in."

There was no discernible movement from Night and yet Kellan could have sworn the prick was smiling. "Good choice, Mr. Blake. I was hoping you'd say that."

"I haven't finished."

"Oh?"

"Sabrina's not going." She'd be fucking pissed off with him, but he wasn't going to be moved on this one. If he was going to go on a mission to investigate whatever the hell they had on Phillip Blake, then he wasn't taking her with him.

She was part of the Blake family and didn't need to be involved with whatever he uncovered—not that he was going to uncover anything—but to be on the safe side. It was better that she stay safe at HQ, where he wouldn't worry about her.

"Hmmm," Night murmured. "I'm not sure she'd agree with that."

"I don't care whether she agrees or not. You just said that no one was indispensable and that presumably includes her."

"And who else do you think's going to be able to get the information I want?"

"Your mission. Your problem."

"That's true," Night agreed. "In which case, I could simply remove you from the mission entirely."

"In which case, I can easily go to Dad and give him the heads-up."

A dangerous kind of stillness gathered in the alleyway and Kellan tensed even further, readying himself in case of violence.

"I can stop you," Night said quietly. "Don't think that I won't. Or that I can't."

Oh, he didn't doubt that, not for a second. "But I won't go without a fight and that's a pain in everyone's ass, don't you think? Easier to get another hacker and make sure Sabrina stays behind."

Laughter echoed around them as a group of people walked past the mouth of the alley, car headlights abruptly spearing through the night. But they didn't illuminate the shadow at the end of the alley. He was left in darkness.

"But didn't you just say that I wouldn't be able to find another hacker with her skills?" Night asked, perfectly reasonably.

"You won't. Which is all the more reason to keep her behind where she's safe. If all you need is someone to download a file off a computer, there are plenty of people who can do that for you. Hell, I'll get Sabrina to teach me how to get past any encryptions and I'll do it myself."

It wasn't an empty boast. He'd learned a few computer skills from her over the past year or so after the accident—since he'd had nothing better to do—and he was pretty confident in them. Physical skills came easiest to him and he was good at them, but he wasn't a slouch when it came to computers either.

And shit, it would be better all round if he took on this mission himself. He didn't want anyone getting in his way when it came to proving his father was innocent.

Night laughed. "You? Fuck, you're confident, Mr. Blake, I'll give you that. But this is well beyond your pay grade."

Kellan stared hard into the darkness. "You want this mission done and done well, then you send me. Alone. Sabrina knows Dad. She knows my mom. I don't want her involved in this bullshit."

Another silence.

"And if it turns out I'm right? That your father is a traitor after all? Can I trust you to bring me the information I want?"

Kellan stiffened. It was a good question though, and one he would have asked himself. "I'm a man of my word. If the information you want is there, I'll bring it to you. A traitor is a traitor."

"Even if it's your father?"

This time Kellan allowed himself a smile. "Especially if it's my father. But it won't be, asshole. He's innocent. And I'll prove it to you."

Sabrina sat on the couch in the deserted 11th Hour HQ, her laptop on her lap, playing a calming game of Minecraft while the other, more powerful computers over in the control area ran the searches she'd programmed into them a couple of hours earlier. Again.

She didn't know why she'd bothered to run them a second time when they hadn't turned up anything the first, but she liked to be thorough, especially when it concerned Kellan.

He'd gone off to see if he could track down Jacob Night a couple of hours ago, and she was starting to get worried for him. Not that Night would do anything to him—though really, she didn't know why she thought that when the guy and his motivations were a complete mystery. So he *probably* wouldn't do anything to Kellan. No, she was more concerned that he wouldn't give Kellan what he wanted, which was a halt to this mission. And if the mission went ahead . . . God, she had no idea what to do.

Well, no, she had one idea. She'd have to somehow, some way, convince Kellan to stay behind while she went, along with Jack or Isiah.

Like that's going to happen.

Yeah, some hope. She knew how protective he was. He'd never accept her going on her own without him.

An old and familiar bitterness curled tight in her stomach.

He got territorial over her, but not because she was anything more to him than a friend. His best friend sure, but never anything more than that.

Sabrina sighed. Dammit. She was definitely getting into one of her moods.

Pushing aside her laptop impatiently, she reached for her phone in her jeans, pulling it out and opening the dating app she used on occasion. Flicking through the matches currently in her area.

She wasn't the most adept when it came to men. Her mother's death and her father's subsequent silent grief had left her a shy and socially awkward kid, and later, a shy and socially awkward teen. She'd been your standard, clichéd nerd, coping with her loneliness by turning to computers and immersing herself in code because code was simple, logical. It wasn't messy and didn't make you feel bad. You didn't have to talk to it or wish it felt the same way about you as you did about it. Plus, if you were good, you could make it do whatever you wanted it to. Coding became her area of expertise, the one part of her life she had control over and her escape from her own unrequited feelings for Kellan, and she'd thrown herself into it completely.

Working in Silicon Valley after she'd left high school had exposed her to more social situations though, and since she didn't have Kellan around—he'd already enlisted—and she was sick of pining for him, she'd decided she'd needed to woman-up and at least try a couple of dates. Also, being a computer nerd *and* a virgin at twenty was a cliché too far even for her.

Since then, she hadn't gotten any more adept talking to men, but at least she knew how to work a dating app. And the apps had the photos and interests of potential matches, which reduced her anxiety when it came to figuring out conversation. She'd also discovered that men really liked talking about themselves, which meant that as long as she kept asking questions, they were happy to fill up any awkward silences.

It worked very well. Mostly.

But looking at the matches now, none of them thrilled her, though there was one nice looking blond guy who looked to be in a bar a couple of doors down from HQ. Maybe she should message him? Without thinking too hard—if she did, she'd lose her nerve—she sent him a text.

"Hey, computer girl."

Sabrina's head jerked up to see Kellan stroll into HQ's vaulting space carrying a couple of pizza boxes from her favorite pizza joint.

The fist around her heart, the fist she'd had no idea was there, abruptly relaxed. He was okay. Night hadn't done anything to him. He was even grinning in fact. Did that mean . . . ?

"What happened?" Sabrina demanded, forgetting her phone for the meantime. "Did you find him?"

Kellan came over to the couch, dumping the pizza on the coffee table in front of it and sprawling down beside her with his usual predatory grace. "I found him. Or rather, he found me."

A pulse of shock shot down her spine. "What? You're kidding. You actually *met* him?"

Kellan was grinning, but there was something sharp in his smile. "Yeah, I met him."

"Oh." She searched her friend's beautiful face, noting the lines of tension despite the smile. Didn't look like the news was good. "And?"

"Short story? He's not going to change his mind. The mission's going ahead."

Her stomach dropped away. "Kel, I'm—"

"It's okay." His smile became sharper, the one he got when he was digging in about something. "I've decided to take it on. He wants to prove Dad guilty? Motherfucker can try."

Shit. Shit. Shit.

Kellan frowned. "Hey, what's wrong?"

Double shit.

Mercifully her phone buzzed at that moment with a text, and she looked down at it in her lap. It was the guy she'd texted earlier.

"Who's that?" Kellan's voice had suddenly got very neutral.

Beneath her shock, a small lick of anger flared inside her. He always got very interested in the guys she dated, wanting to know all about them and making no secret of the fact. He told her it was because he wanted to make sure she was safe from assholes and ax murderers, but it never failed to irritate the hell out of her.

She hated it when he acted like a jealous boyfriend, especially when it was none of his business. After all, she didn't go investigating all the women he slept with. Jesus, that would take her *days*, given the number of women he hooked up with.

"No one," she snapped, reaching for the phone.

She was a second too late, Kellan's long fingers closing around the piece of technology and snatching it out of her lap before she could stop him.

"Hey!" She made a swipe at him, trying to get her phone back, but he simply lifted it out of reach, staring at the screen.

"Who's 'Thunderlover23'?"

"No one. Just some guy." She grabbed at the phone again. "Don't be a dick."

"Speaking of. He looks like a douchebag."

"Yeah, well, since you're not the one texting him, it doesn't matter what you think." She managed to get her hands on the phone this time, snatching it out of Kellan's grasp. "Not that who I hook up with is important right now."

His brows drew down. "You're going for a hookup? Now?"

Great. She might not want to talk about this damn mission, but she wanted to talk about hookups even less.

Sabrina shoved her phone in her pocket and leaned forward, reaching for one of the pizza boxes. "Did you get olives?"

"Do I look stupid?"

"*And* pineapple?"

He gave her a very level stare. "Is the Pope Catholic? And don't change the subject."

"Hey, I wasn't the one grabbing my phone and getting interested in some guy called Thunderlover23."

Kellan narrowed his gaze, giving her the look that never failed to get her heart rate up. The one that made her feel like she was the complete and utter focus of his attention. "What? You want to know about the mission? I told you. Night isn't going to change his mind. That's all there is to it. Now why are you texting this guy?"

Sabrina resisted the very real urge to pick up a piece of pizza and shove it in his handsome, movie-star face. Instead, she turned and flipped open the pizza box, choosing a slice carefully. Taking her time.

She was *not* going to talk about the guy she'd been texting. That wasn't important.

"I thought you didn't want it to go ahead?" She didn't look at him, picking up the slice she'd chosen and taking a bite. God, it was delicious. She hadn't realized how hungry she'd been.

"Good?"

"Hell, yes." She flicked him a glance. "Giovanni's does the best pizza."

His smile became less sharp, more satisfied. He always did like looking after her. "Of course. I'd never go anywhere else."

Sabrina chewed, then swallowed her mouthful. "You didn't manage to change his mind, then?"

"Who, Night?" Kellan reached forward and grabbed a piece of pizza for himself. "No. Asshole wouldn't budge."

She wasn't surprised. Jacob Night had always struck her as the type of guy who once he'd made up his mind, wouldn't change it back again. Well, except for that one time when he'd helped Jack out with rescuing his fiancée, Callie. But apart from that, he didn't.

A lot like Kellan, come to think of it.

"You seem okay with that." She watched him polish off the slice of pizza, then reach for another as if nothing was bothering him whatsoever.

"I decided that if he's going to get someone to get this information anyway, then it might as well be me." He flashed her one of his trademark, sexy grins. "Dad's innocent and I'm going to prove it."

Her heart dropped. Oh crap, this was what she'd been afraid of, Kellan changing his mind and deciding to take this mission on anyway. Because once he'd determined he was going to do something . . .

"Are you sure?" she began hesitantly. "I mean, there's no way you could have gotten Night to call it off?"

Kellan finished his second slice of pizza, then reached for a napkin, wiping his hands fastidiously. "I tried, believe me. But I didn't have the leverage. I mean, I told him I'd walk and take you with me . . ." He shrugged. "The asshole just told me no one was indispensable."

"But surely—"

"I had no leverage, Bree." His ice-blue eyes were suddenly very direct. "This thing's going to go ahead whether I like it or not, and if I don't do it, he'll get someone else who will." Steely determination glowed deep in his gaze. "I can't walk away from this. If this arms ring is selling guns to cartels and civilian lives are at risk, then that makes it doubly important I prove Dad had nothing to do with it. And I can't sit back and let someone else who doesn't give a shit find that information. They don't care whether Dad's innocent or not, but I do. If there's any evidence he's not involved, then I'm fucking going to find it."

This was getting worse and worse.

Her appetite abruptly gone, Sabrina reached for a napkin herself, wiping her fingers and using the time to think about how the hell she was going to respond. "Maybe," she began slowly, "you don't have to do it yourself. I mean, Night requested me to go, so maybe I could—"

"No." The word was hard and flat.

She glanced at him in surprise and found his gaze on hers, that steel in his eyes glowing even brighter.

"You're not going, Bree." He said it with so much certainty it was as if he was stating one of the laws of the universe. "I told Night this would be a solo mission."

Anger flared inside her despite her fear. So. He thought he could unilaterally make decisions for her. Without even discussing them with her first. Goddamn arrogant asshole.

"And naturally you decided to tell me this after the fact." She didn't bother to hide her annoyance. "I love it when you make all my decisions for me. Makes me feel really, really good."

Kellan's straight blond brows snapped together. "You don't want to be involved in this crap. Besides, there won't be anything for you to do because there won't be anything to find."

"If there's nothing for me to do, then why did Night request me specifically?" She clenched her hands in her lap in an effort not to raise her voice, because yelling at him wouldn't help matters. "Faith said they could do it without you, but not without me."

He didn't even have the grace to look ashamed of himself, merely giving her that flat look that told her he'd made up his mind and nothing was going to change it. "I told Night I'd get the information he wanted myself."

"Oh really?" She didn't hold back with the sarcasm. "And how exactly were you going to do that? With your wide range of computer skills?"

His beautiful mouth quirked. "I thought you might give me a few tips."

Sabrina blinked. He could *not* be serious. He thought he could forbid her to go on the mission yet get her to teach him how to extract the information himself? "You arrogant asshole," she said before she could stop herself. "You actually expect a 'few tips' will let you extract information from a highly encrypted computer?"

The grin faded. "We don't know where the information is. We don't even know if there's any damn information to find. And besides, even if it is on a computer, how—"

"If you say 'how hard can it be,' I *will* hit you."

He sat back against the couch, angling his body toward her, studying her face as if she was a difficult mountain he was going to climb and he was trying to find the best route. "You know I didn't mean that."

Anger flooded through her, surprising her with its heat, and she found herself digging her nails into her palms. "Do you have any idea what I do? I mean *really?*"

"Bree—"

"What? You think that all it takes is a few little instructions? A nice list of steps? That it's *easy?*"

"No, of course I don't—"

"Fuck you, Kellan. Fuck you and the horse you rode in on." She didn't know why she was getting so angry. No, scratch that, she *did* know. His arrogant attitude had something to do with it, but mainly it was fear.

Fear that he was going to take this all on himself and discover that his father wasn't the hero Kellan thought he was. He'd had enough crap to deal with recovering from the burns after the helo accident. He didn't need to know his adored father had feet of clay. Not that there was proof yet, but Sabrina had her suspicions. She knew enough about Phillip Blake that she wouldn't be surprised to discover he ran an arms ring too.

The main issue was that she didn't want Kellan to find out about any of it.

"Hey." Kellan leaned forward all of a sudden, frowning, reaching out to put one of his large, warm hands over hers. "I *never* thought that what you did was easy. That's not what I'm saying. All I want is to make sure you stay safe, okay?"

His hand felt so good against hers, his skin warm.

She loved it when he touched her.

She hated it too.

He had her best interests at heart, she knew that. And he'd always been super proud of her technical skills. But that didn't change the fact that she didn't want him to go on the mission. If she could somehow convince him that it was best if she go, while he remained here, then that would be the most ideal situation.

Yeah, like he's ever going to choose to stay here while you go handle it.

Shit. Of course he wouldn't. Kellan wasn't the type of guy to sit around while others did things. And most especially when it concerned his own family.

She wanted to leave her hand there, covered by his, but she couldn't have that kind of temptation, so she pulled it away. "I know you want me safe," she muttered. "But I'm a part of this team whether you like it or not."

"Yeah, and I get that." He didn't reach for her hand again, which disappointed her, merely crossing his arms over his broad chest. "But Bree, you don't want to be part of this—"

"There you go," she snapped, irritated once more, "making my decisions for me again." She met his blue gaze, deciding to say it and to hell with his reaction. "Why can't Jack and I go, and you stay here?"

He grinned, the mega-watt Kellan grin full of warm amusement that usually charmed the pants off everyone. "Seriously?"

Sadly for Sabrina her pants remained firmly on. "Yes. Why not? Why not try being the one waiting around for a change? Might even do you good. You could . . . I dunno, take a vacation or something? Go to Vegas."

He laughed. The prick. "Hey, it's *my* father we're talking about here. You really think I'd let someone else take on the responsibility?"

Of course she didn't think that, and they both knew it. "Well, you didn't want to do it when Faith brought it to us yesterday."

"Yeah, and now I've changed my mind. This is *my* job. He's given his life to the military, to protecting civilian lives, and I'm sorry, but I'm not letting some asshole like Night ruin his reputation because of some fucking file that's not there anyway. I'm also not trusting protecting that reputation to anyone else."

"Not even your best friend?"

It was a low blow, but Sabrina didn't care. If he was bound and determined to take on this job, she wasn't going to convince him otherwise. But she'd be damned if he made her sit on the sidelines. The least she could do was go along and maybe protect him from whatever information they found.

An emotion she couldn't read flickered through his ice-blue gaze. "It's not about trust. This is about making sure you're completely safe, and the only way I can guarantee that is if you're here at HQ."

"But I—"

"You're not going, Sabrina." His voice was hard. "And that's final."

Like hell it was.

She let the subject alone as they finished the pizza, allowing Kellan to move the conversation onto safer topics. But much later, after he'd gone and she was finally alone in the little room off one of the HQ corridors that she'd taken for herself, she got out her phone and texted Faith.

Tell Night I'll be his bitch forever if he backs me to do this job.

Faith replied almost immediately. *What about Kellan?*

Sabrina scowled and texted back. *Kellan can suck it.*

For a moment or two there was nothing but silence from Faith. And then she finally sent, *I'll handle it.*

Which wasn't a yes, but it was something.

CHAPTER 3

"No," Kellan said flatly. "Just fucking no."

Faith merely stared blandly back at him, ignoring his anger. "The decision is not yours, Mr. Blake. It's Mr. Night's. And he's decided that Sabrina is vital to the mission."

Kellan struggled to get a handle on the hot flood of fury that pulsed through him, trying to find his usual control and the smile which usually persuaded people to change their minds on decisions he didn't like.

Such as this one for instance.

Christ, what was it with people being such assholes lately? Night had promised that he'd stop Sabrina from going on the mission the night before, so why the hell had he changed his mind today?

A deathly silence had fallen in HQ, broken only by the sounds of Jack's fists hitting the punching bag in the gym section of the huge space.

Sabrina sat on the couch across from him, her hands clasped in her lap. Her chin was lifted, her hazel eyes full of stubborn determination. Fuck, he remembered that look well. It was exactly the same look she'd given him when she was twelve years old and he'd told her the oak on the grounds of the Blake estate was too tall for her to climb.

She'd been his best friend for two years by then, a quiet, reserved kid he'd managed to coax away from her computer and out of her shell because she'd needed someone and he liked the way she smiled only for him and no one else.

That day though, she revealed her stubborn streak, her mouth getting the same hard line as it did now, her narrow shoulders square, her pointed chin jutting. He'd thought she'd listened to him, that she wasn't going to climb that tree. Yet later that night, she'd knocked on the door of his bedroom to tell him triumphantly that she'd climbed it and it wasn't as hard as he'd made out.

Jesus Christ, he'd have thought that by now he'd have figured out how to deal with Sabrina when she got stubborn, but it seemed like he hadn't. Back then he'd been pissed with her. He was the head of the family, a responsibility he took very seriously, and the safety of the people he cared about was important to him. Protecting them was important to him. It still was. Even after everything that had gone down with Pippa had nearly broken him.

He tried the smile again. "Look, Bree, let's think—"

"I'm going, Kel." She didn't raise her voice, merely giving him a very level look. "It's all been decided."

"By who?"

"By me."

His anger twisted, worry threading through it. There were so many things he wanted to point out to her about why this was a bad idea, but all of them were going to make him sound like a douchebag. Not that he cared about sounding like a douchebag when it came to keeping Sabrina safe, but still. She was already pissed at him and he hated it when she was pissed at him.

"Bree," he tried again, directing the smile he saved just for her in her direction. "Let me handle this. Please. Like I told you yesterday, this is my responsibility, not yours. You don't need to take it on board for me, you know that."

It was shitty of him to use emotional blackmail like this against her. But he'd do what he could to protect her, he always had.

The expression in her eyes flickered. Momentarily. And then firmed again. "I do know that. I'm still going."

A muscle jumped in the side of his jaw. He glanced at Faith. The look on her precise, lovely features didn't change. He knew that look too.

"Isiah can't be happy about this," he said, reaching for yet another objection.

"Yeah, I'm fine with it." Isiah's voice came from the doorway, the sound of the door slamming behind him echoing through the room as he strode in. "Just been discussing tactics with Night and he was real clear Sabrina is an essential component to this mission."

Fuck. Fuck. *Fuck.*

Kellan tried a laugh, shoving his hands into his pockets. "Hey, what am I? Chopped fucking liver? I know computers too. Sabrina can run a few things past me and I can deal—"

"And what if any encryption is something you can't handle?" Isiah interrupted. "What if the file gets corrupted or compromised because you don't have the skills?" The older man's gaze was hard as granite. "A good operative knows his or her own weaknesses and adjusts to compensate. I can't fly a fucking helo as well as you, even if you 'ran a few things past me.' Which means any mission that requires a helicopter pilot involves you." He took a couple of steps toward Kellan, then stopped. "This mission doesn't require a pilot. It requires a hacker with God-given skills and that person isn't you. It's Sabrina. We can't risk the success of the mission solely on someone who doesn't have the skillset."

It made sense from a military perspective. It made absolute sense. And his head knew it too. He *knew* he didn't have the same skills that Sabrina did and insisting otherwise was just fucking stupid.

Are you sure it's really about her? Maybe you're secretly afraid all of this is true and you don't want her to know.

Bullshit. It *wasn't* true. His father wasn't selling arms to drug lords and all the rest of this was simply him being her friend and keeping her safe.

Except, it looked like he wasn't going to be able to do that.

Just another thing you're going to fail at if you're not careful.

His jaw felt like granite, every muscle in his shoulders tight. The rhythmic sounds of Jack's fists hitting the canvas made him suddenly want to do the same, work out his anger and worry with a bit of old-fashioned physical exercise.

Or better yet, some physical exercise in bed. He hadn't gotten laid in a while and hell, maybe it was sexual frustration that was making him feel antsy. It probably wasn't, but that seemed like the easiest thing to blame it on.

He could feel Sabrina's gaze on him, stubborn and angry. Jesus, if he made an even bigger deal of this than he already had, she was never going to forgive him, was she? And apart from anything else, Jacob fucking Night had him over a barrel and he knew it.

He drew in a long breath, conscious of three sets of eyes drilling into him. Rolled his shoulders. Forcibly relaxed the muscles in his jaw. "Well, shit," he said, trying to keep his voice even. "Looks like I've got no choice, then."

"No," Faith said crisply. "You don't. Now, do you think we could get on with the planning? This nonsense has already taken up more time than it needs to."

Across from him, Sabrina's expression was still set in stubborn lines, that angry glow in her eyes. She was not pleased with him and she had reason. Didn't make him any happier about the decision though.

He kept his mouth shut as they discussed the best way to tackle getting the information Night wanted. Not that it took very long. Not when the simplest and easiest way to get that info was to pay a visit to his family estate in the Hamptons.

"Do you think we need a reason to suddenly show up?" Sabrina asked him. "We haven't visited for . . . I don't know how long."

He'd come to sit beside her on the couch—his usual spot—but he didn't miss the fact that she tensed up as he sat down. Though maybe if she was still pissy with him, that was understandable. Whatever, she'd get over it soon enough. That was the great thing about Sabrina; she never held onto anything for too long.

"I think I went back about six months ago," he replied, trying to remember. Truth be told, he hadn't felt comfortable visiting, not since the accident. Being with his parents, and his father in particular, only reminded him of the military career he no longer had. And though he'd come to terms with that, it was still difficult to see all the photos everywhere of himself in uniform. Both his parents had been so proud of him and his achievements, and they didn't understand the job he had now, not in any way.

Sabrina gave him a narrow look. He hadn't been entirely honest with her about his reasons for not visiting on a more regular basis, but she'd probably worked it out for herself. She wasn't stupid.

"That could be a problem," Faith murmured. "We don't want them asking questions."

Kellan snorted. "Why would they? A guy can't go visit his parents?"

But Faith was frowning. "They won't ask why you chose now? After six months of absence?"

He shifted on the couch. "No, of course they wouldn't. Mom would simply be glad to see me and Dad—" He broke off, remembering his last visit. His mother had been fine—fussing around him, but fine. His father, though, had been oddly distant and a touch awkward. As if he hadn't known what to say to Kellan, which didn't help the feeling that his dad was disappointed with him in some way.

Yeah, his dad might want to know what had prompted the visit after six months of virtual silence. And then the fact that he was bringing Sabrina along with him . . .

"Okay," he admitted reluctantly. "We might need a reason if they start asking questions."

"They will if I'm with you," Sabrina said, echoing his thoughts.

Isiah, who'd been sitting in his favorite spot—the recliner—looking through the job file, suddenly looked up. "Why if you're with him? I thought they were like family to you."

Sabrina took an audible breath and glanced down at her hands. "They are. I'm just . . . not family to them though. At least not in the same way."

Kellan blinked, a dart of surprise going through him. Shit, this was news. Since when did she think that? Sabrina had always been family to the Blakes. *Always.*

He stared at her. She kept her gaze on her hands, her sharp, pointed profile showing lingering traces of that mulish determination. "Hey." His voice was a little rough. "You know that's not true."

She lifted a shoulder. "Whatever. That doesn't change the fact that they're going to want to know why we've suddenly decided to come to the East Coast for a vacation."

He wanted to push her, ask her why she felt she wasn't family. After her father had taken off, his mother had insisted she be taken in by the Blakes since she had no one else, and Kellan's father had agreed. They hadn't treated her any differently from him. She'd been part of every family celebration, every family vacation, and every family event since. Plus, he knew she had a special bond with Charlotte, his mother. Why the hell would she feel she wasn't family?

But this *wasn't* the time for asking those kinds of questions, no matter how badly he wanted to ask them.

"You can't be with me simply because you're my friend and we do things to together?" he asked.

She gave him a sidelong glance. "Since when have we ever visited them before? Together?"

Never. You never take her when you visit.

The dart of surprise deepened into shock. It was true. He never had. Not that she'd pressed to come with him. In fact, now that he thought about it, she'd never even asked. All of which meant that both his mom and dad were going to be more than a little surprised when he turned up with her in tow.

He gritted his teeth. This goddamn mission was starting to become way more complicated than it needed to be. "A surprise visit isn't going to necessarily equal 'Hey, Dad, I think you're the head of an illegal arms ring, and where's your computer at so I can check?'"

Isiah snorted. "Don't be a dick, Blake. The fewer questions the better and you know it. Which is why I suggest you have a good story up your sleeve."

The tension gathered tighter in his shoulders. A good story meant lying to his parents and then he'd be snooping around their house as if they were criminals . . . And what if they found out what he was doing? They'd be so angry, so hurt.

He hated the thought.

Calm down. You'll find nothing, they won't know, and that'll be it. And then that asshole Night can suck it.

Slowly and deliberately, Kellan laced his fingers behind his head and leaned back against the couch, stretching his legs out. "Okay, so . . . a good story." He glanced at Sabrina and raised a brow. "Any suggestions?"

Sabrina kept her gaze on her hands in her lap. They were clasped together so hard it was a wonder she hadn't cracked the bones.

She could feel Kellan beside her, his long, muscular body stretched out, the heat of his thigh so near to hers. He had his hands behind his head and she didn't need to look at him to know that his T-shirt would be pulled tight around his powerful biceps and across his broad chest, outlining all that delicious, cut muscle.

Focus, idiot.

Her heartbeat was loud in her ears, her own muscles tight, expecting a fight. She knew he wouldn't be pleased with Faith's flat declaration that she was going on the mission whether he liked it or not, yet he hadn't made as massive a deal of it as he could have done.

He wasn't happy, sure, but she could live with that. She just hadn't thought as far as needing a reason for a sudden visit to the Blake estate. Because whatever he thought, they were going to need one.

He hadn't seen his parents for months and the times he *had* visited, he hadn't brought her with him. Not that she would have gone anyway. Charlotte had gotten strange with her after his accident, as if she blamed Sabrina for the helicopter crash. As if Sabrina hadn't upheld her end of the bargain in protecting him.

Crazy, when that had happened while Kellan was on deployment and she'd been in Silicon Valley testing systems security for one of the huge tech firms. Even so, there was a part of her that had agreed with Charlotte, that had felt some responsibility for him, even though she'd had nothing to do with his decision to join the military. That feeling was still strong now, so maybe she'd always feel that way.

Regardless, Charlotte would be puzzled by her turning up with Kellan and she'd definitely be expecting some reason. Actually, knowing her, she'd probably jump to the worst conclusions too, that something was wrong. And Sabrina did *not* want her to think that, not after what she'd already gone through with Phillip and his affairs.

Except . . . what?

"Pity you haven't gotten engaged to anyone." Sabrina stared down at her fingers. "Or gotten anyone pregnant. That would be the perfect cover given how your mom is about family."

Kellan's laugh held a brittle edge. "Yeah, true enough. Though Mom would want me to be engaged to some Manhattan WASP, not a San Diego beach bunny."

"Does it matter who it is?" Faith asked. "It's a cover story, that's all."

"No, I guess it doesn't." Kellan let out an audible breath. "Shit, I might as well announce that I'm marrying Sabrina."

There was a short silence that felt so loud her ears rang.

He was joking. Of course he was joking. She could hear the telltale thread of humor in his voice. It was an off-the-cuff thing, a casual mention. A punch line.

He definitely didn't mean it.

Sabrina clasped her hands tighter and she was sure she heard her knuckles crack. There was a pressure along her shoulders too, an itch along her skin. He was looking at her.

"Actually," he said slowly. "Now that I think about it, that's not a stupid idea."

A burst of shock swept through her, the ringing in her ears getting louder. Faith was talking and so was Isiah, but Sabrina couldn't hear either of them. She didn't want to look at the man sitting beside her. The man who'd just given voice to her most private fantasy. Where she was married to him and had everything she'd always wanted, from the day her mother and two siblings had been swept away in a flood in their car, and her father, unable to deal with his grief, had uprooted her from her life and set out on an eight-month road trip that had ended up at the Blake's estate.

Home. A family. Someone to love. All the things she'd lost.

But no, she could never have that, at least not with Kellan. Not when he'd never seen her that way.

She blinked, trying to get the shock under control and her brain to stop flailing around. Faith was frowning at her and she realized she'd been asked a question, and Faith was waiting for an answer.

"W-What?" she mumbled, her lips feeling numb.

"I said, what do you think?" A crease appeared between Faith's brows. "You don't look happy with the idea."

Do not look at Kellan. Do not.

Sabrina licked her suddenly dry lips. "I mean . . . uh . . ."

"Come on, Bree." Kellan leaned forward, his elbows on his knees, turning toward her. "It'll be a little weird I admit, but it *is* a good story and it'll cover us both."

Crap. She was going to have to look at him, wasn't she?

Hoping the shock wasn't plastered all over her face, she forced herself to meet his blue gaze.

His straight blond brows were raised and there was a half smile playing around his beautiful mouth, as if this was all a big joke that he wanted her in on. And a wave of anger hit her. "So, first you didn't want to even do this mission, then you didn't want me to do it. Now, not only are you completely happy for me to come, you want me to pretend to be your fiancée and lie to both your parents."

She knew she shouldn't have said it, that it sounded shrill even to her own ears, but she couldn't help herself. His uncharacteristic changes of heart were giving her whiplash, and this cover story was only making things worse.

His brows arrowed down, the smile vanishing. "Yeah, I know. But I told you why I have to do this. And whether I like it or not, Night is insisting you come, so I'm sucking that up too. As for Mom and Dad . . . You were the one who said we need a reason for a visit. And as reasons go, this isn't a bad one since it explains why we're both coming."

"But it's not true. Charlotte will—"

"Mom will be shocked, yes. And Dad too, probably. But it's not real. We'll maintain the fiction while we're there, then give them a month and we'll let them know we changed our minds."

"Whatever story you go for," Isiah said, putting his hands on the arms of his recliner and pushing himself out of it, "figure it out. I'll go sort out the jet."

Sabrina ignored him. Her palms felt sweaty, her heartbeat way too fast, and she was very conscious that Faith was looking at her with sharp speculation in her eyes.

"Charlotte will hate the idea," she said, keeping her gaze on Kellan's. "Like you said, she wants you with some Manhattan WASP girl."

"So? It's not real, so it doesn't matter. And anyway, leave Mom to me. I'll handle her."

Easy for him to say. He didn't know the reality of the relationship between herself and his mother. And one thing she did know; Charlotte would *hate* any liaison between her and Kellan. That was not Sabrina's place.

Don't make this a big deal. He's right, it doesn't matter. Not when it's only pretend.

Yes, that was true. So very true. And if she continued to protest, it was going to look even weirder than it already was.

Kellan's mouth curved, his smile returning. The one he used to coax her into doing something she didn't want to do. "Come on. It'll be fun."

Fun. Ha.

She took a silent breath, then let it out, consciously releasing her knotted fingers, then wiping her palms down her jeans. "Sure, why not? Just don't ask me to kiss you, 'cause that's not happening."

He blinked, an arrested look crossing his face. Then, just as quickly, it was gone and he laughed. "I don't think that's going to be necessary. But you might have to settle for an arm around your waist or something."

"You'll need to settle on a backstory too," Faith murmured as she stared down at her phone. "I'll tell Mr. Night it's all in hand." She rose from the armchair she'd been sitting in and lifted the phone to her ear, moving away from the living area of the huge space and over to where all the computers were situated.

Leaving Sabrina very conscious that she and Kellan were now effectively alone together, and that she was drowning in awkwardness.

Kellan had linked his long fingers together between his knees and was studying her face. "What's up? You don't like this, do you?"

Shit, what was she going to say? Perhaps a partial truth would get him off her back. "I don't like lying to your folks, no. And I'm kind of still pissed at you for telling me I couldn't come."

"Yeah, I got that. But you know me, I don't want to involve people I care about in things that might turn to shit."

"But—"

"But I'm over it now, okay? I mean, it makes sense for you to come."

To give Kellan his due, he was a guy who could admit when he was wrong about something. And he didn't sulk about it either. "Well, good," she said, hating the awkwardness between them and knowing that was all her, not him.

His gaze sharpened, his smile fading again. "I am going to insist on one thing though."

Crap, he was serious now, which usually meant he was going to be stubborn about whatever it was. "What?" Her pulse kicked up a notch at the hard look on his face. Which was weird.

"I'm in charge of this mission, okay? It concerns my family, which makes it my responsibility."

Someone had to be in charge since that was the case with every mission the 11th Hour undertook. And she couldn't argue for it to be her, not when she didn't have either the experience or the training.

"Okay, fine." She shrugged, making it no big deal. "Doesn't worry me."

The pressure of his intense blue gaze didn't relent. "You know what that means, though, don't you? I get to call the shots and you can't argue with them."

She rolled her eyes, ignoring the strange flutter way down deep inside her. "How is that different from any other day?"

"I'm serious, Bree." He didn't smile this time, his chiseled jaw hard.

The flutter inside her increased. Dammit. She had no idea why his take-charge ways turned her on, especially when they also irritated her intensely. "Okay, okay," she muttered. "I get it."

He narrowed his gaze a moment, as if checking to make sure she was fully on board, then his features relaxed. "Good. Guess we'd better start thinking of a story, then."

"What story?"

"What do you think?" One corner of his mouth lifted in his inevitable grin. "The story of how we fell in love and I eventually asked you to marry me."

Oh. That.

Well, her story was simple to tell. She'd fallen for him the moment she'd met him, when she'd been a shy, reserved ten-year-old who'd first come to live on the Blake estate along with her father.

Her dad hadn't bothered to enroll her in school yet, so she'd been left to her own devices while he'd worked on the estate gardens. It had been that initial afternoon, the day her father had started work, and she'd wandered out over the western lawn, staring in awe at the terraced rose gardens. And a tall blond boy had come up behind her, imperiously asking her who she was and what she was doing here.

She'd been frightened and had nearly run away. But then, as if he'd known he'd scared her, he'd smiled, and just like that, she'd had the immediate feeling that everything was going to be okay, no matter what.

That had been the moment for her. That had *always* been the moment for her.

But she couldn't tell him that.

Sabrina shifted on the couch, unable to sit there any longer, hating how awkward she felt and how much she suddenly needed to put some distance between them. Because she couldn't think. She just couldn't think. "Not now," she muttered, pushing herself up off the couch. "Tonight."

"Tonight? But we need to get this—"

"I'll text you," she said over her shoulder, not looking back as she headed for the door.

"Bree." He sounded surprised. "What the hell?"

But Sabrina didn't turn around and she didn't stop.

She needed some Kellan-free space and she needed it now.

CHAPTER 4

Kellan held a beer bottle loosely between his fingers, staring moodily out the windows of his Bayside penthouse apartment at the lights of San Diego Bay and beyond, across the darkening sea, to those of the exclusive beach community of Coronado.

When he'd first come to San Diego over a year ago, he'd bought this apartment because of the view. He liked looking at the ocean and the boats in the harbor, liked being able to look at Coronado, remembering his SEAL training at the naval base there.

Usually, it soothed him. Like this beer he had now was supposed to soothe him. But for some reason neither the view nor the beer were working the way they were supposed to. He still felt just as pissed off and antsy as he had done this morning at HQ, after Faith had told him that Sabrina's presence on the mission was nonnegotiable. After he'd had the bright idea of her posing as his fiancée when they visited his family.

After she'd abruptly walked out with barely a word.

Slowly, he raised the bottle to his mouth and took a sip,

frowning at the lights of one of the ferries as it made its way toward Coronado.

Something was definitely up with her and it irritated him that he didn't know what it was. He could understand her getting annoyed with him when he'd tried to stop her going on the mission, but the way she'd suddenly gotten up and left HQ that morning? In the middle of a planning session? That wasn't like her, and he wasn't sure what had prompted it.

He and Faith and Isiah had spent the rest of the morning planning logistics and getting everything in place, since Night wanted it done ASAP. And Kellan had expected Sabrina to return to HQ and join in with the planning. Yet she hadn't.

He'd texted her a couple of times to ask her what she was doing, and she'd responded simply that she had a couple of things to do and that they could finish the planning without her. She'd come over to his apartment that night and he could fill her in.

Both Faith and Isiah were unimpressed with that attitude, but Kellan had reminded them that Sabrina wasn't military and whatever was up with her—because something clearly was—he'd get it out of her that night.

Again, it wasn't like her to take off. She liked being involved and didn't normally shirk any responsibilities she had, so whatever it was that had caused her to disappear the way she did, it had to be pretty major.

He sipped again from his beer, trying to figure it out. Had he said something? Done something? Was it the mission? Or was it something else she hadn't told him about?

He didn't like that idea, didn't like it at all. Sabrina was pretty open and honest with him, and she always told him when things were bothering her.

Hypocrite.

The voice whispered in his head, insidious, reminding him of his own secrets, but he ignored it. There were reasons he'd never told Sabrina about Pippa. Why he'd never told *anyone* about Pippa except his dad. Very, very good reasons. And he was okay with continuing to not tell her about it, because it didn't have anything to do with the present. All of *that* had happened years ago. Still, if there was something bothering her *now* that she wasn't telling him . . .

He scowled at the view. She should tell him. Wasn't that what friends were for? She'd helped him out so much after he'd been recovering from the helicopter crash and then when his military career had become a smoking ruin, just like that helicopter, she'd been there for him. It was only right that he be there for her, in whatever capacity she needed him.

Except she had to tell him what was up first.

As if the thought had brought her right to him, he heard the buzzer go, and he turned, moving around his large leather sectional sofa and dodging the boxes still stacked in various places—boxes he hadn't unpacked since he'd gotten here—to get to the front door where the control pad was. He didn't bother looking at the screen, hitting the button that unlocked the front door so she could get into the building, then pulling open the door to his apartment so she could walk straight in.

"Hey," she said a minute or so later, sounding slightly breathless.

He'd gone to stand by the windows again, irritation needling at him no matter how much he tried to ignore it. He didn't actually want to be annoyed with her, but his mood about this whole mission was coloring everything and he couldn't seem to put it aside.

At her breathless "hey," he turned around.

She was in the process of shutting the door behind her, a four-pack of beer dangling from the slender fingers of her other hand. Her long chestnut brown hair was in its customary ponytail that fell to midback, the light gleaming on her curls. When she turned to face him, her wide, generous mouth was curved in a smile, but there was definitely something guarded in those green-gold eyes.

He should have asked her if there was anything wrong immediately, but that wasn't what came out. "Where were you?" he asked instead, and it sounded like a demand instead of the mild question it should have been.

She looked surprised at his tone, then her straight dark brows arrowed down, her expression turning defensive. "What do you mean, 'where was I'? I had some stuff to do, I told you that."

"Yeah, and you were supposed to be with Faith and Isiah and me, planning this mission. You were supposed to be involved."

Her throat moved as she swallowed and he found he was staring inexplicably at it. She had a long, very elegant neck, her pulse beating fast beneath pale freckled skin.

Why was it fast? Was she afraid?

Her gaze flickered away from his. "I know. I'm sorry."

Frustration curled in his gut, though he tried to keep his voice level. "What's going on, Bree? You left so suddenly and then you didn't come back. And planning is an important part of the mission, you know that."

An expression he couldn't read rippled across her pointed features, then she turned, moving over to the kitchen that was situated in one corner of the massive, open-plan area.

"Like I said," she murmured, putting the beer down on the counter that separated the kitchen space from the living area. "I'm sorry. I know it's bad form not to be there, but . . ." She stopped, her face angled away from him.

Worry tightened in his chest and abruptly he forgot about his own frustrations and annoyances. "But what?" He moved over to the counter and put his bottle down, then turned around to lean against the white marble. "Something's up. Want to tell me about it?"

Her head was bent and one curl had come loose from her ponytail, hanging over her face and preventing him from seeing her expression. He reached out and caught the errant lock of hair with his finger, gently tucking it behind her ear. The glossy curl felt silky against his fingertip, the skin of her ear warm as he brushed against it. And strangely, he could have sworn he felt a shiver go through her as he did so. Which was weird.

The thought made him uncomfortable, so he pushed it away, concentrating instead on her face. Her long dark lashes were fanned out across her pale cheekbones, her attention very firmly on the marble of the counter.

Sometimes remaining quiet could get her to talk, so he didn't push, letting the silence settle between them.

Eventually she let out a breath and lifted her head, meeting his gaze. "I'm nervous about this, okay? Yes, I know I pushed for it and don't get me wrong, I'm still all in. But . . . You're right. I should have been there and I wasn't because I got a little freaked out, to be honest."

That all made perfect sense. This was her first field mission and it involved people she knew, people she cared about. It was going to involve some playacting on their part too, and Sabrina had never been a great actor, just as she had never been that good of a liar. This would all be new to her, and yeah, he could see this being a big deal.

"Understandable," he said. "But you know you can talk to me about all of this. Taking off like that isn't going to help."

She turned around to lean back against the counter like he was. "I thought you might take that as an excuse to stop me from going and I didn't want that."

He snorted. "Like I could. Night wants you on this mission and what he says goes. Besides, I told you I was good with it now."

"Yeah, I guess so."

She wasn't convinced, obviously. Well, he couldn't do much about that. But he could help with her nervousness.

Reaching for the beers she'd brought, he grabbed one out of the pack and handed it to her. "Come on, drink this while I fill you in on what you missed."

Sabrina sighed, then took the beer, twisting off the cap and taking a deep swallow as he told her what Isiah and Faith and he had worked out.

They'd leave tomorrow on the jet, flying direct. All of them had thought it better to preserve the element of surprise, agreeing not to call ahead to let the Blakes know he and Sabrina would be coming. A day or so should be all that was needed to find the file—or not find it more likely—but they couldn't leave too quickly otherwise more questions might be asked.

Get in, get out, without drawing questions, basically.

"That sounds . . . fine," Sabrina said, nodding as she sipped at her beer. "I mean, it shouldn't be too difficult getting some time alone to search Phillip's study, see if we can find out whether he's got another hard drive stashed somewhere, or a laptop."

"Yeah, and I can distract him if it looks like he's going to stay holed up in there. Or we can check it out once he's gone to bed."

Talking about skulking around his family home felt wrong, but then he couldn't tell his father he'd been sent to investigate him. Not after he'd told Night that he wouldn't. And then there were the lies he'd have to tell about this engagement business.

The thought didn't sit well with him, but what other choice did he have?

No, he was going to have to stay silent and pretend to his dad that he was there only to visit. At least until he and Sabrina had searched for that goddamn file. A file that wasn't even going to be there, because it didn't exist in the first place.

"Okay." A hesitant note entered her voice. "I guess we need to talk about this whole engagement thing then, right?"

He glanced at her, not missing the uncertainty in her eyes. "You nervous about that too?"

Sabrina fiddled with her bottle, picking at the label. "No, not really."

Like she thought he wouldn't notice. "Bullshit. You can't hide this stuff from me, Bree. Remember? I know you. Is this what's really freaking you out?"

Another flicker of an expression he would have named as hurt crossed her features, though it couldn't be hurt, could it? Because what would she be hurt about?

"Maybe." Her fingers kept picking at the label on the bottle.

Definitely nervous.

Kellan reached out and took the bottle away from her, putting it down on the counter. Then he took her hands in his, turning so he was facing her. The tips of her fingers were cold, her eyes wide and very green all of a sudden. "It's no big deal, okay?" He made the words sound as reassuring as possible. "It's only a little playacting. Hell, you don't even have to do anything. You can leave the talking to me."

She said nothing, only stared at him. He found his gaze drawn once again to the pulse at the base of her throat and how fast it was. And he became aware, all of a sudden, that they were standing quite close to each other and that he could smell the familiar scent of her, laundry liquid and that faint feminine musk that was all Sabrina.

She was in her usual jeans and an emerald T-shirt, nothing special or out of the ordinary, but . . . There was something about the deep green color of the cotton that made her skin seem creamier and the dark brown of her hair richer.

Christ. Why the fuck was he thinking about the color of her T-shirt? Or her skin and hair for that matter? This was Sabrina.

His best friend. And he didn't notice stuff like that. At least, he hadn't before, so why he was doing it now was anyone's guess.

But the way she was looking at him . . . There was something in her gaze, a kind of glow, a sort of heat. And he suddenly noticed that there was more gold than green in her eyes now. Little shimmering flecks he'd never seen before . . .

So why are you seeing them now?

Kellan blinked. And just like that the glow he'd thought he'd seen was gone. Her dark lashes swept down and she pulled her hands from his, pushing them into the pockets of her jeans and turning toward the windows. "I could leave the talking to you," she said, the words coming out breathless. "But they're going to ask me questions all the same. Jesus, Kel." She stopped near the couch, the big floor-to-ceiling windows at her back, and turned, looking around at the boxes all stacked on the hardwood floors. Her cheeks had gone pink. "When the hell are you going to unpack all of these? They've been sitting here for six months."

Something had happened just then. A moment of weirdness between them. And he didn't know what the fuck it was all about, but one thing he did know: He sure as hell didn't want to think about it.

The feel of her cold fingertips against his lingered strangely, so he pushed his hands into his pockets as well, leaning back against the kitchen counter again. "You know why. I can't be fucked unpacking. And don't change the subject."

Her head came up, her chin lifting. "I'm not. It was only a question."

"Which I've answered." Shit, and now he was sounding short with her. Gritting his teeth, he forced himself to relax, to smile. "So, tell me when was the first time you knew you were in love with me."

Sabrina turned away again, wandering over to the windows.

"The first time I knew I was in love with you . . . okay . . ." She stopped at the glass, her back to him. Her silhouette was tall and narrow, her curves slight, though by no means unfeminine.

Why the fuck are you noticing her curves?

Kellan blinked again. Holy shit. He might have blamed the beer for all this weirdness, but he'd only had one.

"Maybe when I was helping you recover from the crash," Sabrina went on, completely oblivious to the chaos in his head. "All that time spent together getting you well and we realized our true feelings for each other, blah, blah, bullshit."

It was a good story and it made sense.

"Okay," he said slowly. "So over the course of the past year, we gradually realized we were in love and I popped the question, completely surprising you . . . where?"

"On the beach." She didn't even hesitate. "It was a beautiful day and it was early in the morning. There was no one around. We were walking hand in hand, and then you suddenly dropped down on one knee in the sand and asked me to marry you."

Kellan shifted against the counter, uncomfortable for some reason. "You've clearly thought about this."

She didn't move, her attention directed out the window. "I've had all afternoon."

There was an odd note in her voice, one he couldn't place. "Why the beach?"

"Because it's special to me. That's where you first kissed me."

She hadn't been kidding. She really *had* thought about this.

His discomfort deepened, though he couldn't have said why.

"Of course the beach," he said, ignoring the feeling. "I know how much you love the place."

"Do you?" She turned around, the oddest expression on her face. Almost . . . accusing. "Do you really?"

* * *

Kellan's blond brows rose, surprise rippling over his perfect features, and Sabrina abruptly wanted to die.

Shit. Why the hell had she asked that? It had come out sounding both defensive and demanding at the same time, and apart from anything else, she hadn't meant to say it.

God, she was supposed to be smart, but sometimes, around him, her brain didn't seem able to function very well.

She'd just gotten . . . mad. No, scratch that, she'd been mad the moment she'd stepped into Kellan's familiar apartment. Mad and awkward and scared and all kinds of other emotions that she shouldn't be feeling when she visited him. His apartment had always been a safe space for her and now it wasn't, and that made her afraid and angry, and yeah, mad with herself for letting all of this get to her the way it was.

To be fair, it hadn't started well. Then there had been that strange moment when he'd taken her hands and she'd felt her heartbeat speed up and her breath catch, the way it always did. And she'd seen something spark in his blue eyes. Something she'd never seen there before. She'd had to pull away, though, too uncertain about what that spark was, and not wanting to give herself any hope that it wasn't the friendship he always gave her.

Yeah, that hadn't helped. And then the questions about the engagement pretense . . .

She hadn't been able to look at him, the story of their pretend love affair coming out of her mouth with frightening ease.

She'd let that get to her. And his arrogant assurance that of course the beach hadn't helped, because he'd said it like he knew, and he didn't. Not about her early morning walks on the sand, where no one else was around but the sea. Or about how she loved the peace of it, the feeling of sand between her toes, and the sound of the waves. Once or twice she'd asked him to come with her, but he'd always had other things to do, and then she'd decided that the beach would be her special place. Her Kellan-free zone.

He didn't know what that meant to her. But there were a lot of things he didn't know about her and for some reason that hurt.

"What? That you like the beach?" There was a puzzled look on his face now. "I mean, I know you go for walks in the mornings."

It should have appeased her that he'd noticed, yet it didn't.

Turning away, Sabrina gave him her back as she stared out at the view over the bay, the lights of Coronado glittering in the darkness like a sprinkle of precious gems.

Crap. She should have forced herself to go to that planning meeting, then maybe this wouldn't have been so difficult. She felt guilty about that, but she hadn't been able to face it, especially not talking about this pretense in front of sharp-eyed Faith and equally sharp-eyed Isiah. They'd have guessed her problem within seconds flat and then she'd have died of embarrassment.

"Okay then," she said lamely. "So the beach is my special place."

There was a silence, uncomfortable and awkward.

That's your fault.

Yes, it really was. It had nothing to do with him. He didn't know what was in her heart, and he didn't know because she hadn't told him. And she wouldn't. Which meant it was up to her to fix the awkwardness.

"I'm sorry." She curled her fingers into fists in her pockets. "I guess this whole engagement thing really is weirding me out." There, that was a bit of truth for him and perhaps would make things a little easier.

"Ah." His voice was deep and soft, and she wished she wasn't quite so sensitive to it. "I wondered."

She knew he'd pushed himself away from the counter because she could see his reflection in the glass, tall and broad, coming toward her with that easy, predatory grace. He came to a stop behind her, close enough that she could smell his clean, fresh scent, feel the seductive heat of his body.

"It'll be okay," he said quietly. "I'll make sure it won't get weird. God knows it'll be the only fun part of this goddamn mission."

Fun. This was fun to him.

Get a fucking grip. If you don't want him to know what a pathetic ass you are for him, you can't mope around like this.

That was true. She *did* need to figure out how she was going to handle herself; otherwise, this whole thing was going to be a nightmare. And seriously, if the worst part about it was having to pretend to be Kellan's fiancée and not searching for a file that would incriminate Phillip Blake, then she needed to get her head read.

Yeah, she needed to handle it and handle it now.

Steeling her spine and gathering all her considerable determination, Sabrina turned around. He was standing close, a frown of concern pulling his brows together, those incredible ice-blue eyes on hers.

Her heart caught like a piece of silk on a blackberry bush.

Handle it.

"Fun." Her voice sounded tinny. "You're right. It should be fun. In that case, we should probably practice."

One brow arched. "Practice?"

"Yeah. You know. Holding each other. Being affectionate. Engaged couples don't slap each other on the back or never touch, if you know what I mean."

His frown deepened, his gaze turning searching. But he nodded. "It's true, they don't."

This was a dangerous game she was going to play, but she couldn't see any other way around it. She had to learn how to deal with herself around him. So maybe like any other phobia, gradual exposure was the key. Hopefully maybe even the cure, if she was lucky.

"No," she went on. "They hold each other. Kiss each other." Her heartbeat was going into overdrive now, no matter how she tried to get it to slow down. "So, you know, maybe it wouldn't be a bad idea to practice that."

His brows twitched. "What are you saying?"

Sabrina took a deep, silent breath. "I'm saying that if you wanted to kiss me, I would be fine with it. In fact, I think we probably should do it. To be convincing to your folks and all."

If he was surprised, he didn't show it, his expression unchanging, and she felt herself quiver way down deep inside.

If he refused, she didn't know what she'd do. Maybe punch him. Especially since he'd never know how much it had cost her to even suggest it.

But what if he doesn't say no? What if he says yes and he kisses you and it's amazing and you'll never be able to—

"Okay," he said slowly, interrupting her flailing thoughts. "Are you sure though?"

Oh. God. He was okay with this. And now that he was, she *wasn't* sure. In fact, the one thing she *was* sure of was that it was a really dumb idea. But she'd said it now. It was too late to pull back. Besides, she needed to do this. Inoculate herself, as it were.

If the kiss turned out bad, she could put this stupid crush she had on him behind her. And if the kiss turned out great then . . . Well, at least she could say she'd kissed him. At least she'd have that.

Nice justifications.

Sabrina shoved the thought from her head. "Yes." She tried to make the word as steady and certain as she could. "I mean, it's going to look odd if you don't kiss me, right? And if we leave it till we're there, it might turn out to be unconvincing. So . . ." She stopped, not able to quite bring herself to say it.

Kellan had no such problems. "So you want me to kiss you now?"

She swallowed. The look on his face was curiously guarded but definitely not repulsed, which was a start. And he wasn't laughing as if the whole thing was a big joke, which was also good.

Yet she could feel herself tensing up, her shoulders aching and her stomach churning. The space between them felt weighted and heavy, and no matter how hard she tried to ignore it, the awkwardness of the moment was choking. "Sure," she forced out. "Might as well, right?"

That silvery-blue gaze searched her face and there were no smiles turning his beautiful mouth now. He stepped forward, closing the space between them, and all of a sudden he was right there in front of her. And even though she was tall, she found herself having to tilt her head back slightly to look up at him.

Every instinct she had screamed at her to take a step back, get some distance, but she held her ground. No, she *had* to do this. For her own peace of mind it was necessary.

Yet . . . God. He was so broad, the cotton of his black T-shirt stretching over his wide shoulders and muscular chest, and he was so warm. The smell of him familiar. Being close to him was like a drug to her, intoxicating, dizzying . . . She could barely stand it.

He lifted a hand, cupping her jaw in his palm, and the feel of his hot skin against hers was so unexpected and intense she nearly flinched.

"You okay?" There was concern in his voice and in his gaze. "We don't have to do this now if you don't want to."

His eyes were the most fascinating color, a clear, light, silvery blue, like the sky on a perfect winter's day, and his lashes were surprisingly thick and darker than his hair. Even the lights of the room couldn't mask the gleam of gold in them. She could see that same golden gleam along his jawline too, defining the sharp, hard line of it.

Beautiful. He was beautiful. But then she'd always known that.

His hand against her cheek was burning hot and if he didn't kiss her now, she was going to chicken out, and she couldn't let that happen. Hell, if he asked her if she was sure one more time she definitely *would* punch him.

Yet it didn't look like he was going to move, which left her with only one option.

Don't think about it. Just do it.

Sure. She'd kissed other men after all, so how hard could it be?

Pulling both hands from her pockets, she lifted them and slid her fingers into the thick silk of his blond hair. Then she tugged his head down until his mouth met hers.

She'd fantasized many times about kissing Kellan Blake. About when and where and how. But she'd never been able to fully imagine what it would feel like because she'd never let her mind go there, not really. It had always been too much, so overwhelming, she didn't even want to think about it.

But now it was real. Now she was actually doing it, kissing Kellan. And the moment his lips touched hers, she knew she'd been right all this time. It *was* too much.

His mouth was warm and soft, making electricity arc the entire length of her body, shooting down her spine and grounding out through her feet, freezing her in place.

He didn't move either, both of them standing there like statues.

She could feel the tension in him, his muscles as tight as her own, which was a total giveaway. He didn't want this, and she'd made a terrible, terrible error.

Her heart lurched and she started to pull away, the words of apology already flooding her mouth.

But then the hand on her jaw slid to the back of her head and his fingers were suddenly in her hair, holding on. Preventing her from pulling away any farther. And that warm mouth on hers began to move, a slow, gentle exploration, testing her.

She shuddered, her brain struggling to make sense of what was happening.

His tongue ran along the seam of her lips, wanting in, and she found herself opening her mouth, letting him inside. And then the whole world tilted on its axis as the flavor of him exploded in her head.

Dark. Rich. Alcoholic. Hotter than fire. Better than she'd even imagined. Better than any other kiss she'd ever had.

And far, *far* more than she could deal with right now.

A choked noise tore from her throat and before she could stop herself, her hands were on his hard chest and she was pushing at him, tearing herself out of his grip, turning and taking a few stumbling steps away from him

Her heart was racing, her mouth burning, and she knew she'd never be able to get the taste of him out of her head.

Mistake, mistake, mistake. Holy fuck, for someone so smart, she really could be incredibly stupid.

He was like a dangerous drug she knew would be bad for her, that she'd tried anyway, and now she'd never be able to forget it. Never stop craving. Never stop wanting.

You goddamn idiot.

"Bree?" His voice was behind her and she could hear the deep surprise in it. "Are you okay? Did I hurt you? "

No. She wasn't okay. And yes, he'd hurt her. But not in the way he meant and not in a way he could heal. But she couldn't let him know that.

Sabrina took a couple of deep breaths, thrusting her shaking hands into the pockets of her jeans, and tried to get her racing heartbeat under control. Tried to ignore the way her mouth burned. Then she forced herself to turn around and look at him.

There was nothing but concern in his blue eyes.

Great, so obviously the kiss hadn't affected him the way it had affected her. Wonderful. Then again, maybe that was a good thing. If there was incontrovertible proof that he didn't feel the same way about her as she did him, then here it was.

And yes, that was good. Very, very good.

"No." Dammit, her voice was hoarse. "You didn't hurt me. It's fine."

He took a step toward her and she found she'd taken a step back before she could stop herself. His eyes darkened. "Bree—"

"I'm absolutely fine," she interrupted quickly, before he could go on or, more importantly, get closer. "Honestly, I just got a little weirded out. But now we've practiced and I'm sure if we have to do it again, it'll all be okay." She stopped and took a breath, hating how shaky it sounded. "Now, is there anything else you need to fill me in on? Because I should get back to HQ and pack."

An expression she couldn't read flickered across his face, then vanished, and she thought he might push her for more answers. But he didn't. "Yeah," he said after a moment, glancing away from her. "That's probably a good idea."

Perhaps it was then that she understood what she'd done, as the tension between them widened, deepened.

That kiss had changed things and nothing was going to be the same again.

CHAPTER 5

Spring in the Hamptons was usually Kellan's favorite time of year, when the crowds weren't as bad and neither was the traffic. But as he and Sabrina drove the rental car from the private airfield where they'd landed that evening, to Southampton, where the family estate was situated, it wasn't the weather he was thinking of.

The flight from San Diego had been tense, and though Sabrina kept acting like there was nothing wrong, he knew there was. They'd spent it going through some of the mission objectives and thinking up a few strategies for how to search for the file without drawing suspicion. The first night, they'd both decided, they'd lay low, letting the Blakes deal with the whole engagement thing, and then maybe Kellan would handle distracting his father, while Sabrina attempted to get into Phillip's study and search it.

Sabrina didn't mention the kiss. At all. Though he knew that's what had to be bothering her because something was and logically it had to be that. She was never normally so determinedly cheerful.

He couldn't blame her though. That goddamn kiss had been bothering him too.

He'd been surprised that she'd suggested it, but it made sense. He couldn't be treating her the way he always did if they were supposed to be in love, and a kiss was part of that. Laying one on her for the first time in front of his family was a stupid idea, so it was logical they practice it first.

She'd been visibly nervous, which had surprised him since it was only him and she must know that he wouldn't hurt her. And anyway, it was pretend. It shouldn't matter.

Apparently though, it did. He saw the apprehension in her gold-flecked eyes as he'd cupped her jaw in his palm.

Maybe then he should have pulled away, let the idea of the kiss go. Yet he hadn't. For some reason he couldn't put his finger on, he'd kept his hand against her cheek, conscious suddenly of her nearness, the way he had been over by the kitchen counter. There had been a flush to her skin, freckles standing out against her skin and the gold in her eyes seemed to glitter like gold dust in a clear river bed.

But she'd been the one to take the initiative, sliding her fingers into his hair and pulling his mouth down on hers. He'd felt her tense at that moment, and start to pull away, and he had no idea why his hand cupping her jaw had tightened, holding her still. No idea why he'd touched his tongue to those incredibly soft lips. Why he'd coaxed her to open for him and she had, the flavor and heat of her flooding his mouth—

Fuck. No. Why was he thinking about it? It was only a pretend kiss with his best friend and it didn't mean a goddamn thing.

Sabrina was chattering about something, but he wasn't listening. His body felt tight. Everything felt tight.

Shit, he should have gotten himself laid before he left San Diego, because clearly some good, hard, head-clearing sex would have made this whole thing a hell of a lot easier.

Silence fell as they finally turned down the street that led to Blake House's gates, yet more unwelcome tension filling the car. This time, though, it wasn't just about the kiss, at least not for him.

He hadn't been home for a good six months, and there was a part of him that didn't want to walk through those doors even now. The weak part of him, the one that couldn't stand those pictures of him in uniform, whole and uninjured. The perfect son. The standard he'd set himself and that he'd now failed to achieve. The hero he was supposed to have been.

You were never going to be that and you know it.

Especially not now, not when his current mission was going to consist of lying to the two people who'd given him nothing but love and support his whole life. Lying and sneaking around, trying to find evidence that one of those people was a traitor to their country.

But no, he couldn't think about that. This was all about proving his father's innocence and if he needed to tell a few lies in order to do so, then so be it. Working for the 11th Hour team may not have been what either he or his father had envisaged for him, but it was still all about protecting people, and in this case, it was his father he was protecting.

"So, are we just going to announce it?" Sabrina asked into the heavy silence as Kellan pulled the car up outside the familiar wrought iron of the gates to the estate. "Like straight up? Or do you want to wait?"

Distracted by his own thoughts, Kellan almost asked "announce what?" Then he remembered. The damn engagement. "Straight up," he said, wrenching his brain back on track. "No point stringing it out." Beside one of the gates, set into a high brick wall, was a keypad and intercom. Would the code have changed? Or was it easier to call up to the house?

Only one way to find out.

"You're probably right," Sabrina muttered, staring at the

gates like they were the gates of hell. "Get it out of the way and all that."

"It'll be fine," he said, automatically responding to the note of apprehension in her voice. "Like I told you before, let me do the talking. All you have to do is act like you adore me."

"Right." Sabrina scowled at the driveway for a long minute, then suddenly her expression turned worried. "Oh, I forgot! We don't have a ring."

He grinned—for a change not having to force it—since the look on her face was pretty much genuine. "Don't worry. We'll just tell them I wanted to choose one of the heirlooms."

A crease appeared between her brows. "Heirlooms . . . Hey, aren't some of them kept in the safe in Phillip's study?"

Actually, now that he thought about it, they were.

For a second all the awkwardness between them dropped away as their eyes met, and Kellan's grin became wider, the two of them sharing in a moment of triumph.

"That's it," he said. "That's a perfect reason to be in there. You're a goddamn genius."

"I know." She smiled, her cheeks pinkening, then gave a little toss of her head, ponytail bouncing. "I mean, my IQ is Mensa level, surely you haven't forgotten that?"

"Not when you keep pointing it out every two seconds."

"I haven't mentioned it once today and you know it." She gave him a look from beneath her lashes. "You just can't handle the fact that I'm smarter than you."

He laughed. Teasing him about the fact that her IQ was bigger than his was familiar, and right now, they could do with familiar. Especially if it stopped this strange awkwardness between them.

And most especially if it stops you thinking about that damn kiss.

Yeah. That most of all.

"Can you fly a helicopter?" His standard comeback.

"No. But I bet it's not hard."

"Talk to me once you've handled a joystick, honey, then we'll decide who's smarter."

"I've handled plenty of joysticks." Sabrina was grinning. Then her expression faltered, the flush in her cheeks getting redder. "I mean gaming joysticks, not . . . I'll shut up now."

Yeah, this was better. This was how it should be. The two of them laughing and teasing each other, making jokes. None of that awkwardness. None of that tension.

He let himself relax. "Good plan. Now you sit tight while I go see if Dad's changed the codes. And if he has, you can put that brain to work figuring out new ones."

"You're not going to call up to the house?"

He'd already decided against it. "Nope. I want complete surprise. Plus, if they're not home that could be an added bonus for us."

A minute later he was by the gates and punching in the code he remembered from years ago. They swung open immediately, which he found vaguely encouraging.

The perfectly groomed gravel driveway made its way to the massive, shaker-style manor, winding through familiar green lawns where he and his father used to play catch, and artfully designed gardens that he'd played hide-and-seek in with his cousins and later, with Sabrina.

The house itself lay at one end of the curving drive, all overhanging eaves and winding ivy around the thick white columns of the veranda. It was grand and gracious, and he'd always loved the place. Mainly for the rolling gardens and the pond down one end of them, since even when he'd been a boy he preferred to be out doing stuff rather than sitting around inside.

He stopped the car right outside the front steps and turned the engine off, he and Sabrina sitting there in silence, staring at the house, contemplating the situation they were about to get themselves into.

"Are you ready?" he asked after a couple of moments had passed.

"As I'll ever be, I guess."

There was something in her voice that made him glance at her, a vulnerable-sounding note. And for a second, as he studied her sharp profile, he realized that being here would mean something to her too, and that he didn't know what that something was.

An odd sensation coiled inside him. As if he was seeing her for the first time, a stranger he didn't know. A woman with sharp features and a pointed chin, freckles dotting her nose and cheeks, glossy curls in a ponytail down her back. A wide, soft-looking mouth . . . Pretty. Yeah, she was pretty. And she had her own memories of this house, of his family. Memories that were pulling the corners of her mouth tight and making her narrow shoulders hunch.

"I'm just . . . not family . . ."

Her voice from a couple of days earlier rang in his head, that same vulnerable note in it, and he suddenly wanted to ask her what she meant by that again. And whether there was something going on, some memory that was bothering her that he didn't know about.

But then she was clicking open her seat belt and taking it off, putting one delicate hand on the door handle. "Come on," she said without looking at him. "Let's get this over and done with."

Kellan reluctantly pushed aside his curiosity, because she was right, the quicker they got this out of the way the better.

He got out of the car, unloaded the bag they'd each brought with them before handing Sabrina her laptop bag, then he went up the front steps, the regal columns laced with ivy on either side, and pressed the doorbell.

There was a silence for a moment, and he could hear Sabrina

breathing softly behind him. Faster than normal. She was nervous.

He half turned to tell her it was all going to be okay, when the grand oak front door pulled open, a small, motherly looking older woman standing on the threshold. Her features were stern, her iron-gray hair pulled back in a bun, but she took one look at him and the sternness dropped away, her face becoming one huge smile.

"Mr. Kellan!" Jane, their English housekeeper, exclaimed, her hands going to her cheeks. "What on earth are you doing here?"

Kellan grinned. "Surprise visit. Can we come in or are we going to camp out on the doorstep?"

Jane laughed, ushering them both into the vaulted foyer with its hardwood floor and the glittering chandelier that dominated the space overhead.

He dumped the bags, then gave the still shocked housekeeper a hug. Jane had been with the family since he'd been a boy and she'd always been one of his favorite people, and he fully admitted that it was because she spoiled him rotten.

Jane emerged from the hug, pink and smiling, her brown eyes darting behind Kellan's shoulder. "And Miss Sabrina too! This *is* a surprise."

"Hi, Mrs. Carson," Sabrina said, lifting an awkward hand.

"When are you going to call me Jane?" The housekeeper's smile deepened. "Mrs. Blake isn't here now, you know." Without waiting for Sabrina to reply, she stepped forward and gave her a hug.

Huh. He'd never noticed before that Sabrina never called Jane by her Christian name. She always called her "Mrs. Carson." He'd assumed it was because Sabrina was chronically shy and preferred being formal. Which was a weird thought to have when he knew that although Sabrina *was* shy, she wasn't formal at all. And actually, why would his mother's presence make any difference?

Puzzled, he studied Sabrina's stiff form as she endured Jane's hug, a forced-looking smile on her face. It was nerves, surely? It had to be. Jane, for all her Englishness, had never stood on ceremony, and he'd thought Sabrina treated her the way he treated her, as a friend.

Apparently not.

Jane stood back from Sabrina and beamed at them both. "So what brings you here? Mrs. Blake didn't mention anything to me nor did Mr. Phillip."

"Well, there's a reason for that." Kellan gave her an easy smile. "Because I didn't tell them we were coming."

Jane clasped her hands together, pleased. "Wonderful! And are you staying?"

"Yeah, a couple of days I think. Where's Mom and Dad?"

"Oh, they're in the white sitting room, but—"

"Jane?" His mother's voice floated down the hallway ahead of them, her heels tapping the parquet. "I heard a car. Who's visiting . . . ?" Her voice trailed into silence as she appeared through the open double doors that led to the back of the house and stopped dead.

Charlotte Blake was small and perfectly formed, and groomed from the top of her blond head to the soles of her not-too-high Chanel pumps. Even in her late sixties she was still beautiful, with blue eyes and an exquisite bone structure that gave the illusion that she was at least ten years younger than she actually was.

There was shock in her eyes as she stared at him that morphed into a wild burst of happiness, before quickly being dampened into something more acceptable. His mother, like his father, did not believe in emotional displays and kept herself under tight control at all times.

His urge was to give her the same kind of hug that he'd

given Jane, but as always, he ignored it. Physical affection was not done in the Blake household.

"Hi, Mom," he said, settling for smiling at her instead. "Bet you weren't expecting us, huh?"

Charlotte blinked, her features rearranging themselves into lines of reserved pleasure. "But how wonderful to see you, darling." She came forward and lifted her face for a kiss on the brow—the only display of affection she'd allow—then stood back, glancing at Sabrina. "And Sabrina too. This *is* a surprise." Her smile faded, her forehead creasing, her hands clasped in front of her. "What brings you both here? Is something wrong?"

Of course, that was his mother. Always thinking the worst.

"No, the opposite in fact."

"Oh?" Charlotte glanced at Sabrina again, then back at Kellan, her blond brows arching.

Here went nothing.

Calmly Kellan reached out and wound his arm around Sabrina's waist, drawing her in tight to his side. There was a moment of resistance, her body stiffening the way it had in Jane's hug, then, clearly remembering her role, she relaxed against him.

Charlotte blinked again, her eyes widening.

"We're here because we wanted to surprise you." Kellan forced a wide grin. "Plus, tell you in person."

"Tell me?" The crease between Charlotte's brows deepened as she stared at them. "Tell me what?"

Kellan met his mother's blue gaze. "That Sabrina and I are together. And that we're going to get married."

It was all Sabrina could do not to shiver as Kellan's voice echoed around the foyer, deep and sure, saying the words that half of her had always secretly longed to hear, while the other half had dreaded hearing it. Watching the shock cross Charlotte Blake's lovely face, before vanishing beneath the perfect mask of reserve she wore. She gave them both a slightly disbelieving smile. "Kellan, darling. You know I don't do jokes very well. Come on, what's the real reason for your visit?"

Kellan's arm was heavy around her waist, holding her firmly against his side. Standing next to him made her feel protected and yet at the same time oddly vulnerable as well.

"No joke, Mom." His voice was full of warmth, steady and sure. "It happened in San Diego while I was recovering. We realized what we meant to each other and . . . well. I asked her to marry me a couple of days ago." He said it so easily, so naturally. As if it were fact and not a total pack of lies.

Sabrina struggled to keep her breathing level, to meet Charlotte's gaze. She couldn't quite manage a smile, but she hoped she at least had a little of that "just engaged" glow to make it convincing.

But Charlotte was frowning, looking back and forth between them as if she couldn't quite believe what Kellan was saying. "Engaged? You and Sabrina?" She sounded appalled.

Sabrina's stomach lurched. She'd always known that Charlotte Blake would never accept it if she and Kellan got together, should a miracle occur and Kellan decided that he felt the same way about her as she felt about him. But before, that knowing had been theoretical. Not so much now. Charlotte *was* appalled, Sabrina could see it in her eyes.

She swallowed, trying to ignore the dip in her gut, a sick feeling that she got every so often, when Charlotte wanted to make it clear that although Sabrina was part of the family, she wasn't a Blake and never would be.

Beside her, Kellan stiffened, the arm around her waist tightening. "Yeah, Mom." The warmth had vanished from his voice, leaving behind it a note of challenge. "Me and Sabrina. Is there a problem with that?"

Instantly the frown lifted from Charlotte's face and she smiled, giving a small laugh. "No, of course not. You simply . . .

surprised me. And I can't deny it's a shock." Her gaze shifted to Sabrina's and Sabrina didn't miss the accusation and hurt gleaming there—masked, but still obvious. "You never told me anything about this, Sabrina dear."

"No, I'm sorry." She sounded hoarse and shaky. "It all happened so fast and I—"

"I didn't want her to say anything," Kellan interrupted smoothly. "I wanted it to be a surprise for you and Dad."

Charlotte's mouth twitched and much to Sabrina's relief, her attention shifted back to her son. "Well, you certainly did surprise me. And your father's going to be very surprised too."

"After which you'll both be extremely supportive of our decision, I hope." Kellan's tone made it clear that it was not a question. "And don't worry, we're not talking weddings just yet. We thought we'd give it a year or so before we start organizing shit like that."

"Language, Kellan," Charlotte chided automatically. She was smiling, but Sabrina didn't think it was because she was happy. No, she was smiling because that was her default when it came to news she didn't like.

Just like someone else you know.

She gave Kellan a sidelong glance and sure enough, he was smiling too. His usual easy smile, yet Sabrina could see the slight edge to it. A muscle jumped in the side of his jaw and there was a hard glitter in his eyes. He was pissed with his mother's response, that was for sure.

Her chest felt tight at that, but she wasn't quite sure why.

"Sorry, Mom," he said, not sounding sorry in the slightest. "Shall we go break the happy news to Dad?"

Beside them, there was a discreet cough and Sabrina remembered that Jane was still standing there.

"Shall I prepare the red bedroom?" the housekeeper asked, beaming, as though the sudden tension that had gathered in the foyer didn't exist.

"Oh, but they're not married yet," Charlotte said. "So I think we'll keep to separate bedrooms—"

"No, we won't," Kellan interrupted yet again, his voice hard. "There'll definitely be no separate bedrooms. Sabrina and I are together, Mom. I'm sure I don't have to point out to you what that means."

Sabrina's mouth had gone dry. She hadn't thought about the whole sleeping issue—couldn't, if she was honest with herself—but looked like she was going to have to think about it now.

Sleeping in the same room as Kellan. In the same bed. Together . . .

Shit. She almost agreed with Charlotte.

Charlotte had gone a delicate shade of pink. "Kellan, please. There's no need for that."

"Maybe she's right—" Sabrina began.

Only to have the rest of her sentence die unsaid as Kellan turned his head and pinned her with that ice-blue gaze. "I don't think you want separate rooms, do you, baby?" He sounded lazy, but the look in his eyes was not.

Baby. He'd called her baby.

Heat whispered over her skin. From this angle, held close against him, she had to tip her head back even farther to look at him, making her conscious of his height and how intimidating he could be.

She hated "baby" as an endearment and she wasn't fond of being intimidated either, so why the hell should she find that hot? Then again, pretty much everything he did made her hot, so maybe that was no surprise.

"I . . . I . . ." she stuttered.

"No," he said softly. "You don't. Not when you know how much I like talking in bed with you."

Talking in bed? What did he mean by that? They'd never . . .

Abruptly realization arrowed through her. This whole mission was going to be a lot easier if they had a private place to talk and debrief.

"Talking . . . Right." She gave him a slight nod to show him she understood. "Of course, uh, h-honey."

Amusement gleamed briefly in his eyes at her slight stutter, which she couldn't decide whether to be offended about or not, but then Jane said, "The red bedroom it is then. Leave your luggage here and I'll get it sorted," and bustled off without another word.

Kellan turned back to his mother, that easy grin still plastered to his face. "So where's Dad? Let's go break the news to him."

Charlotte's mouth thinned. "He's in the white sitting room."

"Great." Kellan loosened his arm around Sabrina's waist and she had a moment of bittersweet relief, but then he reached out and threaded his fingers through hers. "Let's go."

He didn't wait for his mother, striding straight on through the double doors ahead of them and on down the hallway, and Sabrina had no choice but to go with him.

She didn't dare look at Charlotte as they went past, but she could hear the older woman following them down the hall, her heels tapping on the parquet.

Sabrina dragged in another deep, silent breath, the churning in her gut getting stronger. She hadn't realized how much bigger Kellan's hand was until those long, powerful fingers were wrapped around hers, his large palm almost enclosing her hand entirely. A possessive hold.

A lie. A lie. A lie.

Right. Of course. And she couldn't let herself get used to this. But that didn't mean she couldn't enjoy it, right? Besides, the warmth of his skin and the firmness of his grip was reassuring and right now, with Charlotte radiating disapproval behind her and Phillip's reaction in front of her, she needed reassurance.

She found her fingers tightening around Kellan's as they got to the end of the grand wood-paneled hallway, where it opened out into a long, light sitting room with windows along one wall. The view was of rolling green lawns, the gleam of the pond at the bottom of the gardens visible, and close by, the pool and the pool house. The sea lay beyond the gardens and pond, sunlight shifting and glittering off its surface.

The room itself was *Better Homes and Gardens* elegant, deep couches and armchairs upholstered in cream linen with lots of little side tables in dark wood scattered around. On more than one table were vases of Charlotte's favorite flower, white camellias, their petals creamy against the glossy green of their leaves.

It should have been a restful room, but Sabrina had never found it to be particularly restful. Not when the majority of times she'd been in here had involved being the ear into which Charlotte poured her anxiousness about her son and her bitterness about her husband, or the few instances when she'd been asked to serve drinks at one of the Blakes' "informal get-togethers."

She tried to relax and failed as the tall form of Phillip Blake unfolded itself from one of the armchairs down the end of the room. He'd always been an imposing man and even now, over seventy, he still was. Tall and broad, and only just a little shorter than his son. It was obvious where Kellan got his looks though; his father's were the same Hollywood movie-star perfection, even with the lines and wrinkles of age. His eyes were the same color too, though Phillip's generally didn't hold the warmth that Kellan's did. They were flinty, hard. But then the general was a hard man and always had been.

Sabrina instinctively tightened her grip on Kellan's hand as Phillip cast aside the paper he'd been reading and peered sharply over the top of his glasses. Kellan didn't glance at her, but he gave her fingers a squeeze, letting her know that everything was going to be okay.

It helped as Phillip's gaze settled first on his son, then on Sabrina, then back to Kellan again.

"Hey, Dad," Kellan said, lifting his free hand toward his father. "How are you doing?"

"Pretty good." Phillip smiled as he approached to shake his son's hand, his sharp blue eyes searching Kellan's face, before dropping down to where Sabrina had her fingers wrapped around Kellan's. If he had a reaction to it, Sabrina couldn't read it. "This is unexpected," Phillip said, that faint smile still playing around his mouth. "What are you doing here, son?"

"Kellan and Sabrina have an announcement," Charlotte murmured from behind them.

"An announcement, huh? Sounds exciting." The warmth in his smile didn't reach his eyes or color his voice; Phillip Blake had emotional control down to an art form.

Kellan dropped his father's hand, though he didn't let go of Sabrina's. "Sabrina and I are engaged," he said in the same challenging tone as he'd taken with his mother, never taking his attention from his father's face. "We arranged a surprise visit because we wanted to tell you in person."

Sabrina's heart was beating fast and very loudly, and her mouth had gone bone dry. She didn't have a close relationship with Phillip Blake and there were reasons for that, and right now, she had to admit that she was a little afraid of his reaction. Not that he would do anything to her, but that he'd say something outright disapproving. Which would anger Kellan. And God knew, right now, the last thing they—the mission—needed was to have Kellan's already strained relationship with his father get even more strained.

"Engaged," Phillip repeated, his eyes widening slightly. "You and Sabrina?"

Tension had started to gather in the room, Sabrina could feel it. Shit, this was a problem for Phillip as well, as she'd known it would be.

"Yeah, me and Sabrina." Kellan's edged smile was back.

Sabrina braced herself as Phillip looked at her for a long second, something hard gleaming in his eyes. No, he was definitely *not* happy. But then she'd known he wouldn't be. Both he and Charlotte would always want more for their precious boy than the ex-gardener's daughter.

"Well, well, well," Phillip murmured, mercifully glancing back at Kellan. "I have to say, I would never have picked that."

Kellan's whole body tensed. "Why not?" His teeth were white in his smile. "Sabrina and I have been friends a long time. It's almost a natural progression, wouldn't you say?"

The tension in the air got even thicker.

God, this was turning out pretty much the way she'd expected, though clearly not how Kellan thought it would go. But then he'd never fully understood her place in the Blake household, had he? He'd thought she'd been embraced the way his mother had always declared, that she was part of the family, no distinction. Yet despite all the nice sounding declarations, there *were* distinctions, and Sabrina had been made clear what they were from the moment Charlotte had taken her in.

Oh, she was welcome, no doubt about that. And that the Blakes' house was her house. But she could never be a Blake. She would never be a daughter, not a real one. She was alternately the ear Charlotte poured her troubles into when Charlotte needed emotional support, and the poor abandoned stray that had been generously taken in when Charlotte needed to prove what good people the Blakes were.

She was sort of part of the family, but not really. And she must always remember that. She wasn't part of that world and never could be.

Which was fine. She'd known from the start that's how it would be. Yet Kellan had never seen those distinctions. He'd treated her as if she was fully a family member. Which was the beauty and torture of it all, because she loved him for the fact that he didn't see those distinctions, and hated him for the fact that he treated her like he did a sister.

You're fucked up.

Yeah, when it came to him, she totally was.

A heavy silence had fallen and Sabrina opened her mouth to say something—anything—when Charlotte forestalled her. "Kellan, why don't you sit down? I'll get Jane to bring you and your father a beer. You can discuss it, while Sabrina and I have a quiet word."

Oh, fuck. There was no doubt what "a quiet word" was going to entail. Charlotte would want all the details about her supposed love affair with Kellan, all the while radiating those disapproving vibes. Then she'd probably let Sabrina know in no uncertain terms that an engagement with her son was *not* what they had planned for Kellan. Not that they had any say in what Kellan did these days, but still. It would be yet another round of "Sabrina, know your place."

"Not now, Mom," Kellan said flatly, taking his attention off his father to glance at her. "In fact, why don't you and Dad sit down and have a beer and discuss it? Sabrina and I need to get our room organized." The smile had totally gone from his face now, the expression on it just as intimidating as the one on his father's. "We'll come back down once you two are ready to be happy for us."

Charlotte's mouth opened slightly, shock flitting through her blue eyes, while Phillip said gruffly, "Kellan."

But Kellan had already turned back toward the doors that led to the hall, his fingers tightening around her hand. "Come on, baby. Looks like they need a good half hour to rethink their fucking attitude."

And without waiting for her to speak, he strode from the room, pulling her right along with him.

CHAPTER 6

The red bedroom was up the stairs and at the back of the house, its view over the lawns similar to the sitting room downstairs, except it was at one end, and had another window that looked out across his mother's lavender garden.

Despite its name, it was decorated in neutral creams, with a massive four-poster oak bedstead against one wall and a low couch underneath the window opposite. The red designation came from the red velvet throw pillows on the bed and on the couch, and from the beautiful hand-knotted silk Persian rug on the floor.

A hand-knotted silk Persian rug that Kellan didn't give a shit about as he paced back and forth on it, his boots grinding pieces of the gravel driveway into the fabric.

Mostly because he was fucking pissed.

The necessity of lying had put him in a foul temper anyway, and then had come his mother's reaction to the news of his and Sabrina's engagement, which had annoyed him intensely. Then his father had looked at Sabrina like she'd just crawled out from under a rock, and every protective instinct inside him had gone on high alert.

It shouldn't bother him, he knew that, because it wasn't like the engagement was real and it wasn't the reason they were here anyway, but still. It was clear both his parents were highly disapproving and that pissed him off.

Naturally, their very reserved reaction to his unexpected arrival had only added fuel to the fire, though again, it wasn't like he expected parades through the streets and overjoyed tears. His parents didn't like displays of emotion and had brought him up the same way, and there were very good reasons for his own tendency to keep a lock on his emotions, but again, a smile of genuine pleasure wouldn't have gone amiss.

It's never going to be the same, and you know it.

Yeah, he did know it. He was ex-military now, the accident having destroyed their dreams for him, and they didn't know what to do with that. They'd been proud of his military career and now that had gone, they couldn't handle it. He wasn't their golden boy anymore.

You lost that title when Dad found out about Pippa.

Kellan pushed that thought aside. He'd made up for that mistake to his father, more than made up for it. Besides, it had nothing to do with him and Sabrina. Just like the accident didn't have anything to do with him and Sabrina.

"Kel," Sabrina murmured. "It's okay."

She was sitting on the end of the huge four-poster, watching him pace, concern in her hazel eyes. And it only irritated him further that the concern was for him.

"It's not okay," he growled. "You should be pissed too."

"Why? Because they didn't immediately shower us with congratulatory hugs?" She lifted a narrow shoulder. "It doesn't matter. It's not real."

She was right. Yet that didn't do anything to calm the anger that churned in his gut.

He came to the end of the carpet and turned, grinding yet more gravel into the fibers of the silk. "I don't care. They could at least have offered more than 'it's a shock' or 'how unexpected.' And why did Mom want a word with you anyway?"

"I don't know." Sabrina dark lashes came down as she glanced away from him, leaning back on her hands. "We're not here for that though. We're here to find that file."

The way she was leaning had pulled the cotton of her plain red T-shirt tight across her chest, fitting closely to the swell of her small, high breasts, outlining her long, elegant body. And he found he'd stopped pacing and was staring at her.

Jesus Christ, what is wrong with you? Why are you looking at her tits?

Excellent fucking point. He shouldn't be.

Even more angry and this time at himself, Kellan dragged his gaze away, shoved his hands in his pockets, and paced to the end of the carpet before turning and pacing back again.

"Why would getting engaged to you be such a goddamn problem?" he demanded. "I would have thought they'd be fucking over the moon."

"I don't want to say it—"

"So don't."

"But I told you so."

He growled. She'd told him this would be their response. And he'd ignored her.

She sighed. "Let it go. We're stuck with it now. And think of how pleased they'll be when we tell them we called it off."

Again, she was right. But for some reason he *couldn't* let it go. He kept seeing the look of shock on his mother's face, the disapproval he'd felt radiating from her, and the cold look his father had given Sabrina.

It was not what he'd expected. Yes, he'd known their preferences in partner for him—they were old money and they wanted him to marry old money. But he'd thought both his parents viewed her as part of the family and even if they didn't entirely approve, they'd at least be happy for him and for Sabrina.

Apparently not.

They haven't been happy with anything you've done for years, not really.

Well, no. But hadn't he told himself after the accident that as long as he was still challenging himself, it didn't matter what they thought?

"Fine," he muttered, coming to a stop at last. "Let's forget that then. So, you're okay with sharing the room?"

She pushed herself upright, giving him a fleeting glance before looking around, a faint stain of color washing over her cheeks. "Sure. It'll give us opportunity to discuss what we're doing without worrying about being overheard, right?"

"Yeah, that was the plan."

"I'm good with it." She patted the mattress she was sitting on. "You have the bed and I'll take the—"

"*You* are having the bed," he growled. "And *I'll* take the couch."

She frowned. "Don't be stupid. The couch is way too small for you."

Jesus, please don't say they were going to have an argument about sleeping arrangements.

"I'm a goddamn gentleman and you're having the bed," he said flatly. "End of story."

Sabrina opened her mouth as if to argue, but he glared at her until she threw up her hands. "Okay, okay, I'll take the bed. Be uncomfortable, see if I care."

"Hey, you're going to be doing all the work on this mission, so you're going to need the rest." Still angry and not sure what to do with himself, he prowled around the room before stopping in front of the windows and glancing out. Jane had opened one window, the smell of lavender from the garden beneath floating up and scenting the air.

A memory stirred deep inside him, of being in that garden the night of the midsummer party, where Pippa had told him—

No, fuck. He wasn't going to think about that.

Turning away from the window, he found Sabrina watching him, and he thought he saw something hot and bright glow in the depths of her hazel gaze. But whatever it had been vanished so quickly, he wondered if he'd imagined it.

"You okay?" he asked, curious.

"I'm fine." She pushed herself off the bed, going over to where her laptop bag was resting on the couch. "Don't worry about me. Have you called Faith? We'd better let them know we're in position."

A change of subject. Interesting.

"You're not fine." He watched her tug the laptop out of her bag and carry it back over to the bed, very determinedly not looking in his direction. "Mom and Dad were—"

"I can handle it." She sat down on the bed cross-legged, balancing her laptop on her knees as she opened it up. "You should call Faith."

"Fuck Faith," he muttered. "And if you could handle it, why the hell did you squeeze my hand so hard downstairs?"

A familiar stubbornness tightened her jaw. "I did not squeeze your hand."

"You did. When we saw Dad."

She didn't look up from her screen, her fingers moving fast over the keyboard. "I was nervous. You know I'm not a very good liar."

He wanted to tell her he hadn't liked the way his father had looked at her, but he didn't want to draw it to her attention if she hadn't noticed.

You know she noticed, come on. She's not stupid. Or blind.

"Dad was an asshole."

"He's always an asshole." Her fingers stopped dead on the keys and she looked up all of a sudden, meeting his gaze and flushing. "I mean . . . He's not all the time. Sorry, I shouldn't have said—"

"It's okay," Kellan interrupted. "It's the first honest thing I think you've said all day." And the way she'd said it, so casually, as she was distracted by her computer, had the ring of truth to it too.

She thought his father was an asshole.

She's not wrong.

Okay, maybe she wasn't. He could be very charming when he wanted to be, but he was also very demanding and had extremely high standards, as Kellan had good reason to know.

He just hadn't thought his father had been an asshole to her.

The flush in her cheeks went deep red, and she looked down at her computer screen, not saying a word.

"Did he do something to you?" Kellan didn't bother to make it sound like a request. "And you'd better fucking tell me, Bree. Now is not the time to be screwing around with this kind of shit. I'm not in the mood."

There was a brief silence.

Then she said, "What makes you think he did anything?"

Kellan tried to hold on to his patience. "Oh, maybe the small fact that if he hadn't, you wouldn't be calling him an asshole."

"He hasn't done anything."

Kellan waited, but she didn't continue. So he took a few steps over to the bed and stopped in front of it, looking down at her where she sat on the mattress.

Her jaw was tight, her generous mouth in a line, her gaze glued to her screen. And he wanted to reach out and take her small, pointed chin in his hand and tilt her head back so she'd look at him.

His fingers itched, his heartbeat beginning to get faster, and suddenly all he could think about was that kiss in his apartment before they'd left San Diego. The heat of her mouth, the taste of her, so unexpectedly delicious . . .

Jesus, no, he couldn't be thinking about that. Which meant touching her was possibly not a good idea.

His mood, already shitty, was not improved by that fact, so instead, he reached out and pulled the laptop out of her hands.

"Hey!" Her head jerked up, outrage crossing her face. "What the hell are you doing?"

Ignoring her, he shut the laptop and tossed it down on the mattress beside her, then leaned down, putting one hand on the bed on either side of her knees, so his gaze was on a level with hers. "Like I said, I'm not in the fucking mood. So why don't you tell me what's going on for once?"

He knew it was a mistake the moment those big green-gold eyes of hers met his. And the air between them suddenly became thick with the sort of tension that had never been between them before and shouldn't be there now. Yet it was.

And he was conscious of her familiar scent and the quick sound of her breathing, and there was more gold than green in her gaze, glowing bright. She was staring at him, the pulse at the base of her throat fast, her pupils dilating. Her lips were so close. Right *there.* All he'd have to do to taste her again would be to lean forward a little more . . .

Sabrina's gaze dipped. It was only a small slip and lightning fast, but he caught it all the same. He was too close to her not to.

Holy shit, she'd looked at his mouth.

Did that mean . . .

"Your father argued when Charlotte decided to take me in," Sabrina said, her husky voice flat and oddly expressionless. "He didn't view me as part of the family, no matter what Charlotte said, and he made it really clear to me that I wasn't. So that's the reason I think your father's an asshole." There was anger in her eyes now, thick and hot. "Happy now?"

* * *

She hadn't wanted to say all of that, *really* hadn't wanted to say it. She'd much rather have snatched back her laptop and continued working on the program she was in the middle of writing, because that was so much easier than dealing with Kellan and all this emotional bullshit.

But she was angry. He'd bent down and put his hands on the mattress, and now he was so damn close to her. All she could see were those winter-sky eyes, his hard jaw, his broad shoulders blocking out the windows. Blocking out the entire freaking world.

She shouldn't have looked at his mouth, it had been a stupid thing to do, but she hadn't been able to help herself. And he'd noticed, because he noticed damn well everything. And of course things had suddenly gotten very tense and she hadn't known what to do.

Every part of her was screaming at her to back away, get off the bed and put some distance between them. But she was sick of always being the one to do that. Why couldn't he be the one to back away for a change?

So she'd given him the truth he'd wanted, about his father. Not the whole truth, because she'd sworn to herself that he'd never know about that, but a part of it. The part that related to her.

Shock flickered through his gaze, and he pushed himself away from her with a sharp movement.

You made him back down first. Congratulations.

It was a relief and yet she felt the loss of his physical nearness like an ache.

"I know you seem to think they welcomed me with open arms," she went on, because she was angry and the shock in his blue eyes hurt her. "But they didn't. Yes, they gave me a place in the family, but it wasn't the same place as you. And they made sure I knew it."

Kellan said nothing for a long moment, simply standing there staring at her, the look on his face impossible to read. Then he turned away, stalking over to the windows, giving her his broad back. Digging into his back pocket, he hauled out his phone, the sunlight coming through the windows tipping his blond hair gold as he bent his head to look down at the screen. He pressed a button, then lifted the phone to his ear. "Faith? Yeah, we're here."

Sabrina's throat felt thick, her chest tight. She hadn't wanted him to know about this, to break the nice little illusion he'd had about her place in the family. Wanted him to keep thinking that both his parents had treated her no differently than they treated him, since it made him happy to think that.

But a small piece of her wanted him to know the truth. And that small piece of her was glad she'd finally told him, even though it would hurt him. Because why should he be the one who was always left untouched? Why did she have to be the one who was always hurt?

Swallowing back the tightness, Sabrina reached for her laptop again and busied herself with her program as Kellan's smooth voice murmured in the background, giving Faith a debrief and what the plan was going to be.

After a minute, he disconnected the call, putting his phone away as he moved toward the bedroom door. "I'm going to see whether Mom and Dad have changed their attitude. You stay here. I'll get Jane to send you up something to eat."

Sabrina opened her mouth to say that she didn't want anything, but he was gone, the door shutting firmly behind him.

She took a breath, trying to hear his footsteps as he went on down the hall, but he moved so silently she couldn't hear a thing.

No, she couldn't feel bad that she'd told him. It was good that he knew. And anyway, he was the one who'd wanted her to tell him the truth, so she had. It wasn't her fault that he didn't like it.

Yet no matter how hard she tried, she couldn't get rid of the ache in her chest that only got worse the more the day stretched on.

He didn't come back.

About a half hour later, Jane arrived with a sandwich and a glass of milk, as if she was that pale, shy ten-year-old again. Sabrina thanked her and gave a cursory bite of the food and a sip or two of the milk, but she wasn't hungry and didn't finish it.

Taking a break from the program she was writing, she busied herself with setting up her own heavily protected Wi-Fi signal and checking out the local digital environment in case there were any other networks in the area she might have missed from her remote sweep back in San Diego. But there was nothing with the amount of protection that would warrant a second look. Standard home signals in other words.

A few hours passed, the light outside the windows changing and deepening into late afternoon.

Eventually Kellan came back to announce that there would be dinner in the informal dining room, and that she wasn't to worry. He'd had words with both Charlotte and Phillip. They wouldn't be giving her any grief.

True to his word, both Blakes were the very epitome of politeness when she and Kellan came down to dinner. Charlotte asked her a few questions about her job with the 11th Hour, Phillip putting in a couple himself, both of them listening politely as she answered.

The dinner table was smaller than in the formal dining room, the room smaller and more intimate too. She was seated opposite Kellan, with Phillip and Charlotte at either end of the table. There was wine in a crystal decanter and proper silverware, an expensive lace tablecloth, because Charlotte liked to make even informality a little bit elegant.

Both Blakes smiled at her, the conversation flowing easily and naturally. Charlotte's voice was even warm, asking her what San Diego was like, while Phillip engaged his son in military talk.

No one spoke of the engagement, which should have been a relief, but wasn't. Not when Sabrina could feel the tension that lay underneath all the polite words and careful smiles.

Kellan might have told his parents to behave and they were, but nothing had changed. She was still the cuckoo in the nest. A cuckoo who had the temerity to ally herself with the eagle.

It didn't help that throughout the meal she could feel Kellan's sharp gaze on her, watching her. Watching his parents too. Like he was a scout examining a military base for a planned covert operation.

Which, to be fair, he was. Except that she wasn't supposed to be part of the base he was invading. She was supposed to be invading with him.

Eventually the relentless politeness of it all got too much and she wanted out. Putting her napkin down, Sabrina pushed her chair back and pasted a smile on her face, muttering excuses about being tired and needing to go bed.

That got her some surprised looks since it was relatively early, and a few cursory protests, which Kellan handled by also rising from his chair. "Yeah, I think we'll both call it a day," he said, leaving no room for argument. "The flight was long and we need the rest." His blue eyes held hers for a second. "Don't we, baby?"

"Y-yes," Sabrina stuttered. "We do."

Dammit, she was hoping for a bit of time by herself, mostly so she could brace herself for the reality of his presence in the room with her. But it looked like she wasn't even going to get that.

Kellan gave his parents a curt good night, then came over to her and grabbed her hand, pulling her from the room without waiting for a response.

"You don't need to come to bed now," she muttered as he tugged her along the hallway, heading for the grand sweep of the dark oak stairs. "It's still early."

"It's better if we're seen leaving together." He gave her a brief, sharp look. "Besides, I've had about as much as I can stand of both my parents right now."

Sabrina swallowed. "What did you do this afternoon?"

"I went for a run. Then I went and told both of them in no uncertain terms that if they didn't accept you as my fiancée, then they weren't the people I thought they were." He gave a low laugh, no amusement in the sound. "Shit, they're not the people I thought they were anyway."

"I'm sorry." She hadn't wanted to say the words, since it wasn't her fault his parents had treated her the way they had, and she was sick of apologizing all the time. But the apology came out all the same. "I shouldn't have told you about them."

He was halfway up the stairs, pausing to turn and pin her with that sky-blue stare. "Hey, I asked for the truth and you gave it to me."

"I know, but it's not their fault."

A flicker of anger glowed in his eyes. "It's not your fault either."

"I know that."

"Do you?" He searched her face. "Because sometimes you act like it is."

Heat rose in her cheeks, the way he was looking at her making her feel as if the contents of her entire soul were all displayed for him. "I do not," she snapped, vulnerable and hating the feeling. "God, you make me sound like such a doormat." Jerking her hand from his, she let her anger propel her up the stairs past him and down the long wood-paneled hallway.

If she hated feeling vulnerable, she also hated the way she was letting him deal with Phillip and Charlotte. Preventing his mother from having "a talk" and then removing her from the situation at dinner. Like she was a child who couldn't handle herself.

Sure, this situation with him was making her feel uncertain of herself and she'd never been the world's most confident woman, but she *could* handle it. She'd managed herself and her career in Silicon Valley for a number of years, after all. She didn't need him to step in all the goddamn time.

You like it though. You like it when he's protective of you.

Sabrina ignored the thought, opening the door to the bedroom and stepping inside. It was way too early to go to bed, but she didn't care. The quicker this day was over, the better, as far as she was concerned.

She went over to the couch where her case was and flung it open, digging around inside it for the pair of shorts and soft T-shirt she wore when she went to bed.

Behind her, the door closed, making her aware very suddenly that now they were alone. In the bedroom. Together.

"Sabrina," he said quietly.

"I don't want to talk about this right now." Grabbing her sleep gear, she headed toward the en suite bathroom. "I'm going to take a shower. If you wanted the bathroom first . . . Well. Too bad."

She slipped inside, shutting the door behind her firmly, then locking it. Then she went over to the toilet, put the cover down, and sat on it, burying her head in her hands for a couple of moments, trying to calm her heartbeat and stop herself from shaking.

She was letting this get to her way too much. And that was stupid, especially when they had a mission to complete. Maybe it was simply a reaction to being here, being back in this house with Charlotte and Phillip again. Not that either of them had ever been overtly cruel or abusive toward her; no, they'd been kind. Well, Charlotte had been. But it had always been a distant sort of kindness that had left her feeling a little bit empty, a little bit cold.

Kellan was the only one who'd never made her feel that way.

It's him too. You can't deal with him.

But she was going to have to, wasn't she? She was going to have to dig deep and find that determination she'd had back at his apartment when she'd kissed him. And then just . . . get on with what they were here to do.

Feeling a bit better, she debated whether or not to have a bath in the large tub beside the window that looked out over the lavender garden, then decided not to. The massive white tiled and glass shower cubicle looked inviting, and besides, it was less hassle.

Ten minutes later, she crept out of the bathroom dressed in her sleep shorts and T-shirt, only to find the room empty.

Clearly Kellan hadn't wanted to push her into talking about his parents, not when he hadn't even waited until she came out of the bathroom.

She should have felt relieved about that, but she didn't, annoyance winding through her instead. Dumping her clothes on the floor by the bed, she pulled back the quilt and got in. The bed was warm and soft, and she suddenly felt exhausted, wrung out by the emotion of the day and the tension that had colored it.

She'd planned to settle in for a couple of hours, reading, but she must have fallen asleep because the next thing she knew, the room was in darkness, apart from the light shining from the open bathroom door, illuminating the man walking through it: Kellan, naked apart from a towel slung around his lean hips.

His golden skin glistened with moisture, the scars from his burns shiny around his shoulders, the dark ink of his eagle and trident tattoo covering the scars that wrapped around the top of his back. There was another curling around his left arm, something tribal that highlighted the strength of his biceps.

He paused, turning toward her, the light following the hard, cut muscle of his broad chest and abs, gleaming on the scattering of golden hair that arrowed down beneath his towel.

Sabrina shut her eyes, her heart hammering in her chest, her mouth gone bone dry. And he must have thought she was still asleep because eventually he moved, the springs on the couch groaning as he settled down onto it.

She thought she'd never go back to sleep after that, but much to her surprise she did.

Though she dreamed of him all freaking night.

CHAPTER 7

Kellan went for a run early the next morning, needing the exercise to deal with all the weird tension and emotion seething in his gut. An hour later, he returned to the house, heading for the massive farmhouse-style kitchen for some water, only to find his father standing at the counter making coffee.

Excellent timing. He'd been meaning to speak to the old man about getting a ring for Sabrina. Not that his father was going to be thrilled with that, if his reaction to the news of their engagement had been anything to go by, but too bad. They needed some uninterrupted time in his father's study to search for that damn file—if it was even there—and choosing a ring was the best excuse they had to do so.

Besides, he couldn't deny that part of him wanted to push it simply because even though he hated lying to his father, Phillip was being an asshole about the engagement, and Kellan wanted to call him on it. Especially after what Sabrina had told him the day before.

He had no doubt she'd been telling the truth, that his parents hadn't been as warm and welcoming of her as Kellan had always thought, simply because neither of them were particularly warm and welcoming people. And because they weren't, perhaps he should have noticed their treatment of Sabrina earlier.

But he hadn't noticed. He'd just expected that they'd treat Sabrina exactly like they treated him, and it had simply never occurred to him that they wouldn't.

The worst part about it was that it even made sense to him now that Sabrina had said it. His mother had always been very insistent on the importance of family, how a family had to stick together and support each other, while Phillip insisted on loyalty and honoring the family name.

Kellan had experienced those lessons firsthand, and they'd been bitter ones. But he'd learned from them. How necessary it was to put his family first and his own needs second, no matter how strong those needs were.

So mostly he agreed with his parents, yet now, as he leaned an arm against the frame of the kitchen doorway, watching his father fiddle with the coffee maker, he couldn't get the look in Sabrina's eyes out of his head. The anger glowing there and beneath that, a deep and unmistakable hurt.

"He didn't view me as part of the family . . . And he made sure I knew it."

"Hey, Dad," Kellan said into the silence, letting an edge bleed into his voice. "Fancy seeing you here."

His father's head came up and he turned in Kellan's direction. "You're up early, son."

Kellan pushed himself away from the doorway, coming over to where his father stood. "Military training. It sticks around."

Phillip's gaze inevitably slid to the scars on Kellan's shoulders, revealed by the tank top he wore, and Kellan resisted the instinctive tension that crawled through him. Phillip didn't like his scars, yet another reason Kellan had stopped visiting. It was easier on them both if the physical evidence of his failure to be the military hero his father wanted remained hidden.

"Yes." Phillip's voice was so neutral he might as well have screamed his disapproval. "I suppose it does."

Ignoring his father's tone, Kellan gave him an easy smile. "Well, you're not in the military anymore and you're up. And it's not even seven yet."

Phillip returned the smile, though it didn't reach his eyes. "I'm retired. Time to take it easy."

"Seems like a plan. Hey, I wanted to talk to you about something."

"Oh yes?" His father had turned back to the coffee maker, pushing a cup beneath it. For all that his parents had installed a fancy Italian coffee maker, Phillip still preferred good old-fashioned filter. "About what?"

There was no need to beat around the bush, so Kellan didn't. "I haven't gotten Sabrina a ring yet. Mostly because I wanted to give her one of Grandma Jo's."

Phillip glanced at him, his eyes narrowed. "They're heirlooms, Kellan. You can't give her one of those."

Kellan had been expecting this and yet still, the kick of anger inside him made his jaw tighten. "Why not?" He didn't look away. "She's my fiancée."

Phillip stared at him for a long moment. Then he straightened up, his smile fading, his blue gaze hardening. "I'll be honest. Your mother and I aren't happy about this. Not one bit."

"No fucking kidding."

His gaze flickered at Kellan's tone, but all he said was, "Sabrina isn't the girl for you, son."

"Like Pippa wasn't the girl for me, right?"

There was a silence.

Shit, why had he said that? He hadn't meant to bring Pippa up. Christ, he *never* wanted to bring Pippa up. That whole mess with her and the baby was over and done with, and had nothing to do with what was happening now.

His father's expression became granite. "You know why Pippa wasn't the right girl for you. She was married."

An old and familiar pain turned over in Kellan's chest, but he pretended it wasn't there, like he always did. "Yeah, and Sabrina's not."

"That's not the point."

"Then what is?" His smile became sharper. "You're going to have to be clearer, Dad, because I'm having real difficulty figuring out exactly what your problem with Bree is."

"You're not stupid, Kellan." Phillip's voice was flat. "You know exactly the issues your mother and I have with Sabrina. She's a nice girl, but she's not who we want for you. She never has been."

Kellan didn't understand what was with the hot lick of anger that flared inside him. Because it wasn't like this engagement was real, which made his fury pointless. But he hated the implication that Sabrina was somehow not good enough for him.

His parents had always been snobs to a certain extent, but he hadn't realized how snobbish they actually were. Until now.

"She's not good enough," he said, his voice just as flat. "Is that what you're saying?"

Phillip's mouth twitched. "She's the ex-gardener's daughter. And her family . . . Well, let's just say, when I had her investigated, they weren't exactly stellar examples of the institution."

Kellan blinked, a small pulse of shock going through him. "You had her investigated?"

His father stiffened, as if the question had offended him. "I had all employees who came to live here investigated. It's a requirement of any job here."

It made sense and yet that didn't stop the protective anger inside him from burning hotter. She'd been investigated, like a criminal. No, like an employee. Not like a girl who'd lost her mother and her two brothers in a hideous accident, and then been abandoned by her father.

"I can't imagine why you let her live here then." He didn't hold back with the sarcasm. "A poor homeless girl with a shitty family name, sullying the Blake threshold."

His father's jaw had a granite cast to it, his posture every inch the general. "I know you're angry. I get it. But my role is to protect the family, Kellan, and you know that too. I do what I need to do to make sure you and Charlotte are safe."

"Because Sabrina was such a threat."

His father eyed him. "Not all threats look like threats at the time. I would have thought you'd have learned that by now."

He's not wrong,

Yeah, fuck it. Christ, he hated it when his father made logical sense. Because he couldn't argue, couldn't do anything with the emotion that blazed away inside him. Couldn't tell his father he wouldn't have done the same thing if he'd been in his father's position all those years ago, when the mistake he'd made had come back to haunt them.

It still haunts you.

The old pain deepened, a thorn inside him, and he had to turn away, going over to one of the cabinets and taking a glass out of it, needing the movement to distract himself.

"So," he said casually, turning on the tap and filling his glass. "What you're telling me is that some pretty, useless Manhattan socialite is more acceptable than a super smart computer expert?"

Phillip snorted. "I'm not debating Sabrina's accomplishments, which, considering where she came from, are admirable. She doesn't understand our world, Kellan. She's uncomfortable in it, you must have realized that."

Yet again, it made sense. Sabrina had often told him how much she hated all the high society bullshit that the Blakes were entrenched in. The wealth and power of the people the family associated with intimidated her, the social rules surrounding such wealth confusing to her.

"Yeah," he began. "But—"

"In many ways it's almost unfair of you," Phillip interrupted, sensing a vulnerability and going for it. "To drag her into our world and expect her to be happy in it. Have you even asked her if that's what she wants? Or is she doing this just for you?"

Christ. His father always knew how to hit where it hurt the most.

Kellan gritted his teeth, lifting his glass and taking a long swallow of water to cover the burst of frustration that went through him.

He knew what Phillip was doing. Being reasonable and logical was a form of attack the general often employed to get what he wanted. And Kellan had always found it difficult to argue with him, especially when he agreed with all of it.

A memory floated back to him, of sitting in his father's study, despair like acid in his gut as Phillip had pointed out logically, that Pippa was married, that Kellan was only seventeen, that her baby—*his* baby—could not be acknowledged in any way, shape, or form.

That it would be better for the Blake family if Kellan let Phillip deal with the issue privately. So Kellan had let him.

Yeah, because you're such a hero like that.

Kellan put his glass down on the counter so hard it cracked up one side, the sound loud in the silence of the kitchen. He ignored it, turning instead to his father, meeting those cold blue eyes with his own.

"But I'm no longer part of that world myself, am I, Dad? Not after the accident. I'm not your golden boy anymore, which means it doesn't matter where Sabrina came from." He took a step forward, looking his father right in the eye, relishing the slight height difference between them and for once not caring about the lies that were coming out of his mouth. "So I'll be taking one of those heirlooms. And I'll be giving it to her, whether you like it or not. Understand me?"

He didn't wait for an answer, spinning on his heel and leaving his father in the kitchen, striding out and up the stairs toward the bedroom he was sharing with Sabrina, frustrated anger eating away at him.

You fucking idiot. This is pretend and you're acting like it's real.

He was and yet he couldn't seem to stop the feelings from churning away inside him, a protective anger over his friend and a deep disappointment at his parents and their attitude. And maybe the worst part of it was that he wasn't even surprised. Like he'd always known deep down how they viewed Sabrina, he just hadn't wanted to admit it before.

Her presents on Christmas morning were always small and not very personal, and though her birthday was always celebrated, she never had a party. Then there had been that family trip to Europe that Sabrina hadn't come on, his mother telling him that it was because of school work, even though he had the same work. The parties his parents threw for their friends that he was invited to, but Sabrina wasn't. Or if she was, it was only to serve drinks.

Yeah, those small lines of distance, those tiny distinctions, had always been there. And he'd never seen them.

Maybe you didn't want to see them. Just like you didn't want your own child.

The thought slithered through his mind like a snake, but he shoved it straight back out again. No, not thinking about that. Not thinking about *that* again.

He couldn't do anything about it anyway, since it had all happened years ago. And even now, this was moot because he and Sabrina weren't getting engaged. Hell, they weren't even together. Friends. That's all they were.

Pushing open the door to the bedroom, Kellan stepped inside, planning on heading straight into the shower.

Sabrina was still in bed asleep, sprawled on her back. She'd been restless last night—as he had been, stuck on that fucking uncomfortable couch—and now the quilt was pulled down and tangling around her waist. She had her hands flung up above her head, glossy brown curls spilling all over the pillow, and the T-shirt she was sleeping in had rucked up, revealing a lot of pale skin.

Kellan halted, for some reason unable to stop staring at her.

Her T-shirt was pushed up so high he could see the soft underside of her breasts. A little bit more and her nipples would be exposed.

He went hot all over, his heartbeat accelerating as a vision began unrolling in his head, of himself moving over to the bed and bending over her. Gathering her narrow wrists in his hand and pushing them down into the soft pillow, holding them there. Then slowly pulling up her T-shirt to see her tits, touching her . . .

His breath caught and he blinked, becoming conscious that the fabric of his running shorts was oddly constricting.

Yeah. Because you're getting hard.

Oh Christ. He was getting hard for his best friend.

At that moment, a knock came at the door, and he heard his mother's voice on the other side of it. "Kellan?"

Charlotte never found a closed door an obstacle and she didn't now, starting to open it, and he wasn't quite sure what made him close the distance between himself and the bed. What made him sit down next to Sabrina and slide one hand possessively across that bare, vulnerable stomach.

Maybe it was protectiveness, a blatant show to his parents that she was his and they weren't to hurt her. He only knew that when his mother pushed open the door, he made sure he was leaning over Sabrina like a predator over its kill.

"Oh," his mother murmured, sounding flustered. "I didn't mean to interrupt."

Slowly Kellan turned his head and met his mother's shocked gaze, raising a brow. "Anything in particular you want, Mom?"

Her gaze flicked briefly to where his hand rested on Sabrina's stomach, color staining her perfect cheekbones. "I saw your father downstairs," she said, determinedly looking back at him. "He mentioned something about Grandmother Jo's jewelry."

"Yeah and I told him what was going to happen about that." He gave her a lazy grin. "Now is kind of not the time." Beneath his hand, Sabrina's stomach tensed. Okay, she must be waking up.

"Yes, I see that." His mother's expression was tight with disapproval. "I'll talk to you later."

She left, shutting the door emphatically.

Kellan looked away, down at Sabrina, and a small bolt of electricity went through him as he found her hazel gaze staring back. There was shock in it, yet the small golden flecks in her eyes were glittering, bright and hot. Her skin beneath his hand was so soft, so warm. One movement of his thumb and he'd be stroking the tempting underside of one breast.

The pulse at the base of her throat was beating fast, and he couldn't help himself, glancing down at where the cotton of her T-shirt had pulled tight across her tits. Her nipples were hard, the outline of them clear through the fabric.

Holy fucking shit.

Again, he didn't know why he did what he did next. Perhaps it was the disapproval on his mother's face and the fact that he was angry at her. Perhaps it was the fierce protectiveness that suddenly surged through him, a need to show Sabrina that regardless of what his parents thought, he would always be there for her.

Perhaps it was simply that Sabrina's lips were full and red and he wanted to kiss her.

So he did, leaning forward and lowering his head, covering her mouth with his.

Sabrina was barely awake. One minute she'd been deeply asleep, the next she'd felt something warm and heavy on her stomach, and she'd opened her eyes to find Kellan sitting on the bed next to her, still in his running gear, his hand on her abdomen.

There was someone at the door—Charlotte from the sounds of it—and she'd said something. But all Sabrina had been conscious of was that hand resting on her skin, big and hot and heavy. And that familiar ice-blue gaze boring into hers.

Then the door had shut and that searing look dipped to her chest and she'd gone hot all over with shock and embarrassment. Because her body was reacting to him the way it always did: with enthusiastic approval. And now he knew. It was impossible to hide it.

She wanted to cover herself, push him away hard, but before she could move, he'd leaned forward and his mouth had covered hers, and now nothing made any sense at all.

At first confusion at what he was doing made her go rigid, then hard on its heels, heat. A bonfire igniting over every inch of skin she had.

This was nothing like the kiss she'd taken from him back in his apartment. A slow taste, an experiment. This kiss was as if they were already lovers. As if he'd already been inside her many, many times. As if she was his and he could take whatever he wanted from her, and he was as hungry for her as she was for him.

Hard. Hot. Demanding.

He swept his tongue deep inside her mouth and the unexpectedness of it shocked her, thrilled her. Made her shiver all over with reaction. She was tilting her head back before she'd even realized what she was doing, her spine arching into the hot palm resting on her stomach, desperate for his touch.

Then much to her intense disappointment, Kellan abruptly pulled back, leaving her mouth burning, her breathing embarrassingly audible in the silence of the room.

His eyes had gone a deep, sapphire blue and he didn't look away from her. He didn't say anything either, and she knew he was going to kiss her again. She could see it in those incredible eyes. Intent, predatory. Hungry.

Her heartbeat was like thunder in her head, and her hand shot out to push against his chest to stop him before she could think about it, because he could *not* kiss her. He couldn't, not when he didn't mean it and she had no idea why he was even doing it.

Not when her own desire for him was so incredibly obvious.

But almost as soon as her palm connected with the damp cotton of his tank top, the hard surface of his chest beneath it, he was leaning forward, and there was no escape. His mouth was on hers again and she was trembling, burning beneath the demand of it once more.

He leaned forward, his hands coming down on the pillows on either side of her, his chest almost brushing the tips of her breasts.

Her brain wasn't working. Nothing was working. Because his tongue was pushing into her mouth, exploring, demanding. Kissing her like he wanted her. Like he wanted *her.*

Sabrina began to shake, her fingers spreading out on all that rock-hard muscle, the heat of his body seeping into her hand, moving up through her arm, flooding out through the rest of her, igniting her, making her burn.

He was nipping at her bottom lip, licking her, then pushing that wicked tongue of his inside her mouth again, changing the angle of the kiss so he could go deeper, kiss her harder.

A long, low moan of utter need broke from her and she was completely unable to stop it. The sound made tears prickle behind her eyes because he knew now, there was no hiding it. No pretending she didn't want him, that this didn't turn her inside out.

And she could make believe that this kiss was real and that it meant something. But it wasn't and all it meant was that for some reason he'd decided to kiss her. Probably because he hadn't gotten laid for a while and she was the closest available female.

He didn't want *her.* No matter how she told herself he did, and if she let this go on any further it was going to hurt. It was going to break her and right now, with this mission still to accomplish, she couldn't afford to be broken.

It took all her strength, but she did it, shoving hard against his chest and wrenching her mouth from his. "Kellan," she gasped, her voice shaking. "Please stop."

He pulled away, breathing fast, his eyes glittering, his usual fresh scent mixing with the smell of clean male sweat. "Why?" His deep voice sounded even deeper than normal, hoarse and slightly raw.

"Because you don't mean it." The truth tumbled out before she could stop it. "Because it's just for show." Desperately she tried to save herself. "Because you're my *friend!*"

He kept looking at her, that hot blue gaze searching her face, and she couldn't bear it. Shoving hard at him again, she pushed herself past him and off the bed, only to be stopped by a heavily muscled arm winding around her waist.

"Sabrina, wait."

His breath at her ear, his body like a fire against her back. So goddamn close. *Too* goddamn close.

She shut her eyes, struggling to get her lungs to work, to force the raging need back into the cage she kept it in. "If you tell me you're sorry, I'll punch you in the face."

"I'm not going to say that."

"Then if you like your balls hanging where they are, let me the fuck go!"

She didn't think he would, but slowly he withdrew his arm, and she bolted like the coward she was, heading for the bathroom, slamming the door behind her the way she had done the night before.

This time she sat on the edge of the tub, still shaking, arousal and need burning through her like wildfire.

He'd kissed her. Why had he kissed her? His mother had been at the door briefly, so had he been trying to prove some point? It wasn't actually her, because it never had been before and surely nothing had changed. And maybe if she kept telling herself that, one day she'd believe it and it wouldn't hurt. Not that it mattered either way since he was never going to kiss her again, not when all of this was simply pretend.

He wasn't pretending. He kept on kissing you after the door closed.

A shudder went down her spine, her heart twisting inside her chest.

"Bree." Kellan's voice on the other side of the door, low and insistent. "Come out. We need to talk about this."

"No, we don't." God, she sounded like a little girl. "You proved your point or whatever it was to your mother. The end."

He laughed, a rough sound without amusement. "That's . . . not exactly what it was."

"Then what was it?" She gripped the side of the tub hard, then added for good measure, "Not that I care."

He made a growling noise. "I'm not talking to you through this fucking door."

"Then don't talk to me at all."

There was a silence and she thought he'd gone. But then he said, "We still have to get into Dad's study. He's being stubborn about the heirloom thing, which means we're going to have to go in there at night, or I'll have to distract him somehow."

Oh, crap. The mission. Of course.

You can't keep hiding in here. You can't keep running away every time he makes you uncomfortable.

Sabrina swallowed. No, she couldn't and avoiding him wasn't the answer anyway. He'd know by now that she was into him and into that kiss he'd given her. *So* into it. In fact, he would've had to be blind and deaf not to understand, especially after that goddamn moan she'd let escape. And he'd been with a lot of women. He wouldn't mistake that moan for anything other than total pleasure.

Great. Why couldn't this be more like coding and computers? Where everything operated according to rules and logic? Computers were simple, a collection of on/off switches and binary choices. But this wasn't simple. This was emotional and emotions were unpredictable and messy. They didn't obey any rules and logic never worked. And it didn't matter how smart she was, she always ended up feeling stupid.

She hated that.

Still, she had to deal with it. Which meant going out there and facing him. Facing also the fact that she wanted him and now he knew that she did. But she could handle it. Hell, she was going to have to. The alternative was hiding in the bathroom like a teenager, and she couldn't do that, not when she was a grown-ass woman.

Gathering what remained of her dignity, Sabrina pushed herself off the tub and straightened up. Then she went to the door and—taking a deep breath—she pulled it open.

He was standing right in front of it, unexpectedly close, his arms folded, which only highlighted the broadness of his chest and the way the tank top he wore fitted tightly to all that cut muscle. And when his gaze met hers, all the air in the room vanished, because he had that very same look in his eyes as he'd had before he'd kissed her. A deep, predatory sapphire blue.

She tried to ignore the way her heart was slamming against her ribs and her blood pumping hard in her veins. Tried to meet his gaze and hold it. "Do that again and I'll kill you," she said and thank God her voice didn't shake this time.

The look in his eyes didn't even flicker. "It wasn't to prove a point."

"I don't care. Just don't do it again."

"But you didn't want me to apologize."

Oh God. Oh God. "Kellan—"

"You said I didn't mean it." He kept on staring at her, as if she was the only thing worth looking at in the entire world. "You said it was just for show."

No, she didn't want to have this conversation.

Idiot. He already knows. What's the point in denying it now? You wanted to face him, so face him.

Sabrina steeled herself and stood her ground, gathering her courage despite the desperate urge to run the hell away. "Well, isn't it?" she shot back. "It's not like you had a sudden burning desire for me, right?"

The light in his eyes glittered, so blue. "And what if I did?"

Shock poured through her, making her shiver like a burst of cold water sprayed over hot skin. "No," she said, because she couldn't think of anything else to say. "No. Don't lie to me."

"That kiss wasn't a lie."

She was shaking her head automatically. He couldn't be telling the truth. It made no sense for him to suddenly, after all these years of treating her as nothing more than a friend, decide that he wanted her as more. As a woman. Because there weren't a lot of men that did. And she should know since her dating career in the male-dominated industries of Silicon Valley hadn't exactly been stellar.

They liked her, but they didn't want to date her. She simply wasn't the type of woman men were passionate about, and she'd come to terms with that a long time ago.

"No," she repeated. "You don't want me. You wanted to prove a point to your mother. It wasn't me."

His jaw hardened, a muscle flicking along the sharp line of it. "How the fuck would you know?"

"Because you've never wanted me before!" She hadn't meant to say it so loud, but it came out shrill and desperate, reverberating off the walls of the bedroom.

But he didn't even blink at her tone, making it worse instead by looking down the length of her body, deepening her awareness of the fact that she was only wearing her sleep shorts and T-shirt and nothing else.

Then his gaze came back to hers very deliberately, the tension between them gathering like a storm approaching. "What if I changed my mind?"

Anger leapt high inside her.

She took a step forward, pushing a finger hard against his heavily muscled chest. "No, *fuck* no. You don't get to do this. You don't get to suddenly decide you want me after years of treating me like your best buddy." She forgot she was supposed to be pretending that she didn't care. Forgot that she was supposed to be indifferent. Rage was a fire in her blood, giving her a strength she'd never known she possessed. "I have wanted you for *years,* Kellan Blake. Fucking *years.* Do you know what that's been like for me? Do you understand how goddamn hard that's been?" She poked at him again, and he took a step back, his eyes widening in shock. "And all of a sudden you're kissing me and telling me you've changed your mind after all this time? Two words: Fuck. No." She stared into that icy-blue gaze she'd loved for longer than she could remember. "And also screw you, asshole."

He said nothing, searching her face as if he'd never seen her before in his life, tall and broad and so fucking hot she couldn't handle it.

But no, she *was* going to handle it. And she wasn't backing down this time. Perhaps she shouldn't have given him the truth, but too bad. If he was going to pull this shit with her, he had to know her feelings about it. That it wasn't okay. That she wasn't some woman he'd picked up in a bar that he could have sex with for the night and then forget in the morning. She would never be that woman and certainly not for him.

So she said nothing too, merely let him see the truth, stark in her eyes.

"Bree . . ." he murmured and a small flash of triumph went through her at the roughness in his voice. "Fuck, why didn't you tell me?"

"Why the hell do you think? Work it out, genius." She was still trembling, though her anger was starting to fade, leaving her feeling vulnerable and a bit sick. God, she needed to get dressed because standing around half dressed was not helping.

Sidestepping him, she went over to where she'd left her case on the floor by the bed, pulling some clothes out.

She was conscious of him behind her, his silence an indication of how much of a shock her revelation had been to him.

Well, good. About time he felt some of the shit she was feeling too. Being the only one this mattered to was exhausting.

Gathering up her clothes, she turned back.

He was watching her, staring at her as if she was a complete stranger.

But Sabrina had no patience for that crap, not anymore. She walked up to him, lifting her chin. "What? Can't handle it? Join the club, dickhead."

His mouth went hard, the deep blue of his eyes getting lighter, icier. "You should have said something. How was I to know how you felt? I'm not a fucking mind reader, Bree."

"Well, you should have been," she snapped, the hurt beginning to bite now that the protective layer of anger had gone. "I've been reading *your* goddamn mind for years. Maybe you should have tried reading mine for a change."

"I didn't think—"

"No, I know you didn't. And you know what? It's time you did, because I'm sick of being the smart one. Now get out of my way. I need to get dressed."

There was an instant when she thought he wouldn't, where the look in his eyes sharpened and she had no idea what he might do.

Her heart rate began to climb, but then he turned and gestured wordlessly toward the bathroom door, leaving her no option but to walk through it.

CHAPTER 8

Sabrina's anger was still simmering hours later. Kellan had gone off with his father—golfing, of all things—another attempt to change his mind about the heirloom thing, or at least, that's what Kellan had muttered to her when he'd met her in the foyer by the front door.

She'd had an idea already about how to get around that, but there was no time to explain it to him, not that she had the inclination anyway.

Coming out of the bathroom after her outburst, she'd found the room empty, Kellan obviously in no mood to finish their conversation, which was just as well because she wasn't in the mood either.

Instead, she wandered into the other wing of the house, trying to act casual, before creeping down the hallway toward Phillip's study in order to do a quick reconnaissance. The door—predictably—was closed, so after a glance around to make sure no one else was in the vicinity, she crouched down to study the heavy-duty lock to see if it was something she could open. It was a coded keypad, which meant she could hack it, but that would involve crouching outside the door with her computer and that was going to look a little obvious. Far easier to get Phillip himself to unlock the door and let them in.

Except from what Kellan had said, Phillip was not inclined to let them choose an heirloom engagement ring from the safe, which meant getting into his study was going to be a problem.

Luckily for the mission, Sabrina had already thought of an alternative. It wasn't going to be pleasant and she was going to have to be brave, but shit, she'd already told Kellan how she felt about him, so undertaking her plan should be a piece of cake. Especially with her still simmering anger to sustain her.

All she had to do was find Charlotte.

She was about to rise from her crouch when she suddenly heard a click on the other side of Phillip's door, then it began to open.

She'd never moved so fast in her life.

Heart in her mouth, Sabrina bolted around the corner of the hallway and pressed herself up against the wall, struggling to control her breathing.

She could hear Phillip's voice and it sounded like he was on the phone to someone.

"What do you mean the shipment didn't go through?" Anger threaded through his tone. "You were supposed to have paid enough to make sure it did."

A door shut with a heavy thump.

"What?" There was a pause. "Why? I told you this was important. The people waiting for it aren't going to be happy and you know what happens when they're not happy."

Sabrina took a silent, shaken breath, straining to hear.

"Well, you'd better fix it then, hadn't you?" Phillip's voice started to get fainter. He must be walking down the hallway away from her. "No, I can't talk about it now. I'm playing golf with my son."

She desperately wanted to put her head around the corner, check where Phillip was and maybe creep after him, hear some more of that phone conversation.

What shipment was he talking about? And who were the people waiting for it who wouldn't be happy? He'd mentioned a payment to have it "go through" and then warned whoever he was talking to about "what happens when they're not happy . . ."

Perhaps it wasn't anything. An innocuous package he was sending to someone. It didn't necessarily have to refer to an arms shipment or anything like it.

You need to tell Kellan.

No, that was *not* a good idea. An overheard conversation wasn't proof of anything and until that proof turned up—if it ever did—she needed to keep it to herself.

Kellan was so sure of his father's innocence he probably wouldn't think it was anything to worry about anyway. Which meant going with her initial plan to find Charlotte and filing this conversation away to think about later.

Sabrina gave it a few minutes then, peering around the corner to make sure Phillip had gone, she went off to try and find Kellan's mother.

A cursory search soon had her stepping through the glass doors that led to the sheltered lavender garden with its winding paths and bricked flower beds. Charlotte was talking to one of the gardeners at the end of a row, and Sabrina had a weird flashback to when she was a kid, watching her father clearing the weeds from these very same beds.

She'd never been interested in horticulture—not that her father was, he'd just needed the work and could talk a big game when he felt like it—but she'd liked watching him work. There had been something about his hands moving practically in the dirt that was soothing to her, so much easier than when he was at home sitting and doing nothing in front of the television. He'd done a lot of that after her mother and brothers had died. Just sitting there, watching the screen, unmoving.

The memory was not a happy one, so she thought about him doing the gardening instead, inhaling the scent of the lavender and letting it calm her.

After a couple of moments, Charlotte turned away from the gardener, then spotted Sabrina lurking at the end of the path. She smiled her usual, calm smile, then moved in Sabrina's direction.

Sabrina steeled herself and tried to smile back.

"Finally," Charlotte said in satisfied tones, coming to a halt in front of Sabrina. "Now that the boys are away we can chat."

"I was hoping so." Sabrina pushed her hands into her pockets. "I suppose you want to talk about this engagement, right?"

A crease appeared between Charlotte's fair brows. "Well, yes. And I have to be honest, Sabrina. I don't think this is a good idea. You know I think you two being friends is fine. But . . . his fiancée?" Genuine worry glowed in her blue eyes. "Darling, he's not right for you and I think you know it."

Sabrina struggled with the urge to demand why, to get the other woman to name it, out loud. But that wasn't why she was here or what she wanted to talk about.

"Actually," she forced out. "I think you're right."

Charlotte's gaze went wide with surprise. "You do?"

"Yes. It's just . . . he was so insistent. I couldn't hurt him, Charlotte. I'm supposed to protect him, so when he asked me to marry him I . . . couldn't say no."

Instantly Charlotte's manner changed, became warmer, her smile more genuine. "Oh my dear, of course. What a terrible position to be put in." She reached out and threaded her arm through Sabrina's in an uncharacteristic show of physical friendliness, moving toward the house and leaving Sabrina no choice but to come with her. "But how could it have happened? You're his friend. I can't imagine you leading him on."

Sabrina gritted her teeth at the implication it was all her fault. Not that it was any surprise. Charlotte's loyalties were with her son and always had been. "No, I definitely didn't. But I did help him a lot through his recovery and one thing led to another . . ." She paused. "I tried to stop it happening, believe me, I tried. But Kellan is so stubborn when he wants to be."

"Yes," Charlotte agreed. "He is. Not to mention very attractive and persuasive when he wants to be too. No wonder you were swayed. Still giving in to him wouldn't have helped."

"I'm sorry." Sabrina put as much contriteness as she could in her tone. "I tried, I really tried."

Unexpectedly, Charlotte patted her hand. "Like I said, he's persuasive. And there's nothing to be done about it now except tell him the truth." She stopped outside the French doors and gestured for Sabrina to go in first.

"That's what I was hoping to talk to you about." Sabrina stepped inside, then turned as Charlotte came in after her. "He very much wanted to announce it to you and Phillip and he very much wanted to give me an heirloom ring. And I thought if I let him have those two things, then when we get back to San Diego, I'll make him angry somehow. Make sure he's the one to break things off. That way he gets what he wants, and when it's time for the engagement to end, it's his decision. He won't even know I never meant to say yes in the first place."

Charlotte was silent, giving her a long, considering look, and Sabrina met it. "I only want what's best for him, Charlotte," she said with utter conviction. Because it was true. "That's all I've ever wanted for him. He doesn't know anything about Phillip and the baby, and he never will, not from me. I've never told him a word. But this engagement, it was my mistake. And I'm sorry it's caused problems." She put a note of pleading in her voice that wasn't entirely unfeigned. "Please let me make it right somehow."

Charlotte let out a soft sigh. "You're a good girl, Sabrina.

I can't deny that hearing about this engagement was terribly shocking and . . . Well, I did expect more from you."

The subtle hurt slid under Sabrina's skin, joining the rest of the splinters that Charlotte had put there over the years. She ignored it.

Charlotte went on, "I don't blame Kellan—men are like that as you know—but I can see what you've gotten yourself into. And of course I'll help in any way I can."

Sabrina forced herself to give the other woman a grateful smile. "Oh, thank you. You can't know how much that means to me.'

"Good." Charlotte's expression became satisfied. "So, what do you need me to do? "

"If you could convince Phillip to let us choose a ring, it would mean so much to Kellan. You can tell Phillip that the engagement is my fault, that I'm going to make Kellan break it off once we get back to San Diego. And that, once I've chosen the ring, I'll make sure I 'forget' it when we leave, so I won't even take it out of the house."

Charlotte frowned and Sabrina didn't have to feign the hope on her own face. It was totally how she was feeling. She didn't let herself feel the pain that Charlotte's reaction to the engagement had caused, even though she'd expected it. Even though it was even necessary for this particular ruse to work. She'd always known she'd never be good enough for their son and she was okay with that.

Why do you care so much about what they think anyway?

She shouldn't. The Blakes were horrible snobs, not to mention hypocrites of the first order and yet . . . They'd taken her in when her father had abandoned her. They'd given her a home. And no, it wasn't perfect, but then, what home was? There were always going to be problems.

Besides, apart from anything else, they'd given her Kellan. And she would be forever grateful for that.

Charlotte's frown deepened, but then she nodded. "Yes, I can see how important that would be for Kellan. Okay, I'll see what I can do with Phillip." She abruptly gave Sabrina a conspiratorial smile. "I'm sure I can convince him that allowing Kellan to choose a ring for you is a good idea. Especially if he knows this whole thing isn't real in the first place."

Sabrina didn't hide the relief that crossed her face. "Oh, that would be wonderful if you could. Thank you so much."

"Let me handle it. It'll be fine." Charlotte paused. "How . . . is he?" she asked hesitantly. "He doesn't call anymore and it's been months since his last visit. I wondered . . ." She stopped, her clasped hands tightening.

And like she always did, Sabrina felt a burst of sympathy for the woman. Phillip Blake's infidelities had only made Charlotte more desperate to hold on to what she had and that was her son.

"He's okay," Sabrina said gently. "He's good. He's enjoying San Diego and the outfit we're a part of."

Charlotte's mouth tightened. "That ex-military unit? I know Phillip doesn't approve but . . ." She paused again, then sighed. "Leaving the Navy was so devastating for him . . . I only want him to be happy."

Sabrina almost forgot herself and reached out to the other woman. Almost patted or hugged her, which Charlotte would not have appreciated one bit, so instead she curled her hands into fists into her pockets. "I know you do," she murmured. "You want what's best for him."

Charlotte gave her a brittle smile. "Of course I do. And if you could encourage him to visit more often, I'd be grateful."

"I will." Not that it would make any difference. She had a feeling Kellan's lack of family contact was very deliberate, not that she'd talked to him in any depth about it. Or when she had, he'd soon changed the subject.

Seems like there's a lot you two don't talk about.

No kidding.

"Well," Charlotte said briskly, collecting herself. "I'll see what I can do with Phillip when he gets back." She gave Sabrina a steady look. "You're doing the right thing, Sabrina. I'm glad you came to me about it." She made no attempt to hide the relief in her eyes, and Sabrina could only nod. Could only pretend that the mass of sharp-edged emotion that sat in her gut wasn't there. And didn't cut her to pieces every time she thought about it.

So she didn't think about it.

This was for the mission; that was the important thing. Everything else was irrelevant.

Her feelings included.

Kellan hated golf and the game he'd had to put up with that afternoon—when he was already feeling surly—was torture. Especially since he'd spent large portions of it trying to be friendly to his father in an effort to change his mind about letting him choose a ring. They had to get into the study somehow, and sure, he could have wrecked the locks on the door, but that would be very obvious and only make his father suspicious.

No, Phillip was going to have to let them in.

The guy was a stubborn bastard and an outright fight wasn't the way to go, so Kellan had tried to be subtle about it, engaging his father in some political talk, which was the old man's favorite topic of conversation.

By the time he and Phillip returned to Blake House, his father was marginally less stiff, energized by a good old-fashioned political argument.

Pity Kellan couldn't say the same for himself, but then he hadn't been concentrating on the argument anyway, not when his head was too full of Sabrina and that kiss he'd taken that morning up in the bedroom.

That and her furious declaration.

"I have wanted you for years, Kellan Blake. Fucking years . . ."

He couldn't stop thinking about it. About the passion in her voice and the golden glitter of fury in her eyes. The deep color in her cheeks as she'd poked him hard in the chest.

At first, he hadn't wanted to believe it, because how could she feel that way about him? She'd never said a word and he'd had no clue, no clue at all. Yet there was no doubting her fury or the pain that lay underneath it, written plainly all over her pointed features.

She'd wanted him. For years.

Desire had still been pumping through him from that kiss he'd taken from her, and he hadn't quite taken it in until she'd pushed him. Until she'd yelled in his face. And then shock had hit, killing the desire stone dead.

Hours later, he was still shocked. Still couldn't get his head around it. Still didn't know how to deal with it or what to do about it.

But her confession did explain a few things, such as her weirdness around him and this whole fake engagement situation. And the way she'd opened her mouth to him up in the bedroom, let him kiss her hard and deep. The way she'd arched up into his hand and given that erotic little moan of desperation, making his cock get hard. Making him want to take even more . . .

"Ah, you're home." His mother's voice echoed in the foyer as he and his father entered, quickly pouring cold water on his heated thoughts.

Not that he should be thinking them. At all. He shouldn't have even kissed her and blaming it on his mother's presence seemed a pathetic excuse.

Her passionate face kept appearing in his head, those words she'd said echoing in his ears. "*I have wanted you for years . . .*"

He'd never known. Never even had one inkling.

And if you had? What then?

Well, he'd . . . Fuck, what would he have done? Maybe nothing. Before this stupid engagement idea, he'd never thought of her as anything more than a friend, but things had changed. And his feelings about her were . . . murky.

His mother was saying something, but he hadn't been listening and he almost had to shake his head to get rid of the Sabrina thoughts that were dominating his attention.

"Sorry, Mom, what did you say?"

"I said, I need to talk to your father about something. Mind if I steal him away?" She was giving him a meaningful look as if Kellan should know what she was talking about. But of course he didn't.

His father wasn't listening either, having pulled off his golf cap and was in the process of giving instructions to Jane about what to do with the clubs, as if Jane didn't know and hadn't been told fifty million times over the past decade already.

"Sure," Kellan said. "Take him away. I need to do a workout anyway." Christ, he had to do something to get rid of the tension that was crawling through him, and the run that morning hadn't even put a dent in it. And now he was going to have to figure out how the hell he was going to handle the situation with Sabrina.

Not to mention the mission that they were supposed to accomplish.

He began to head in the direction of the stairs and the bedroom so he could get his workout gear, when his mother laid a hand briefly on his arm and murmured, "It's okay. I'll get him to change his mind."

Puzzled, Kellan stared down at her, about to ask her what the hell she was talking about, but she was already going over to where his father was fussing over his golf clubs, putting a hand on his shoulder and saying something in his ear.

Change his mind? Change his mind about what?

Whatever it was, Phillip allowed his wife to lead him down the hallway toward the living room, pausing only to give Kellan a nod as he passed—his father's version of a companionable clap on the shoulder.

Okay, so something was going on. Perhaps Sabrina knew?

He carried on upstairs, but she wasn't there, so he got into some fresh workout gear anyway and headed back down and out of the house to the pool area, where the gym was also situated in a separate little studio.

He'd talk to Sabrina later, once he'd figured out what to do.

Halfway through a tough workout on the rowing machine, his phone buzzed and he stopped, glancing down at the screen.

It was Isiah, which meant he was going to have answer it.

"What's your progress?" Isiah asked in his usual rough way.

Kellan moved over to a shelf where some towels were stacked and picked one up, scrubbing it over his face one-handed. "We need access to Dad's study," he said shortly. "And we're still trying to secure that."

"What? You can't just walk in?"

"No." Kellan looped the towel around his neck. "He keeps it locked and the locks are electronic and heavy-duty. Already checked."

"Can Sabrina hack them?"

"Probably, but timing is an issue. If we can't get Dad to give us access, we'll have to make an attempt at night."

Isiah grunted. "That a problem?"

"No. I just don't like sneaking around the house I grew up in like a fucking criminal." Kellan moved over to the floor-to-ceiling windows that looked out over the pool area and glared out of them. "I'll find Night the damn information—if it's even there. But I'm going to do it my way, understand?"

"Remember who you're talking to, Blake. I'm the CO, not you."

Kellan gritted his teeth. He'd never been that good at thinking of Isiah as his CO, mainly because the 11th Hour wasn't a military unit.

And you're pissed off that it isn't.

Maybe he was. But shit, getting pissed off about it wasn't going to change the fact that the military wasn't his life anymore and never would be.

"Yeah, yeah," he muttered, his tone gritty. "I hear you. *Sir.*"

"This situation is urgent, Blake, make no mistake. Night's just discovered that a shipment of rocket launchers bought by one of the cartels was then stolen by a private militia. And those bastards started on selling them. Which means that every day you wait to find that file is another day these weapons get into the hands of people who shouldn't have them."

Already tense, Kellan's muscles tensed even further at the reminder. "Yes, I understand."

"Which means civilian lives are put at risk," Isiah went on, driving the point home—unnecessarily, in Kellan's opinion. "Every day, innocent people are going to die, because your father—"

"I said, I understand," Kellan ground out, guilt needling at him. Jesus, he shouldn't be letting this thing with Sabrina take up so much of his head. Especially not given what was at stake.

He *had* to find proof of his father's innocence so Night and the rest of the team could get on with finding out who was really responsible.

"Good," Isiah said, expressionlessly. "Then you've got another couple of days max." Without another word, Isiah disconnected the call.

Kellan cursed under his breath as he turned and went back to the rowing machine, dumping his phone on the floor beside it.

If he and Sabrina could get into his father's study, they wouldn't even need a day, not when all he had to do then was search it. They just needed Phillip to change his mind about the ring. Either that or Kellan would have to think of some other reason for getting into that study.

He was ten minutes into another workout and still turning shit over in his head, when the door of the gym opened and Sabrina came in.

She had her hands in the pockets of her jeans, her shoulders hunched the way she always hunched them when she was nervous. But her hazel eyes were very direct when they met his, gold glimmering in them.

He shouldn't have noticed the way her skinny jeans, dark blue and frayed at the knees, clung to her long, slender legs or how the emerald-green sweater she wore was tight enough to reveal her high, round breasts. The color brought out the green of her eyes too, made her skin look all creamy and soft, and somehow brought attention to her luscious red mouth.

No, he shouldn't be noticing all these things about her. But he noticed all the same.

"Hey," she said awkwardly, coming to a stop in front of the rowing machine. "Got a minute?"

Slowly he let the machine recoil, then leaned forward, resting his elbows on his bent knees. "Sure."

Her gaze dipped to his bare shoulders and arms, and her cheeks got even pinker, making her freckles stand out.

"I have wanted you for years . . ."

The sound of her voice stuck in his head again and even though he still hadn't come up with a plan of how to deal with it, he said, "Are we going to talk about what you said to me earlier?"

Her chin came up. "Why? I told you my feelings. What else is there to say?"

An unexpected defiance gleamed in her eyes and he felt it connect with something deep inside him. Something that liked it very, *very* much indeed.

And for some reason it hit him right then, that if she hadn't pushed him away when he'd kissed her, if she hadn't told him about her feelings for him, he might not have stopped with a kiss.

There's no "might" about it. You wouldn't.

No. He wouldn't. He'd wanted her. He'd wanted to be inside her.

You want to be inside her right now.

A sudden, intense need to move filled him and he reached for the bars of the machine again, because if he didn't do something he was going to get to his feet and go to her, pull her into his arms. Give her what she wanted, what they *both* wanted.

So do it? Why are you hesitating?

Because she was his friend and if he did that, things would change. A line would be crossed that they could never cross back over again. And he wasn't sure he wanted to do that.

"So?" she demanded when he didn't say anything. "That's it?"

He pulled hard on the machine, the sound of the fan spinning filling the gym. "Hey, you were the one that said there was nothing more to say."

"But you brought the subject up, Kellan. You must have had some point."

You're being an asshole.

Of course he was. She'd fucking laid the truth on him and now he didn't know what to do. Christ, when it came to war, he always had a plan, but wanting his best friend? Yeah, he was shit out of plans right now.

"My point," he bit out, pulling on the machine yet again, "is that you're not the only one."

"Not the only one to what?"

He paused and looked at her then, because there wasn't any point hiding this from her, not after the honesty she'd given him. "You're not the only one who wants something."

She blinked, looking bewildered for a moment. "You want something?"

"You think I kissed you to make some point." He let the machine go, making it recoil with a hiss. "Well, I didn't. I fucking kissed you because I wanted to. Because you were sleepy and sexy, and you were looking at me like you wanted me. And fuck, Bree." He stared right at her, letting her see the truth in his eyes so there could be no doubt. No doubt at all. "I wanted you too."

Her mouth opened. Then shut. Then she blinked again, the color fading out of her cheeks, leaving her pale. "I don't . . . You can't . . . I mean, that's. . . ." She stopped.

He didn't look away. "Don't ask me why things changed, I don't know. I only know that they have. And I can't stop thinking about that kiss. I can't stop thinking about *you.*"

Sabrina turned her head away, her chest rising and falling fast. She looked like she was desperate to break and run but was keeping herself from doing so through sheer force of will.

Stubborn girl.

He got off the machine and took a step toward her, but she shook her head once, sharply, so he stopped.

Every line of her was tense, her profile set. "What do you expect me to do with that?" The question was as tight as the rest of her. "Drop everything and fall into your arms?"

"I don't know. Maybe. Yes." His heartbeat had accelerated, need gathering inside him. He couldn't believe this was hitting him so hard and so fast, but it was. And suddenly all he wanted to do was to give her what she wanted. "You want me, Bree. Well, you can have me."

She looked at him, the green in her eyes intense. "No, Kellan. I can't *have* you. We're friends."

His breathing was getting fast too. Fuck, he felt a little wild, a little out of control, which was a very bad thing. The only other time he'd felt like this had been back when he was seventeen and look what had happened then.

Yet still he said, "So?"

"So?" she repeated, anger threading through her husky voice. "Jesus Christ, what do you think's going to happen when we get back to San Diego? That we'll go back to being friends? That we pretend this . . . thing between us never happened?" She took an unsteady sounding breath. "Because I'm telling you right now that I can't do that. I will *never* be able to do that."

Tension was tight in his chest, in his gut, across his shoulders. He wanted to reach for her, but he knew that would be a mistake. In fact, this whole fucking thing was a mistake, judging from the look on her face.

He hadn't thought this through, he hadn't thought *any* of this through. It had blindsided him completely and now he was left not knowing what the fuck to do, and he hated that. His whole career had been about either giving orders or following them, but there were no orders now. No plan of action showing him the way forward.

All he had was his stupid dick getting hard for a woman who'd never showed up on his radar before and who now was the only fucking thing he could think about.

A woman he couldn't have.

"Okay," he said, his voice like gravel. "You've made yourself clear. Friends it is. Now why are you here?"

Something flared in her eyes, something like hurt, which made no sense. But all she said was, "I came to tell you that I talked to your mother. She's going to get Phillip to change his mind about the ring. So when he tells you it's okay for us to choose one, act like you've never been so grateful in all your goddamned life, okay?"

"How did you manage that?" He couldn't quite keep the surprise out of his tone.

"I'll tell you later." Sabrina turned for the door. "You go back to working on your muscles."

"Later?" He took another step toward her. "Tell me now."

But she ignored him, walking out without even a backward glance.

CHAPTER 9

Kellan sat back in his chair, watching as his mother got up from the dining table. She gave him a smirk, then looked meaningfully at Sabrina. "Come through into the sitting room, dear. Let's leave the boys to chat."

Ah, so that's what she was doing. Giving him and his father some quiet time, no doubt so Phillip could tell him he'd changed his mind about the rings.

Unable to help himself, he glanced at Sabrina. She gave him the slightest of nods, but her smile was for Charlotte. "Of course," she murmured, getting up from her chair.

Kellan narrowed his gaze at her and his mother as they moved toward the door to the dining room. Charlotte seemed . . . almost excited, looping her arm through Sabrina's in a friendly way that was a total contrast to how she'd treated her the day before.

In fact, Charlotte had been in a strangely good mood the entire meal, even going so far as to talk about planning a small engagement party, which seemed odd given how shocked and appalled she'd been when Kellan had first announced it.

Even tonight, she'd insisted that everyone dress for the occasion as they were going to be having a "small celebratory dinner."

Kellan had spent the rest of the afternoon—after a fruitless search for Sabrina to continue their conversation and not finding her—in the hangar checking out the sleek Bell 407 his father had bought and didn't particularly want a "celebratory dinner," not given his mood. But he'd pulled on the suit pants and plain white shirt he'd bought with him anyway, though he didn't bother with a tie, because he hated the damn things. Only to come down to the dining room—the formal dining room this time—to find Sabrina sitting at the table wearing the only dress she had. He'd seen it before, a gold silky thing with little straps that left her shoulders bare, but he'd never realized until now how it hugged her slight curves. Or how it made her skin glow. How it highlighted the fragile elegance of her shoulders and collarbones.

She'd left her hair loose down her back and it seemed he'd never realized before either, how glossy her curls were, a rich chestnut brown that his fingers itched to touch.

It was difficult to concentrate on his meal, difficult to pay attention to his mother, difficult to pretend he was happy about an engagement party, when Sabrina was sitting opposite him and he was wrestling with the fact that he'd never understood how lovely she was until now.

And then, when he'd finally forced those feelings down, his mother's behavior made him realize something else. That Sabrina had somehow managed to forward the mission while he'd done absolutely nothing since he'd gotten here.

It made him feel useless. Made him feel like he was flailing around in the dark, while she was busy making plans and achieving things. Irritation crept under his skin—not at her because Christ knew someone had to get the mission under control and at least she was doing something—but at himself.

Her intellect was superior, yes, but being out in the field was *his* area of expertise and he wasn't used to being superfluous.

He didn't like it. He didn't like that it was his fault either. He'd let his relationship with his parents get in the way, let his goddamn dick and its sudden preoccupation with Sabrina dominate his thinking.

So much for being a SEAL badass.

Yeah, but then again, what the fuck was he supposed to do? There were no bad guys here to fight—if he didn't count his father and he didn't—and there was no danger pressing in. And if there was no danger, there was no one who needed his protection. Only Sabrina. And the thing she needed protecting from was himself.

He was out of his element, and yeah, he fucking hated it.

"So," Phillip said, putting his napkin down on the polished oak of the long, formal dining table and easing back in his chair. "I've rethought some stuff. You really want one of Grandma Jo's rings for Sabrina?"

Kellan eyed his father. "That was the idea."

"Well . . . maybe you should choose one."

He tried to look surprised. "But I thought you were against it?"

Phillip gave him the same charming smile he saw on his own face every morning in the mirror. "Charlie had a talk with me about it. She said it would make you happy, right?"

"Yes. Very happy." He smiled back, like he meant it, though to be fair, at this point, he really did. "It would mean the world, Dad."

His father gave a nod as if that was the answer he'd expected. "Family is important. And maybe I was a little hasty saying no." His gaze sharpened. "We only want what's best for you, son. We always have."

What's best for him . . . Yeah, he'd heard that before. The night his father had told him that the woman he'd been having an affair with at the age of seventeen was married. And that there was no possible way that Kellan could keep the baby that had resulted from that affair.

"We only want what's best for you," Phillip had told him. "You're only seventeen. How can you look after a child? And a child with a married woman at that. You have your whole life ahead of you, son. Don't throw that away on one youthful loss of control."

His father had never lied to him before, had only ever had his best interests at heart, and so Kellan had listened to him. Had believed him. Had let his father handle the mess he'd made and had given up his child, because it had been better for everyone concerned, including the baby.

Keep telling yourself that.

Kellan ignored both the memories and the thought, feeling his smile turn brittle. "Sure, Dad. But . . . I mean, what changed your mind? You and Mom were unhappy about Sabrina yesterday and yet now you're okay with it?" He should leave it alone, he really should. Yet he couldn't seem to keep from pushing.

His father shifted on his chair. "Like I said, Charlie and I had a talk. And Sabrina makes you happy, doesn't she?"

The question hit him strangely, in that there was no need pretend his answer, no need to lie. "Yes," he said, for the first time telling the absolute truth, feeling the words resonate somewhere deep inside him. "She does."

"Well then." Phillip's voice turned gruff. "There's no more that needs to be said." He pushed his chair back abruptly. "Come on. You go get Sabrina, then meet me upstairs in my study."

Kellan couldn't move for a second, those words still resonating, the realization of them moving through him. Because Sabrina did make him happy. She always had.

Of course she does. That's why she's your friend, right?

Yeah, friends. That's what they were. She was always there

for him, giving him her particular brand of honesty, all the while making him feel as if he mattered to her. As if he was important to her. And not because he was *the* Phillip Blake's son and had expectations to live up to, but because she liked him for himself.

He'd never had to prove himself to Sabrina and he liked that, liked it a lot.

"Are you coming or what?"

Kellan realized his father was waiting for him and had been for at least a minute. Fuck, he really needed to get his head back in the game. He was supposed to be focusing on proving his father's innocence, not on what Sabrina meant to him.

Shoving back his chair, Kellan nodded, then got his feet. "I'll see you up there."

Following Phillip out of the room, he went down the hallway to the sitting room, finding Sabrina on the couch next to his mother, who had a magazine open on the coffee table in front of them and was talking about wedding themes.

Jesus. What *had* Sabrina said to her?

"Bree." He couldn't quite keep the edge out of his voice, irritation at his own uselessness creeping inside him again.

Both Sabrina and his mother looked up.

He extended a hand. "Come upstairs. I've got something to show you."

Sabrina's eyes widened in surprise, though for whose benefit he had no idea. "What? Now? But I was just—"

"Don't worry about me, dear." Charlotte gave Sabrina a small, private smile, then patted her knee. "Go on. Better do as the man says."

Sabrina sighed, then got to her feet, moving over to where Kellan stood. It looked like she was going to avoid holding his hand, but he wasn't having that. She'd somehow taken control of this entire mission and he wanted some of that control back. He needed it; otherwise what the fuck use was he?

Before she could go past him, he caught her hand, threaded his fingers firmly through hers. She stilled, the flecks of gold in her eyes flaring, but he didn't let go. "Don't be shy, baby," he murmured, staring down at her, challenging her to pull away. "It's only me."

Her mouth firmed and she glanced over to where Charlotte was watching them covertly from the couch. Her laugh sounded forced to Kellan, but her fingers relaxed in his hold and she allowed him to pull her down the hallway.

"We don't need to hold hands now," she muttered as they reached the stairs. His father's office was on the second floor, in the opposite wing to where their bedroom lay.

"Too bad." He firmed his grip on her as they made their way up the wide oak steps. "This is an important moment. It's got to look right."

Her fingers had gone stiff again. "I guess so."

"Are you going to tell me what you said to them? Or are we going to play games about it all night?"

"Can we have this conversation *after* we've gotten what we need to? I think that's a bit more important right now."

She was right, which pissed him off. He was failing at this, he could feel it. She was doing everything right while he was . . . Fuck, he didn't know what he was doing. Making a complete goddam ass of himself.

He didn't reply, his jaw tight and aching as they walked the rest of the way to his father's study. She didn't say anything either, the silence between them thick with tension.

Normally he would have smiled, would have thought of something to say to diffuse it, but now he couldn't think of a single thing. Seemed like he was fucking up their friendship too.

The door to the study was open, but Kellan paused outside it and turned to her. "You got a—"

"Do I look stupid?" she interrupted. "Of course I do."

His irritation coiled like a cut snake. Of course she'd have brought a USB drive with her already and of course she'd know instantly what he was talking about.

She knows what she's doing. Do you? You're even acting like there's something to find after all.

A muscle ticked in his jaw, but he said nothing. Merely gave her a curt nod before turning and walking into the room, Sabrina following in after him.

Phillip Blake's study was the epitome of a rich man's private office space. Wood paneled the walls along with heavy bookshelves, all full of beautifully bound and expensive-looking books. There were paintings of landscapes on the walls and a large antique oak desk down at one end. A computer screen and keyboard sat on it, along with a few other neatly lined up office supplies.

A couple of comfortable-looking armchairs upholstered in deep green leather were positioned in front of the desk, where his father was also standing, bent over a tray of something that sat on the desktop.

Instinctive tension gathered between Kellan's shoulder blades. He remembered being in this office many times, called in to shake his father's hand in congratulations for his many successes, and less often, to take a chastisement for his failures.

It was here he'd been told about Pippa. About Pippa's husband.

He took a breath. Shit, he needed to *stop* thinking about the past. It didn't have anything to do with this fucking job and the quicker they got said job over and done with the better.

His father straightened and turned as they entered, giving them a slight smile. He moved to the side and gestured to the black velvet jewelry tray on the desktop. "Here you are, son. I got them out of the safe for you."

"Phillip?" Sabrina was doing a good job of sounding shocked. "What's this all about?"

Phillip gave Kellan a nod. "Ask your fiancé. Right, would you like some privacy?"

"That would be great, Dad." Kellan forced a grateful smile on his face. "I owe you for this."

His father gave another tight nod—a sure sign that he was uncomfortable with the level of emotion in the room—then strode past them, pausing to give Kellan another brief smile.

Sabrina didn't move until Phillip had gone, the door closing behind him. Then instantly she was over at the desk, completely ignoring the tray of jewels, as she sat down in front of the computer. "It won't be on this PC," she muttered. "It's too obvious. And I checked already remotely. Look around, see if you can see a laptop anywhere."

Kellan pushed his instinctive annoyance at being given orders aside, switching into military mode. She wasn't wrong; if his father did indeed have the incriminating file on a computer somewhere, it wouldn't be on his desktop.

"If you already checked that one, why are you bothering with it?" he asked as he began a systematic search of the study.

"Just in case. I'll download the contents so at least we have some evidence of where the file isn't, right?"

"True." Christ, she really was thinking of everything.

Sabrina reached up and slid her fingers under the neckline of her dress, pulling something out of it. A tiny memory stick.

Kellan abruptly forgot his foul mood and everything else, grinning at her. "Jesus, where were you hiding that?"

Her answering grin was brief and bright. "My bra. Where else does a badass computer hacker hide her stuff?"

"Badass is right."

"Okay, shut up now and let this badass work." She glanced back at the computer screen, but a smile continued to play around her mouth.

This is how it should be.

Something shifted inside him. Determination. Because yes,

this *was* how it should be between them. Friends teasing each other. Giving each other shit, easy in each other's company. Not tense and angry. Not distant. Not complicated.

Because he'd had enough of complicated to last a lifetime.

Kellan turned back to his search and pushed all those too-complicated feelings way down deep inside him. And made sure they stayed down.

Sabrina tried to keep all her concentration on what she was doing and not on the way Kellan was moving around his father's study, all lethal grace and fluidity as he conducted his search.

Didn't help that he was wearing those deliciously tailored charcoal suit pants that fit him to perfection, and a crisp white cotton business shirt with the sleeves rolled up. She loved it when he got all business-y. The fabric of the shirt highlighted his muscled shoulders and the golden skin of his forearms, and then there was the way his pants sat low on his lean hips, then tightened around his thighs . . .

Shit, she should *not* be thinking about him. Not after everything that had happened that afternoon. And most certainly *not* when she had stuff to do.

"I kissed you because I wanted to . . ."

She blinked at the computer screen, the words he'd said to her in the gym going around and around in her head.

"I wanted you too."

She couldn't think about what he'd said, the shock of it shuddering through her like an earthquake. How many years had she fantasized about him saying those words to her? Or something like them? And now he had. Now he—

Sabrina bit her lip hard, the jolt of pain stopping the thoughts dead in their tracks.

She had to concentrate on this, not him. They wouldn't get this chance again and if she screwed it up . . .

Shoving the memory stick she'd taken from her bra into a port on the computer, the program that would give her access to the hard drive started immediately. It was a sneaky bit of code she'd written herself, back when she'd been in Silicon Valley, and it had come in very useful on various 11th Hour missions. It worked like a charm now, and soon she had access to the hard drive, downloading the contents of it onto the stick.

Not that there was anything on this computer, but you never knew what could be hidden in the code. Phillip didn't have the expertise to do it himself, but that didn't mean someone else didn't have it, and she wanted to be sure.

"So what did you say to Mom?" Kellan asked, his deep voice breaking the silence.

Sabrina lifted her attention from the screen. He wasn't looking at her, currently conducting a search of the bookcases and for a second she was mesmerized. His movements were quick, economical, his focus intense, searching with military precision. And a weird disassociation hit her, as if she was seeing him from the point of view of a stranger. A tall, impossibly handsome all-American guy, a star quarterback, the Homecoming King.

Yet no Homecoming King moved the way Kellan did. With such predatory intent and lethal grace. Dangerous. He was dangerous.

She forgot that sometimes. Hell, she mostly forgot about that all the time. But he was. He'd once been one of the best helicopter pilots in the military and then had switched branches to become one of their most elite warriors. Now he was part of the 11th Hour and had been on many dangerous missions, but she'd never seen him in the field. She'd never seen him in action.

You're not really seeing it now. All he had to do on this mission was to talk to Phillip.

"Bree." His ice-blue gaze caught hers. "Are you going to tell me or what?"

She blinked, realizing she'd been staring. Shit. "Uh . . ." Might as well tell him now. "Okay, so I told Charlotte that I had no intention of marrying you and that I'd only said yes to make you happy. I also said that when we got back to San Diego, I was going to make sure you broke off the engagement. So it didn't matter if you gave me one of the family heirlooms because it wasn't real anyway."

He went still, searching her face. Saying nothing, his expression impenetrable.

She tore her gaze away, looking down at the screen. "Anyway, she said she'd talk to Phillip and change his mind. And clearly she did."

More silence.

Then he said, "Good plan. Well done."

She glanced up again in surprise, not expecting the simple praise. But he wasn't looking at her, continuing on with his search.

There was a warm glow in her chest, the way she always felt when he'd told her she'd done something well, and her cheeks felt hot. She'd never been praised as a kid, certainly her father had never done so, while Charlotte hadn't been interested. It hadn't been until she'd gone to high school that she realized that all her fiddling around first with her father's ancient computer and then with the laptop she'd been given by Charlotte for her school work had been useful. And more, that she was good at working with code. She'd been praised plenty by her teachers and then by the people she'd worked with, but none of them made her feel the way Kellan did with a few simple words.

God, she was a lost cause.

He wants you, remember that.

No. She wasn't thinking about that. Not right now.

The computer had finished downloading, so she whipped the memory stick out, and looked back at Kellan. "That's done. Find anything?"

"Not yet." He straightened, then turned, prowling over to the desk. "Maybe there's nothing to find." But he ran his long fingers over the wood of the desk anyway, searching, exploring.

Her mouth went dry and she had to stop watching him, her skin suddenly sensitive, as if he was running those fingers over her body.

Fucking hell.

She focused on pulling out some drawers and having a cursory look through the stuff in them, papers mostly and stationary supplies.

Kellan went still again, staring down at the jewelry tray that neither of them had paid any attention to. Then he muttered a curse and moved over to one of the bookshelves behind the desk. A tap against one of the shelves and it swung out, revealing the door to a safe sitting behind it.

"Oh," Sabrina said, feeling stupid. "Of course. That should have been the first place we looked."

Kellan didn't say anything. He grabbed the knob on the front of the safe and leaned in, pressing his ear to the metal, listening as he twisted it back and forth.

She held her breath.

A minute or two later the door of the safe swung open. Kellan gave her a single, brilliant look, his mouth curving in a smile of pure triumph, reminding her sharply of the boy he'd once been.

She grinned back, sharing the triumph with him, and for a moment they were simply friends again, all those truths about each other forgotten.

Then he turned his attention to what was in the safe, and Sabrina felt a chill creep over her, as if a cloud had covered the sun. She shook herself, trying to hold on to that moment of just friendship, getting out of the chair and going over to the safe where he stood, trying to peer over his shoulder. An impossibility considering he was taller than she was.

But then he made an odd-sounding noise and turned around, holding something up in his hand: a portable hard drive. The expression on his face was hard to interpret, but his eyes were burning blue with intensity. "If Night's file is anywhere, then it'll be on here."

Sabrina swallowed. "Okay, well. Give me the drive. I'll have to plug it into the desktop and download it onto my memory stick. Or else we just take it with us—" She broke off, her heart hammering as a knock came on the door.

"I guess we'll just take it with us then." With a quick movement he stuck the hard drive into the back pocket of his suit pants, shut the safe, and swung the fake shelf back where it belonged. "Shut down the desktop," he ordered brusquely, moving over to the desk, "then get over here."

She obeyed without hesitation, logging off, then shutting the thing down, before going over to the desk where he was standing.

"Just go with it," he murmured cryptically, before putting his hands on her hips and lifting her up so she was sitting on the desktop next to the jewelry tray. Then he tugged his shirt out from the waistband of his pants and began to pull open the buttons.

Sabrina stared at him in shock, unable to look away from the expanse of tanned skin, black ink, and light scattering of golden chest hair. Getting the shirt fully open, he pushed his hips between her thighs, causing the material of her dress to ride up. "Kellan," she began, her breath catching.

Another knock came on the door.

Kellan reached for her, burying his fingers in her hair and tugging her head back. "Put your hands on me," he murmured and there was no mistaking the tone of command in his voice.

She had no idea what was happening, but he must have had some reason for doing this and she trusted him, so she did what she was told, lifting her hands to his bare chest. They trembled, she couldn't help it, and when they touched his skin, they trembled even more.

Kellan bent and gave her a swift, hard kiss that made the blood roar in her ears and her mouth feel like it had been scorched. Then he lifted his head just as the door opened and Sabrina heard a soft exclamation.

Kellan turned sharply in the direction of the doorway, his expression adjusting to one of surprise. Then he gave a sheepish sounding laugh and ran a hand through his hair, spiking it up. "Oh, sorry, Dad. We got a little sidetracked."

It wasn't until he'd turned that Sabrina realized what he'd been doing. The hard drive in the back pocket of his pants was very noticeable, so he'd hidden it by untucking his shirt, pretending that they'd been making out.

"Hmm." Phillip did not sound impressed. "Do you want another five minutes?"

"No. I think we've chosen, haven't we?" Kellan glanced down at her, a deep blue flame burning in his eyes. "Show him which one you want, baby."

Oh great. Now she was going to have to grab some random ring and pretend like it was the greatest thing in the world. Difficult to do when her head was still spinning from that kiss, the feel of his hot skin still burning against her fingertips

Then he made things even worse by smoothing down the fabric of her dress, the warmth of his palms on her thighs drawing a shiver from her before she could stop it.

"Oh . . . uh . . ." she murmured stupidly, staring at the jewels glittering on the black velvet of the tray. She was about to pick the first one her fingers landed on, when a flash of deep blue caught her eye. It was a simply set ring with a plain silver band, nothing else to detract from the intense azure of the stone that sat on top of it.

She grabbed it reflexively and held it up. "This one."

Kellan's gaze met hers, blue as the sapphire she held, though she tried not to notice that. "Good choice." He reached out and took it from her. "Hold out your hand."

Oh hell. He was going to put it on her, wasn't he?

She tried to calm her raging heartbeat, to not let any of her feelings show on her face as she did what she was told. And she kept her gaze on her hand as he slid the ring onto her finger.

The stone glittered, as real as this stupid engagement was fake.

Emotion pulled tight in her chest, Kellan sliding a fingertip under her chin, and she knew he was going to kiss her again, to cement the moment. But she didn't think she could take another one, so she pulled her head away, then slid off the desktop before he could say a word. "What do you think, Phillip?" she asked brightly, waving her hand at Kellan's father and ignoring the frown that drew Kellan's brows together.

"It's very nice," Phillip replied, his tone neutral.

"Isn't it?" She moved past him, heading toward the door, not risking a glance back at Kellan. "I'm going to show Charlotte."

Then she fled, because apparently she wasn't that brave after all.

CHAPTER 10

Kellan spent the rest of the evening making meaningless conversation with his parents. After Sabrina's apparent rush from his dad's study, he'd managed to follow her quickly enough to catch her at the top of the stairs, letting her know he was going to put the hard drive in their bedroom so she could examine it later.

She'd nodded wordlessly, then carried on down to show off the massive sapphire to his mother. He'd joined them a few minutes later, having gotten rid of the hard drive, his mother waxing lyrical about the ring. Sabrina had excused herself not long after that, pleading a headache.

He stayed downstairs because if she was studying that drive there was nothing he could do to help. Yet he couldn't shake the restless, antsy feeling. His brain kept cycling around to the drive in the safe, going through all the reasons his father would keep it there, and not one of them was reassuring. In fact, it made him feel sick. Half of him had been sure he'd find nothing, while the other half had been caught up in the action of the moment, the searching, the triumph of being able to get into the safe, the thrill of doing something after days of inaction.

And then Sabrina, her eyes gleaming gold as he'd opened the safe, her smile making him feel like he'd done something right after doing everything wrong since he'd gotten here. Then her hands on his skin, the brush of them against his chest as he'd played up them making out as an excuse for his shirt being untucked . . .

He was getting hard just thinking about it, which was definitely not a good thing. He should be thinking more about the implications of that hard drive in the safe and what it meant for his father, not Sabrina.

Christ, where the hell had his control gone? He'd never let a woman get to him the way Sabrina was getting to him right now, not after his obsession with Pippa had ended so badly, and he could not understand what was so different now. Was it simply the whole "friends" thing? The fact that he shouldn't touch her? Was he really that much of a cliché?

His mother was speaking to him, telling him some society gossip and asking his opinion on whether or not he'd like an engagement party, but he wasn't in the mood to bolster the lies he'd told already. Eventually he excused himself before his temper gave him away, taking a long walk in the darkness around the Blake House grounds to get rid of some of his restlessness.

It didn't work.

Finally he found his way to the TV room, with its giant screen, and distracted himself with a stupid action movie about cars.

It was late by the time he got upstairs, and the bedroom was dark, Sabrina huddled under the quilt and by the sound of her breathing, fast asleep.

He desperately wanted to wake her up, see if she'd found anything, but he couldn't bring himself to do it, so instead he had a shower before flinging himself down on the uncomfortable couch and trying to get some shut eye.

That didn't work either.

He didn't know how long he lay there in the dark, his brain working overtime, sleep eluding him, but he did know the moment Sabrina's breathing changed.

Going still, he listened to it getting faster and faster, turning into small, frightened-sounding gasps. A nightmare clearly.

He waited for her to quiet, but she didn't, and eventually he sat up, looking over at the massive four-poster. She was lying very still, but the sounds she made sent a cold current running through him, his chest tightening with worry.

It didn't sound like an ordinary nightmare and the few times they'd slept in the same room together—as kids when they'd "camped out" on the estate lawns—he hadn't remembered her making these kinds of sounds.

He got off the couch and moved over to the bed. She was curled into a ball, the fingertips of one hand lying on the pillow, so he reached out to touch them gently, shocked to find they were ice cold.

Kellan stopped thinking then, his brain flicking instantly into protective mode, and he didn't bother waking her. Instead he tugged back the quilt and climbed into bed beside her, lying down and gathering her into his arms, pulling her tight against him. He hadn't worn a shirt to bed, the only thing he had on was some boxer underwear to spare her blushes, but even through the cotton of the soft T-shirt she wore to bed, he could feel how cold and clammy she was.

God, this must be some nightmare.

She was motionless, her breathing still choppy and gasping, then, as if the warmth of his body had begun to penetrate, she shivered all over. Then she moved, turning toward him, her arms winding tight around him, clinging to him for dear life. She pushed her face into his neck and he could feel her frantic breath against his throat. "Kel . . ." Her voice was almost a sob of relief and the constricted feeling in his chest constricted even further.

"It's okay." He slid a hand down her back, stroking her, wanting to soothe her any way he could. "You're safe, Bree. I'm here with you."

She gave another sob, holding on to him even tighter, curling one leg up and nearly around his waist in an effort to fit herself closer against him.

He kept on stroking her back, murmuring that she was okay, that she was safe, because he hated the fear in her voice and the fact that she was shivering, and he had to do something. He might have been fucking useless on this job, but if there was one thing he could do for her, it was to be her friend. Ease her fear and protect her from nightmares.

Slowly, as he stroked up and down her spine, the tensions began to ease and she stopped shivering. Her skin warmed, her breathing getting easier and he thought she might move away, loosen her hold on him, but she didn't.

He lay on his back, staring up at the canopy of the bed, with her curled against his side and the scent of her, laundry powder and Sabrina, began to thread through his awareness.

He could feel her, the soft press of her tits to his side and the heat resting against his thigh. A very specific heat, made all the more intense because of the way she had her leg thrown across his.

Oh, Jesus Christ. That was not something he should be noticing and yet he was fucking noticing. In fact, it was difficult to be aware of anything else. The heat of her pussy was right there, right fucking *there,* and the only thing separating the luscious warmth of her from his bare skin was her little cotton shorts.

No. Just *no.* He needed to think about something else. He *had* to.

Then everything got exponentially worse because he felt her breathing change against his throat, getting a touch faster, and he knew it wasn't fear this time, he just fucking knew. Her hips moved, confirming his suspicions, and he felt the shift of her against him like an electric shock grounding the whole way through his body.

He caught his breath, shutting his eyes as his goddamn cock hardened. No. He was better than this. He had more control than this. And apart from anything else, this was *so* not the time. Hell, she'd just had a nightmare and he was trying to comfort her not anything else.

But then her breathing hitched and he felt her give a delicate little shiver as her hips moved again. More insistently.

Oh. Fuck.

The blood had begun to pump hot and fast through his veins, and his stupid fucking dick was getting even harder. And all he could think about was moving the hand on her spine lower, to curve over her butt and reposition her. Perhaps over his cock, where she could rub against him and make them both feel good.

No. Hell no. He had to stop this right now. Before he couldn't.

"Bree." His voice was hoarse in the dark. "I'm going to go back to the couch—"

"No." Her denial was so soft he almost didn't hear it.

"What?"

"Stay. Please." She pressed closer to him, the desperate note in the words making his heart miss a beat.

"I can't." He had to force himself to speak, because pretty much all of him was aching to stay right where he was.

"Why not?"

"You know why not." His pulse had picked up speed and a delicate, musky scent had begun to wind through her usual laundry powder smell.

He knew what that was. Jesus, he was fucked. So fucked.

"I don't care." She sounded husky, ragged. "I need . . . God, I need . . ." Her hips shifted yet again, and he could hear her breathing shudder. "I want to feel something good, Kel. Please . . . Help me . . ."

A true friend would have gotten out of the bed and left her alone. Or turned on the light and talked her through it. A true friend would have had more control.

But he wasn't a true friend. He couldn't be, not when he was so hard he ached. Not when his control was in shreds. And not when he'd been such a useless waste of space this whole mission. Right now, right here, was something he could do and do fucking well.

He could make her feel good. He could make her feel amazing.

Excuses. You just want to fuck her.

Yeah, he did. And he shouldn't.

But he was going to anyway.

"I know what you need," he said into the hot dark between them. "You need me." Then he closed his hands on her hips and he shifted her the way he'd wanted to, positioning her so that hot little pussy of hers was pressing down on the aching ridge of his cock.

Sabrina inhaled sharply, a shudder shaking her slender body. "Oh . . . *Kellan* . . ."

Plenty of other women had said his name like that, hoarse and desperate, but the sound of it in Sabrina's mouth hit him like a bolt of lightning.

He could barely breathe. The damp heat between her thighs was soaking through the cotton of his boxers, the slight pressure killing him. Then she moved her hips again, shifting them against him, and he had to grit his teeth to stop the growl that almost tore from his throat.

Holy fucking shit. She was so hot. He could feel that she was wet too, the material of his boxers getting damper and damper, and that movement of her hips was driving him crazy. He was so hard he hurt.

Her breathing against his throat was ragged, her fingers curling against his chest, the brush of them against his bare skin scorching him. And his own hips were rising, meeting the movement of hers, grinding against her the way she was grinding against him.

It was agony, pure fucking agony.

"Kel . . . please . . . *God* . . . Oh, please . . ." Her voice was husky, the desperation in it bordering on frantic.

More. She needed more.

His pulse hammered in his head, the need to bury himself inside her getting stronger and stronger. But he was going to lose it if he did, and right now he didn't want to lose it. He wanted to give her what she needed and him being an animal was not that.

Gripping on to his control with everything he had, Kellan slid his hands down over the soft curve of her ass, and farther down, brushing the fabric between her legs. She gasped, her whole body trembling as he touched her. And holy shit, he'd been right. The fabric of her sleep shorts was soaking.

He was panting now, sliding his fingers beneath the material, brushing the slick folds of her pussy. She groaned, her hips lifting in clear invitation, trembling harder. Hot. Fuck she was *so* hot. She was scorching him. And she was unbelievably wet.

All for you.

This time he didn't stop the growl that escaped him, because yes, fucking, *yes*. This *was* all for him. *She* was all for him. And it was wrong—she was his goddamn best friend, for Christ's sake—but he didn't care. He wanted this. He wanted her.

He stroked her slowly, relishing the feel of her wetness on his fingers, then, even more slowly, he slid one finger into her. She gasped again, her hips shuddering, the sound of his name a hoarse and broken prayer against his throat.

The scorching heat of her pussy around his finger was blinding him, the feel of her internal muscles pulsing as he slid it deeper, stealing all the breath from his lungs. He wasn't going to last, was he? He was going to take her and take her so hard . . .

He eased another finger inside her and she jerked, a sob coming from her as he pushed deep before slowly drawing both fingers out, then easing back in again.

"Kellan . . ." She was panting like he was. Desperate like he was. "I can't . . . Oh God . . . this is . . . *please* . . ."

He lifted his hips as he thrust his fingers inside her, grinding his cock against her clit and she gave another choked sob. So he did it again. And again. Until her whole body was shaking against him and she was making small mewling noises, her face turned into his neck.

And he couldn't wait any longer.

He'd brought nothing with him in the way of contraception because being in bed with Sabrina was the very last thing he'd expected from this trip, but he forced the question out. God knew he'd already paid the price for impatience once and he wasn't that far gone to ignore it now.

Yet.

"Do you have a condom?" His voice was so rough it sounded nothing like his. "Because I don't."

Please God, let her have *something* because he didn't know what he'd do if she didn't.

Her reply was hoarse. "It's okay . . . I'm on the pill."

Relief filled him, so strong he felt dizzy. Thank *Christ*.

Ignoring her groan of protest, he pulled his fingers from her and jerked the cotton of his boxers down, freeing his painfully hard dick. He slid his hands over her butt once more, reaching between her thighs, spreading the soft folds of her pussy, holding it open for him. Then he shifted her again, positioning his cock, nudging the head of it against her wet flesh. Flexing his hips. Pushing inside her.

She cried out as he felt the stretch of her around him, the

give of her flesh as he pushed deeper, blinding heat gripping him tight. Sensation burst through him, a tide of desire and need drowning him.

"Kellan . . . Oh God, *Kellan.*" Sabrina stiffened and then she began to sob, her whole body shaking and shaking as she came all over his cock.

And he felt something break loose inside him.

He gripped her, not waiting until her shaking had subsiding, not fucking waiting anymore. And he turned them both, taking her beneath him, pressing her down into the mattress, his dick still buried deep inside her.

"My turn," he murmured, staring down at her in the darkness, his breathing ragged. "My fucking turn."

Sabrina was shaking and shaking and she didn't think she'd ever stop. Her head was still ringing—shit, her entire body was still ringing—from the aftereffects of that orgasm, and she could feel herself building already toward another one.

Not surprising when her most private sexual fantasy was happening to her right now. Right the hell *now.*

Kellan was inside her. The man she'd loved for years, her best friend, was *inside* her. He was everywhere, his long, powerful body stretched over hers, his hands on the pillow on either side of her head. Looking down at her. She had her legs wrapped around his lean waist and she could feel him pushing deeper.

Big. God, he was big. She groaned at the delicious stretch of him, at the length of him, thick and powerful, filling her so completely it felt like there wasn't enough room for him and the breath in her lungs.

She stared up at his shadow in the dark, panting, wanting to see him. Desperate to see him, because how else would she know this was true? How else would she know this was really happening and wasn't just some extension of that horrible nightmare? A twisted nightmare, where her fantasies came true only to find that it had all been a lie come morning.

"Turn on the light," she demanded, her voice shaky, unrecognizable even to her own ears. "I want to see you."

He didn't say a word, merely leaned over to the nightstand and flicked on the light.

She blinked against the sudden brightness, but then her sight cleared and there he was, and she couldn't stop staring. Those broad shoulders were above her, his muscled chest and taut stomach over her, the ink of his military tattoos dark against his golden skin. And his face, God, his face. Fierce. Set in lines of unmistakable hunger. His eyes so blue and flames in them, burning for her.

This was real. This was happening.

His gaze dropped down her body, then he shifted, gripping the hem of her sleep shirt and lifting it, pulling it off her. Shivers chased over her skin as she lay back, naked but for her sleep shorts. He stared down her body again, lingering on her bare breasts and then down farther, rearing back so he could see between her thighs, to where she was stretched and slick around him. He made a deep, rumbling noise of pure male approval that made everything in her shiver.

That was for her, wasn't it? It was her doing that to him, making him sound like that. Making him hard like that.

"Look at you," he said thickly. "All wet for me." He drew his hips back, sliding out of her, then pushing back in, his attention firmly between her thighs. "Fuck, that's hot." He did it again, thrusting harder this time. "Christ, Bree. You feel so fucking amazing."

Heat swept over her skin at the way he was looking at her, and she almost burst into flames with embarrassment. But he felt amazing too, the slide of him inside her so good she couldn't concentrate on anything else.

But then he stopped, his gaze lifting to hers, the fire in his eyes burning higher. And he looped his arm beneath her knee, lifting her leg up and up until it was hooked over one heavily muscled shoulder, before doing the same to her other leg.

She groaned aloud, the position tilting her hips, letting him slide even deeper, stretch her even wider. She began to shake, not knowing what to do with her hands, but then he solved that problem too, by putting his palms on hers and holding them down on the pillow, interlacing their fingers.

"Eyes on me," he ordered, a dark thread of hunger running through his voice that had her shivering. "Eyes on me while I fuck you, Bree."

The dirty words did things to her, made her sweat, made her breathless, the look in his blue gaze making her burn.

And she did what he told her, she kept her eyes on him as he began to fuck her with strong, powerful thrusts that had her gasping. His hands pressed hers down into the pillow, the sound of their bodies meeting, the slap of his flesh on hers, and the bed creaking loud in the room. His breathing was ragged and every time he thrust, he made a deep hungry sound that somehow made everything more erotic.

The pleasure began to build inside her, relentless, unstoppable, and she twisted beneath him, desperate to fall over the edge again, if only to get some relief. He bent his head then, covering her mouth with his own, his tongue pushing hungrily inside as he surged into her over and over.

His kiss was feverish, half savage, and she returned it, biting at him, nipping him as her hips lifted against his, trying to increase the sensation, chasing the friction.

All embarrassment had left her now, and there was no weirdness. No sense that what she was doing was wrong. She felt nothing but free.

Then he shifted, freeing one of his hands and pushing it between her thighs, finding her clit and pressing down hard. And she came again, sobbing into his mouth, feeling his body gather as he thrust harder. As if he'd had a leash on himself and was only now letting go.

He drove into her, the power in his leans hips making her shake, and dimly she was aware of when he stiffened and he said her name desperately, his fingers tightening around hers as the orgasm came for him too. Then his heavy body came down on hers, pinning her to the mattress, his breathing ragged. His weight was almost crushing, but she didn't want to move. She felt anchored, his body on hers protective, banishing the lingering shreds of that damn nightmare.

Then abruptly he pushed himself up on his hands, looking down at her, another of those fierce expressions on his face. Her chest tightened. Was he going to tell her this was all a mistake? Because she didn't know what she'd do if he said that. The decision she'd made when she'd told him to stay hadn't been a mistake, no, that had been very purposeful.

That nightmare, one she hadn't had for years and years, had left her feeling so cold, and when she'd woken to find his arms around her, holding her, she couldn't bear for him to leave. And then it had become apparent that she was affecting him badly, and everything had suddenly become very simple.

He'd offered her himself earlier. And so she would take him.

Except maybe now that hadn't been such a good idea?

He eased back, withdrawing from her.

She shivered at the sensation, half of her tensing, waiting for him push himself away from her and leave the bed.

But he didn't. Instead he looked down at her for a long minute, that blue flame flickering in his eyes. Then her stomach lurched as he shifted again, putting his hands firmly on her and turning her over onto her stomach.

"W-What are you doing?" Her voice was breathless and she knew she sounded half afraid. But she couldn't stop the plea from coming out. "Don't go."

"I'm not going anywhere." His hand came down to rest on the top of her spine, pressing there lightly. "You think I could actually leave when you're naked and under me? Jesus Christ, baby. It's like you don't know me at all." His free hand moved down her body, finding the waistband of her shorts and tugging them down. "Okay, *now* you're naked."

But she was still struggling to process the fact that he'd called her *baby.* And not for any kind of show. "Baby?"

"Yeah." His hand on her spine stroked down slowly, making her want to arch into his palm. "You got a problem with that?"

Good question. Did she?

Why are you questioning anything right now when he's in bed with you?

"No," she said huskily. "I don't."

"Good." His hand moved back up her spine, then down again in another long stroke. "Now, lie still."

"Why?" She turned her head on the pillow, wanting to see what he was going to do, only for that stroking hand to suddenly grip the back of her neck in a firm, dominant hold.

"Do as you're told," he growled, his breath warm in her ear. "It's my fucking turn and I'm taking it."

Oh God, why did she love that roughness in his voice? And the way his hand was gripping her? Why did it make her shiver all over with delight? She had no idea, only that something inside her wanted his dominance because it felt like a claim. Like possession.

She had never been wanted by anyone. Until now.

"Take it then," she said thickly. "And stop talking."

"No." His teeth grazed her shoulder, nipping her and she jerked at the small pain, amazed at how much it turned her on. "You love it when I talk, especially if it's dirty."

"I don't," she whispered, not because it wasn't true, but because she wanted to argue with him.

"You do." His mouth brushed over the back of her neck, moving down her spine. "Don't lie to me. I saw the look in your eyes when I told you to watch me fuck you. That got you hot."

She shivered again as he trailed kisses over her skin, his hands stroking her sides. "No."

"Yes." His fingertips grazed the curve of her ass, stroking the tops of her thighs. "You fucking loved it, Bree."

"I . . . maybe." She groaned then, the sound ripped from her as his palms pressed against her inner thighs, pushing them apart, the sensation of being held open filling her with a dark and dirty pleasure. "Oh God, what are you doing?"

"Lift your hips for me," he ordered. "Yeah . . . that's it." The bed dipped as she felt him move. "What am I going to do? I'm going to eat you out. Put my tongue in that gorgeous little pussy of yours, taste you." His breath was on the backs of her thighs, his fingers spreading her open again. "Fuck, I can't wait. I bet you taste delicious."

She was shivering again, helplessly, gasping as she felt the wicked slide of his tongue through the folds of her sex, stroking up to her clit and circling it delicately. He made another one of those sexy, hungry-sounding growls, the vibration of it against her flesh making her cry out.

His fingers pushed at her, urging her up on her knees, before spreading her out even more, allowing his mouth full access to her pussy. "Mmm," he murmured, warm breath over her achingly sensitive skin. "I was right. You taste so fucking good. And I can taste myself too, baby. Christ, it's so fucking hot. That's us. That's us together."

She wanted to say something back, something dirty in return, but his mouth was on her again, his tongue pushing into her, and all she could do was bury her hot face in the pillow and sob with agonized pleasure.

The stubble along his hard jaw brushed against the sensitive skin of her thighs, making her so aware of who was doing this to her, and suddenly it seemed all too much. She tried to lift her hips away from him, but he growled like the predator he apparently was. "Don't you fucking dare. I want that pussy on my face." And without waiting for her response, he pulled her back down, holding her firmly against his mouth, his tongue sliding into her again.

Her fingers curled into the sheets, her mouth open against the cotton, her mind slowly imploding under the weight of the pleasure he was giving her.

She was going to come again, for the third time that night, and she didn't think she'd survive it. But she wasn't going to get a choice, because then she felt his fingers sliding over her, finding her clit and circling, teasing as his tongue pushed in deep.

It wasn't so much a climax as a cataclysm that felt like it was ripping her in two, making her scream into the pillow, her hips shuddering and jerking in his grip. And even then he didn't let her go, continuing to feast on her, making satisfied growling noises as she sobbed through the aftershocks.

She didn't think it was possible to want anything more after that, but her body didn't agree, tightening again with need as he rubbed his jaw against her inner thighs.

"That's it," he murmured, brushing his mouth over where he'd just rubbed his jaw, the bed dipping again as he moved. "Get ready for another round."

Sabrina collapsed facedown on the mattress, her body heavy, boneless. "I don't know if I can." Her voice was scratchy and half muffled by the pillow. "I think I'm dead. You've killed me."

"If three orgasms is all it takes to kill you, then you need to toughen up." His hands were on her hips again, lifting her slightly. "Here, let me help you with that." The heat of his body was pressing against the backs of her thighs and her butt, and she felt the head of his cock nudge the entrance to her pussy.

She groaned. "Kellan . . ."

"It's okay, baby." He gripped her hip with one hand, stroking down her spine with the other, easing forward slowly, so fucking slowly. "You can take me one last time."

Yes, she could. She damn well could. And then she was, gasping as he pushed deep inside her, beginning to move. The hand on her back moved to her neck and then into her hair, his fingers curling around it and holding on, drawing her head back. And the pressure against her back increased as he leaned forward, pressing her down into the mattress as he kissed her exposed neck, then bit the delicate tendons at the side.

She shuddered, his hold and the feel of his teeth on her skin making everything pull deliciously tight inside her.

Then he began to move, lazily at first, as if he had all the time in the world, deep and slow. She panted, arching against him, wanting that hard chest pressed to the length of her spine. Wanting his skin on hers.

"There, I knew you could do it," he whispered against her neck. "I knew you could take it. You're amazing, Sabrina. You're just fucking amazing."

"So are you . . ." She could barely think now. "You're . . . oh God, Kel. You feel so good."

He bit her again as if to reward her, moving faster, harder. The long, slick slide of his cock in and out of her was driving her insane. So she began to move too, arching her spine, lifting her hips and shoving herself back onto him.

"Yeah, that's it . . ." His voice was ragged, breathless. "I love that, Bree. I love the way you're fucking me."

She was loving it too and she especially loved the desperate note in his voice, the raggedness. *She* was making him sound like that. Her wicked, dangerous, hot best friend and she was making him pant.

Finally. Fucking finally.

She shoved back harder, causing him to groan and his hand in her hair to tighten. Urging him deeper, faster. And he gave it to her, driving forward, driving her into the mattress, a savage growl escaping his throat with every flex of his hips.

She hadn't thought she'd be able to come again, but then he took her hand and guided it beneath her, down between her thighs to where they were joined. And she could feel him moving in and out of her, feel the stretch of her sex around his. It was so hot, so dirty that she couldn't stop shivering, and then, when he guided her fingers to her clit, getting her to touch herself in time with his thrusts, everything began to tighten inside her.

Oh God, she was going to come again and come hard.

Then she did, the climax surging through her, overwhelming her. This time the only sound she made was a broken whimper as she exploded around him, shuddering and panting, collapsing down onto the bed, barely aware of anything but the unrolling pleasure inside her.

He must have been waiting for her because as soon as she came, his own movements became wilder, falling out of rhythm, and then he gave one last deep, endless thrust, a groan breaking from him. "Fuck . . . *Sabrina* . . ." And his body shook against hers, his hips shuddering, his breathing harsh in the silence of the room as he came.

She closed her eyes, relishing the sound of her name and the desperation in it, loving the way he fell against her. So heavy, so hot, his body covering hers, surrounding her with his heat and his scent, the freshness cut now with the musk of male arousal and sex.

There was a silence in the room, broken only by their harsh breathing. Then a moment later, Kellan withdrew from her and shifted. She almost opened her mouth to tell him not to, that she wanted him to stay, but it soon become apparent that he wasn't going anywhere as his arm wound around her waist and his fingers splayed out on her stomach, turning her onto her side and drawing her in close.

The tension that had started to creep through her vanished, the possessiveness of his hold making her relax. The warmth of his body up against her back was so perfect that she couldn't stop herself from nestling back into him.

He made another of those satisfied sounds, his fingers on her stomach stroking her gently. "So," he said after another long moment of silence. "Are you going to tell me what that nightmare was all about?"

Oh. That. She should have known he wouldn't have left that alone.

She sighed. "Oh, it's one I used to have a lot after Mom and my brothers died. I just haven't had it since I was a kid."

"Want to share?"

"Not really." She didn't like to think about it too much. Certainly she hadn't thought about it since she'd stopped having them around the same time she'd met Kellan. And she definitely didn't want to think about why she'd had one now.

"It's okay, Bree." His mouth grazed her shoulder. "I'm right here. I'll keep you safe. Tell me."

Her throat tightened at the reassurance in his voice. She didn't want to tell him and yet she had enough secrets she was keeping from him. And he was here, holding her . . . The nightmare couldn't touch her now, could it?

"Sometimes . . . I dream I'm still in the car with Mom when it went off the road and into the river. And the water is coming in. And she's pulling at my seat belt and smashing the window, pushing me through it." Cold fear wound through her. "And I . . . I don't want to go. I want to be with her. But the current is pulling me away and all I can see is her face disappearing . . ."

He knew how her mother had died. She'd told him once, back when she'd been a teenager. About how the car had gone into the river and how her mother had saved her. About how she'd been the only one to survive. But she'd never told him about the nightmares, mainly because she'd stopped having them. And she didn't like to talk about it. Even now it was hard.

His arm tightened even further. "Oh . . . Bree . . ."

"It's okay," she said shakily. "I haven't had that nightmare for a long time. I just . . . don't know why I had it again."

There was a silence.

Then he said softly, "You don't want to be in the river with her, baby."

She took a little breath, the words hitting her hard. Well, of course she didn't want to be, not really. And she knew that. Didn't she?

He fitted her more closely against him, as if he was aware of exactly how the heat of him drove away the cold. "And she wouldn't want you to be either. That's why she pushed you out of the window. She saved you. She wanted you to be here." His mouth brushed the back of her neck again. "With me."

Unexpectedly, the prickle of tears started behind her closed lids. "I don't know," she heard herself say, even though she hadn't meant to. "Sometimes I wonder why she did. Dad didn't stay for me . . ." She stopped, emotion sitting like a stone in the center of her chest. God why was she saying all this stuff? It had happened years ago, it shouldn't matter now.

"No." Kellan's voice was flat with denial. "He left because he couldn't deal. You know that. It wasn't you. It never was."

"I know," she said thickly. "Just . . . sometimes . . ."

"Don't." He held her so tightly, like she was precious to him and he never wanted to let her go. "Don't think like that." There was a fierce note to the words. "I'm glad she saved you. I'm glad you're here and that you came to us. That you came to me. Because fuck knows, my life would have been a hell of a lot poorer without you in it."

She swallowed, the emotion in her chest shifting around, making those damn tears pressing against her lids seep out. He was so good to her that it broke her just a little bit. "Thanks,

Kel." She put her hand over his, where it rested on her stomach. "And sorry. I didn't mean to spoil the moment."

"You're not spoiling anything. Shit, I was the one who asked what the nightmare was about anyway." He nuzzled the side of her neck. "I'm here for you, okay?"

"I know."

"Make sure you do." He shifted even closer and she became aware that there was something long and thick pressing against her butt. God, he was hard again. But all he said was, "You should sleep."

"Are you sure? You don't feel like you want me to sleep."

He gave a low rumbling laugh that vibrated against her back. "Oh, don't worry about me. But just so you know, I'm keeping score, and currently it's my two orgasms to your four." His breath ghosted over her skin as he kissed her nape. "I'm planning on getting those last two out of you in the morning."

The promise in the words almost tempted her to turn over and pay him back right then and there.

But then, contrary to all her expectations, she fell asleep with his arms around her.

He woke her in the early morning, whispering in her ear, "I want your hands on me, baby. Now. Right now."

And sleep fell away from her almost instantly. She turned and pushed him down on the mattress, and did what he asked. She put her hands on him and finally she got to explore all that hard, cut muscle, all that smooth golden skin she'd been fantasizing about for so long. With her fingers. With her tongue. Making him as desperate for her as she was for him.

"Suck me," he ordered, losing patience and pushing her head down. And she let him, taking the long, thick length of his cock in her hand, loving the velvet feel of his skin covering all that hardness. She stroked him, tested him, then she bent and took him in her mouth, the taste of him salty and delicious.

His hands twisted in her hair as she sucked him, as she made him shudder, made him growl her name in that deep voice, turned ragged and broken by her mouth and what she was doing to him.

She loved that too. Loved having this lethally dangerous man shaking beneath her.

He came down the back of her throat with a cry and she swallowed all of him, relishing every second of it. Then she stroked him back to hardness again and moved on top of him, straddling him, then sinking down on his cock, making them both groan at the aching pleasure of it.

His hands gripped her hips and he showed her how to ride him, how fast and how hard, then how slow and how deep. Until it got too much and there was no room for anything but fast, faster, harder. Until the climax ripped them both to shreds.

"I think we're even now," she murmured when she'd recovered enough to speak.

"No," he growled. "You're still one up. Not that I give a shit." He reached up and pulled her down, holding her tight, nuzzling against her neck. "Because we're doing this again, Sabrina. Just so you know. Again and again."

The words were a relief, because she wanted to do it again and again with him too. But there was a part of her that was scared, that wasn't sure she wanted to get in any deeper with him than she was already. She didn't want to argue though, not when he was beneath her, holding her, his warm body better than any mattress.

So she only nodded wordlessly, her head pillowed on his hard chest, listening to his heartbeat as she drifted off to sleep again.

CHAPTER 11

Kellan was awakened the next morning by someone shaking his shoulder.

"Kel, wake up," a feminine voice demanded.

Sabrina.

A rush of heat went through him, his morning hard-on suddenly getting a hell of a lot harder, and he automatically reached out, his hand encountering warmth and feminine curves.

He gave a growl of appreciation and pulled her against him. Or at least he tried, until she went stiff with resistance and shook him again.

"No, we don't have time for that," she said impatiently. "Wake up. I need to show you something."

Kellan opened one eye.

Sabrina was sitting on the bed next to him, unfortunately dressed again in her sleep shorts and T-shirt, her laptop held on her knees. Her cheeks were pink and her hazel eyes were glowing, and he could still feel her fingers on him from earlier on that morning, still feel her mouth wrapped around his cock.

"You need to be naked," he murmured, tightening his arm around her waist, unable to drag his gaze from her lips.

She made another impatient sound. "And you need to focus. I've been decrypting what was on that hard drive."

Instantly all thoughts of sex vanished, a pulse of adrenaline overwhelming the earlier heat.

He released her and sat up, scrubbing a hand over his face. "Okay, tell me. What did you find?"

"Right, so it was weird. The thing was encrypted, like I said, but decrypting it was . . . Well, let's just say that I was expecting it to be much harder. Anyway, that's not the only thing that was strange. There's only one file on it and it's a list of dates and what looks like map coordinates."

Kellan frowned. Did that mean . . . ? "That's it? That's the file that Night was looking for?"

"I mean . . . it must be. There's nothing on his desktop, which must mean that hard drive."

Something tight inside Kellan gathered a little bit tighter. Shit, he was hoping for something more conclusive than that. Like, say, nothing at all. "We need to look up those coordinates," he said flatly. "Figure out what they refer to. They could mean nothing."

"Well, I did look them up. They refer to various different places in Central and South America. Colombia, Guatemala, Peru."

His gut clenched, a sick feeling settling inside it. Jesus. All places that had a healthy drug trade ruled by the South American cartels. "Great. So it's entirely possible that the coordinates relate back to this arms ring bullshit then."

The glow in Sabrina's eyes dimmed. "Yes, it could."

Ah . . . fuck. So this was it? Did finding this file mean his father was guilty?

And if he is, what other lies has he told you? What have you been protecting all these years?

But he couldn't accept that. Wouldn't. His father had to be innocent. He had to be. Because the alternative was that Kellan had given up his child all those years ago, to protect a liar. A hypocrite. A man who'd sold guns to kill innocent people.

That's not the reason.

No, he wasn't thinking about this anymore. What he needed was to figure out what the hell the info in the file meant, so he could prove his father's innocence once and for all.

"Was there anything else in the file?" The question came out sharp, but he didn't bother to soften it. "Anything at all?"

If his tone bothered her, she didn't show it. "There was a name. Only the one, which I thought was really strange. Andrew Elliott. That mean anything to you?"

Oh yeah, it meant something all right.

"Elliott's one of Dad's cronies. Used to be ex-military and now owns a massive manufacturing company. He's filthy rich, comes from one of New York's society families." Kellan narrowed his gaze at her. "That was the only name?"

"Yeah and like I said, it's weird. Why name anyone?" Sabrina frowned, chewing on her bottom lip, which Kellan found incredibly distracting for a second. "The encryption was easy to break too. Which is odd for a file as important as Night seems to think it is."

She wasn't wrong. It was odd. But he'd already come to a decision about what to do. "We need more," he said. "I need absolute proof of Dad's innocence to take to Night."

"Well, the hard drive was in his safe . . ."

"So? Doesn't mean Dad knows what's on it or what it means." The protestation sounded hollow, even to his own ears, but he ignored it.

Sabrina gave him a look he couldn't quite interpret. "We should call the team and let them know we have the file. Downloading the information is all we were supposed to do."

"No. I told Night I was going to find proof and that's what

I'm going to do." And goddamn, finally a plan was slowly resolving itself in his head. It wasn't what Jacob Night wanted, but that was too bad. Kellan wanted proof and he was going to get it. "I think I need to pay Andrew Elliott a little visit."

She blinked. "What? Like, actually talk to him you mean?"

"Yeah, that's exactly what I mean."

Energized, Kellan pushed himself out of bed and strode over to where his bag was on the floor by the window. At last he had something to do instead of sitting on the sidelines. Something that wasn't fiddling about with files and computers, or having difficult conversations with and lying to his father. He'd always preferred the direct approach and going and talking to Elliott was as direct as it got.

As he bent to grab some clothes, he was conscious of Sabrina's gaze following him, and predictably his cock liked that idea very much. For a second he debated whether or not they had some time to revisit a few memories from the night before, but then decided that there would be plenty of time for that later. And there *would* be later.

Last night with her had been . . . Well, he couldn't think of when he'd had better, hotter sex in all his life, and now they'd taken that first step, he'd be fucked if he took it back. Sure, he'd wondered about crossing the line with her earlier, and whether that was a good idea, but it was too late for recriminations and backtracking now. He didn't want to anyway.

And certainly not after her confession of her nightmare and the terrible vulnerability in her voice when she'd wondered why her mother had saved her. As if she truly didn't know.

He'd wanted to wrap her up in his arms in that moment, run his hands all over her slender body, show her exactly how glad he was that her mother had saved her. And he might have if she hadn't already had four orgasms in a row and sounded exhausted.

He'd settled for holding her close instead, keeping his arms around her as she'd fallen asleep, so she'd know he was there.

Because he was always there for her and always would be. Even now they were more than simply friends.

"So what?" Sabrina asked doubtfully as he grabbed some clothing. "You're going to simply stroll up to him and ask him why his name would be in a mysterious file you found on a badly encrypted hard drive in your father's safe?"

"Sure, why not?" He turned and gave her a grin. "You know I like the direct approach."

"He's not going to just tell you, Kel."

"In which case, I'll give him some incentive." He didn't bother hiding the dangerous note in his voice. "This is the only lead we have and I'm following it."

"But this is going beyond the mission."

"So? I told Night I'd get him the intel and I will. But not until I get proof that Dad's either innocent or guilty."

She was still chewing on her lip, gazing at him uncertainly. "We have a time limit. They want that intel ASAP."

"Yeah. Which is why I'm going to borrow the helicopter. Elliott's in New York, so I'll fly direct."

Her brows drew together, a gold gleam in her eyes. "'I'll?' Don't you mean 'we'll'?"

"This is my deal. You can stay here where—"

"No, hell no." She put the laptop to one side and slipped off the bed, crossing over to where he stood. "I'm coming. I'm part of this mission, remember?"

Christ. He didn't want to take her, not when things could get messy and/or dangerous. Plus, he didn't want her to see him get lethal with Elliott if the situation called for it. He'd rather she kept on thinking of him as one of the good guys.

"It could be dangerous, Bree," he said, looking down at her. "Especially if Elliott turns out to be involved."

"So? Believe it or not, I can fire a gun. Faith got me some lessons when I joined 11th Hour."

Shit, really? This was the first he'd heard of it. "When? And why didn't you tell me?"

"Because you didn't need to know. Plus, I didn't want you telling me that I didn't need lessons since I wouldn't be going out in the field."

He let out a breath. "I wouldn't have said that."

"Yes, you would." She gave him back nothing but determination. "Anyway, I can defend myself if need be. And you might need me. How are you going to get to see this guy? You're going to rock up in your helicopter going, 'Hey, Andy, can I have a word?'"

Kellan stared at her, his heart beating faster at the gold glinting in her eyes, at the fierce look on her face. He wanted to protect her—he'd always wanted to—but shit, she'd fucking taken charge of this mission since they'd gotten here and she'd proved herself. So . . . why not take her?

Apart from anything else, he had a feeling she'd make it very difficult for him if he insisted she stay here and there was no time for arguing anyway.

Also, there was the matter of how he was going to borrow his father's helicopter for a trip to New York, especially since flying off randomly to go visit one of his father's friends would no doubt generate suspicion.

But taking his fiancée out for a surprise trip to the Big Apple? Yeah, that would work.

Not forgetting that you might need her.

He sighed. "Okay, okay. You can come. But from here on in, I'm in charge of this thing and you do what I tell you." The gold in her gaze gleamed a little brighter at that, and his breath caught. "Shit, Bree. Don't look at me like that."

Her gaze dropped, to where he was hard and getting harder, and since he was naked, it was pretty fucking obvious. "Why not?" Her voice had gotten husky.

"Because you said there was no time for that. And you're right, there isn't."

She swallowed and look away from him. "Of course there isn't."

Oh no, he wasn't having that.

Catching her chin between his fingers, he turned her back to face him, looking down into her eyes, knowing already what she was thinking and wanting to nip that in the bud straight away. "No time doesn't mean no, okay? Because I meant what I said last night. I'm not done with you, Sabrina Leighton. And I might not be done with you for a fucking long time."

Color flooded her cheeks, her freckles standing out, her eyes suddenly very green as they searched his. As if she didn't believe him. As if she thought he was lying.

So he gripped her chin tighter and leaned down, covering her mouth with his. But not hard or fierce like the night before. This time he went slow and deep, tasting her, convincing her without words, showing her the truth.

She made a soft noise in her throat, leaning into him, her hands coming to his chest, spreading out on his bare skin. And he knew he was going to have to stop this in its tracks or else they weren't going to leave this room.

He lifted his head, almost forgetting himself when she rose on her tiptoes, trying to follow him to keep his mouth on hers. But he kept a tight grip on her, holding her still. "That's not a threat," he said softly. "That's a promise. Understand me?"

Her throat moved as she swallowed. "Okay. It's just . . . I'm not done with you yet either."

Gently, he stroked her bottom lip with his thumb, relishing the soft feel of it. "Good. You'd better not be."

Sabrina gave him a look from beneath thick dark lashes, then before he could move, she closed her teeth around his thumb and gave it a nip.

The slight pain shot straight to his cock and he inhaled sharply.

But she was already stepping away, acting like nothing had happened. "Right, so I guess you have a plan for getting to this Elliott guy? Because we're going to need one."

He did have a plan. And it was a pretty good one, even though her soul cringed at what he was going to expect of her.

He'd made her sit down and see if she could hack into Andrew Elliott's company and access his secretary's computer, get into his diary, which indeed, she could. They'd discovered that Elliott was attending a charity gala at the Met that night, which Kellan thought was the perfect opportunity to have his little "chat" since it didn't include having to mess around with making appointments or breaking into his house—something Kellan had seriously suggested and she had nixed on the grounds that it was a stupid idea. She didn't like the sound of the gala any better, but unfortunately it looked like it was the best way to get access to the guy.

Pity she hated parties and society parties in particular. It brought back memories of hovering on the outskirts of the parties the Blakes had thrown. Feeling out of place, not one of the family, and yet not a friend either. Not an acquaintance, yet not a stranger. A misplaced person who belonged nowhere.

Yeah, she did not want to go. Then again, there was no way Kellan was leaving her behind. She had no idea what this Elliott guy would say to him, but if it had anything to do with Phillip she had to be there. Not that she had any idea of how she was going to stop Kellan finding out about his father's guilt. If indeed he was guilty, and since that conversation of Phillip's that she'd overheard, she couldn't kick the feeling that he was.

He'd betrayed his marriage vows and had another child. A child she'd seen with her own eyes. So why wouldn't he betray his country? Plus, her mind kept going back over the way he'd talked about that "shipment" and the people who "wouldn't be happy." On the surface so innocuous and yet . . .

She kept those doubts to herself. Kellan couldn't know. She'd promised Charlotte that would remain a secret.

A couple of hours later, Kellan having spoken to his father about taking his fiancée for a trip to New York in the Bell and received the go ahead, Sabrina found herself out on the lawn near the hanger where the helicopter had been prepared and was now ready for takeoff.

Flying to New York in a helicopter to attend a gala? What the fuck is happening to you?

She had no idea. All she needed was some damn princess gown and her Cinderella transformation would be complete.

You already have the handsome prince.

Sabrina's throat tightened as she approached the helicopter, watching as Kellan moved around it, fluid and purposeful, making last-minute checks.

No, she didn't have the handsome prince. Sure, she'd had him the night before but she didn't *have* him. At least not in the way she wanted. It had been great sex—life-changing sex if she was honest with herself—but nothing more than that. He'd told her he wasn't done with her, and she still didn't quite know what she was going to do about that, because she wasn't done with him either. She'd never be done with him. But one day, he'd be done with her. And that would break her heart.

He was always going to break your heart.

Yeah, that was true. So maybe she should take what she could get while the going was good.

Kellan came around the front of the helicopter, spotted her, and grinned. And that aching heart of hers—the one he was going to break one day—tightened. Because he had that boyish excitement about him that he always got when he was about to fly and it never failed to make her breath catch.

He loved to fly and after the accident he'd told her he wasn't going to let one helo crash end his flying days. So as soon as he'd been medically cleared, he'd gotten straight back into a helicopter again. And he'd been keeping those flying skills sharp in San Diego by flying the small collection of 11th Hour helicopters when he could.

He leaned back against the machine as she approached, tall and gorgeous in jeans and a blue T-shirt the same color as his eyes, a battered leather jacket thrown over the top.

"Are you ready?" That heart-stopping grin was playing around his mouth, his gaze brilliant. "Your chariot awaits."

She gave him a dubious look. "So what are we going to do about clothes for this gala thing? I don't know if it's a jeans and T-shirt kind of event."

"Don't worry about that. We'll go get something from Barneys."

Ugh. Shopping.

She pulled a face, but he only laughed at her. "A tux for me and a dress for you. It'll take five minutes, I promise."

"Can't we just hire something?"

He gave her a slightly incredulous glance. "Uh, no. We can't. Not for a gala at the Met." Pushing himself away from the machine, he turned back to it, then pulled open the passenger side door, reaching in, then bringing out a helmet, holding it out for her. "Come on. Let's go."

Ten minutes later they were in the air, Kellan's strong hands on the joystick as they flew. She'd flown with him many times and yet she never failed to get a kick out of watching him pilot a helicopter. He was so confident, so sure. As if the machine would do anything and everything he wanted it to, without any problems at all.

But staring at those long-fingered hands of his wasn't good for her peace of mind, so she tried to concentrate on something else.

Like this mission maybe?

Oh yes, that.

"So," she said into the microphone on her helmet, "did Phillip ask any questions?"

"Nope. He was all good. Even cleared us a spot in a downtown helipad to park this thing."

She wanted to ask him if he thought Phillip suspected anything, but there was no reason to ask that. No reason that Phillip would suspect anything, other than her own doubts about him. So she kept quiet and asked instead, "How are we going to get into this gala when we don't have an invite?"

Kellan glanced at her and grinned. "I'm Phillip Blake's oldest son. I don't need an invite."

There was something about him, a kind of bright, crackling energy that hadn't been there the past couple of days they'd been at his parents' house. But she knew what that was.

"You're liking this," she said quietly. "Doing something, I mean."

"Sitting on my butt on a mission isn't my style." Another of those brilliant glances. "But like I told you last night, you did fantastically. We wouldn't have gotten Elliott's name if not for you."

The warmth in her chest grew and she had to distract herself by looking out over the city they were fast approaching while sunlight glinted off car windows on the freeway far beneath them. "Thanks, Kel. That means a lot."

"Well, it's true."

The radio crackled and she waited while he answered a couple of calls from other pilots also in the air, confirming their position.

A feeling of awkwardness overcame her as he finished up, and she didn't know what else to say. Part of her wanted to talk about what had happened the night before, to ask him about where this was going and what exactly did he mean when he'd told her he wouldn't be done with her for a "fucking long time." But another part of her didn't want to broach the topic, too afraid of his answer.

It was silly to talk about that anyway, especially when they had more important things to be doing.

"You okay?" he asked after a long moment of silence, clearly sensing something was up. "You're very quiet."

His voice through the headset crackled, but she felt the deep vibration of it all the same and it made her hands knot in her lap. "I'm fine."

But he knew her too well. "Oh, come on, you're not. It's last night, isn't it?"

She let out a breath. There was no point in trying to hide it. And they needed to talk about it. "Yeah."

"I told you it wasn't over. That I want more."

"I know, but it's still . . . strange. I mean, you're my best friend and now . . ." She stopped, suddenly feeling like an idiot. "It's just sex, right? It's not as if this is going to change things between us or anything."

Kellan's brows drew down. "I'm beginning to think that sometimes you don't listen to me when I tell you stuff. Or that you don't believe me. Don't you remember me saying I'm here for you?"

She remembered. It still made her want to cry. "I heard."

"So? I never say shit I don't mean, you know that. So when I say I'm here for you, I am." He glanced at her and she could feel the sharpness of that gaze go right through her. "And that's regardless of whether we're sleeping together or not. Understand?"

She wanted to believe him, she really did. And if there was anyone in this world she could count on, it was him. Except . . . "Lots of people have left me, Kel," she said quietly and with way more honesty than she'd intended. "And sometimes that makes it difficult to believe that anyone would want to stay."

His expression softened. "Hey, I get that. But have I ever once left you? Have I ever once not been your friend?"

Her throat tightened. Of course he hadn't ever left her. He'd always been there when she needed him. "No."

"That's right. So you need to believe me when I tell you stuff like that, okay? You need to trust me that nothing could make me stop being your friend."

She had to swallow back that lump in her throat, ignore the emotion that pulled tight in her chest. That one that made her want to tell him how she really felt, that the love that filled her heart wasn't a friend kind of love. But she couldn't tell him that, so she didn't. She smiled instead. "Okay. I believe you."

"You trust me too?"

"Always."

"Good." It sounded like he was going to say more, but then he received another few radio calls as they approached Manhattan, and the moment for more conversation passed.

Not that Sabrina was unhappy about that. She should never have broached the topic in the first place and especially not now, in the middle of a mission. Maybe later, when they had more time.

Or maybe not at all. You were going to take what you could get, remember?

Oh yes, that's right. She was. In which case, thinking and worrying about this was pointless—at least right now it was.

Sabrina stayed quiet as fifteen minutes later Kellan brought the helicopter in to land on one of the East River helipads. Another fifteen minutes later, she found herself sitting next to him in a car with a driver that Kellan had apparently organized for them before they'd left Southampton. Their first stop before getting to the gala, he informed her in that flat no-argument tone, was Barneys.

Yay, shopping. Not.

She'd never been interested in clothes—not when circuits and codes were more fascinating to her—and she still wasn't. But that didn't seem to matter since Kellan, stalking past racks of gowns, trailed by a fawning sales assistant who seemed to think he was some kind of minor god, clearly had his own ideas about what she should wear.

She wondered if she should argue with him, find her own damn gown, but after fifteen minutes, where he efficiently quartered the whole floor, eying up various designers' offerings, he eventually stopped in front of a mannequin wearing a shimmering strapless gown in deep green silk.

"That one," he said.

Sabrina opened her mouth to tell him that it probably wouldn't fit—even though she rather liked it—not to mention the fact that it was likely to be horribly expensive and she'd never wear it again, but before she could get the words out, he'd turned to the sales assistant and had given her Sabrina's size, instructing her to bring the gown to one of the fitting rooms.

Sabrina shut her mouth with a snap, a small thrill shooting through her. Though whether it was annoyance at the sheer arrogance of him or delight at the way he was taking charge, she couldn't quite tell.

"I can find my own gown, you know," she said, following him as he turned and strode toward the fitting rooms.

"You hate shopping." He didn't even turn. "I thought I'd make it easier."

She scowled. Definitely it was annoyance now, though she wasn't sure exactly why. "How did you know my size?"

Kellan sat in a fluid sprawl on one of the armchairs near the fitting room, his long denim-clad legs out in front of him, powerful arms crossed over his chest. He glanced up at her, a flash of ice blue. "Bree, I've known you for fifteen years. I know what dress size you are."

She blinked at him, the annoyance starting to melt around the edges, as if she liked that he knew. "But I don't know your pants size."

His mouth curved. "Really? After last night?"

She could feel her cheeks getting hot. "*That* is not your pants size."

"'Big' is the word you're looking for." There was a gleam in his eyes, which made her cheeks get even hotter.

Damn him. Teasing him was normal, but this was different. This was sexual and out of her wheelhouse. She'd never gotten the hang of flirting and it felt especially weird to do it with him.

"I can find my own dress, you know," she said, deciding to ignore the whole pants size argument. "I don't need you to start choosing for me."

"I thought the less time we spent here the better." He tilted his head, eying her. "Plus, I didn't think you were interested in choosing gowns."

"I'm not."

"So what does it matter if I choose it for you?"

She shifted on her feet, not able to come up with a single reason other than the fact that it was making her prickly.

"Hey," he said softly. "The quicker we do this, the quicker we get this damn mission over and done with. And then we can figure out where we go from here, okay? I only wanted to make sure this gets done and fast." He leaned forward all of a sudden, a lazy hand coming out and catching behind her thigh, his long fingers spreading out, the heat of his skin seeping through the denim of her jeans. The wicked gleam in his eyes turned even wickeder. "Mainly so I can get you back into bed."

Her breath caught and she had an almost overpowering urge to grab that hand and move it higher, to the curve of her butt, see what he'd do, whether his breath would catch the way hers was doing now. A reminder to herself that it wasn't all one way, not anymore.

But then the sales assistant returned and Sabrina found herself being led toward a fitting room, her arms full of shimmering green silk, a pair of strappy sandals that matched the dress perfectly dangling from her fingers.

Once inside, she reluctantly stripped off her jeans and T-shirt, and then, after a glance at the gown, her bra as well since it was strapless. Then gingerly she stepped into the gown and pulled up the fabric, wriggling a little bit.

Outside the fitting room, she could hear the tinkling laugh of the sales assistant and the rumble of Kellan's deep voice. It made her scowl, which was stupid. She'd had to get to grips with jealousy a long time ago and she'd thought she'd had it handled, but clearly one night with him and she was back at square one again, hating all the women who flirted with him. The beautiful women he tended to favor, mostly because she was not beautiful and never would be.

Fighting the emotions that clawed at her and trying to ignore the sound of the sales assistant's laugh, Sabrina managed to get the zipper of the gown done up herself. Then she stood for a moment in front of the mirror, staring at her reflection and blinking.

A tall woman stood there, encased in green silk that fitted her curves to perfection and highlighted the pale skin of her shoulders. The color of the gown caught the green sparks in her hazel eyes, intensifying the color.

She looked . . . good. Which was a surprise since she hadn't expected to.

"Come out." Kellan's voice came from outside the door. "I want to see what it looks like."

You look fantastic, you know you do. Why not show him?

She swallowed and moved to the door, her heartbeat thumping as she pulled it open and stepped out.

Kellan was standing in front of the fitting room door his arms folded. And as she came out, something flared deep in his blue gaze. He went very still, staring at her as if there was no one in the entire store except the pair of them.

It was very, very obvious that he liked what he saw.

The uncertainty inside her fell away in that moment and she lifted her chin. "What do you think?" she asked, knowing full well what he thought and yet wanting to hear it anyway.

"You really want to know?" He sounded rough. "Okay, this is what I think." And he took two strides toward her, catching her face between his palms and tilting her head back, his mouth covering hers.

He kissed her, long and deep, and she shivered, wanting more.

But then he pulled back, staring down into her eyes. "I want to fuck you very badly right now, Sabrina. So maybe you'd better keep your distance from me tonight, otherwise I have no idea how I'm going to concentrate on this goddamn mission."

The words rolled over her skin like a caress and suddenly the sales assistant didn't matter anymore. None of those women mattered anymore. She was the one he was looking at now and that's what counted.

She raised a brow. "So I look okay then?"

He smiled, the kind of smile that made her heart turn over and over inside her chest. "Baby, you look magnificent."

She blushed like a rose. "You have good taste in gowns."

"In women too, apparently." He stepped back and didn't hide the fact that it was reluctant. "Keep the dress on. We'll go find a tux for me and then . . ." His smile was slightly feral this time. "It's showtime."

CHAPTER 12

Kellan reached behind him to make sure the Glock he'd brought with him was sitting firmly against the small of his back, then he glanced over at Sabrina, who was sitting in the car next to him. She had her hands in her lap and was looking out the window, her bottom lip caught between her teeth.

For a moment, he simply stared at her. At the elegant curve of her neck and all that lovely pale skin on show, her narrow shoulders rising gracefully from the green silk of her gown. They'd stopped by the makeup counter on the way out of Barneys where she'd reluctantly let one of the sales assistants do her makeup. The woman had done a great job, keeping things simple, but highlighting Sabrina's beautiful hazel eyes. There was green shimmer on her lids and gold eyeliner, deepening the green of her irises and making them seem vaguely feline. Her hair was caught up in a loose knot at the back of her head, with a few glossy chestnut curls hanging down, drawing attention to her lovely neck and vulnerable nape.

He wanted to put his hand there, grip on to her. Maybe bite

her. Kiss her. Feel her shiver under his mouth the way she'd done in the store.

His cock hardened and he grimaced, forcing himself to drag his gaze away. Yeah, coming into a gala with a hard-on was not the best look, so maybe he should stop staring at her.

Except it was difficult. Way more difficult than he'd envisaged if he was honest with himself. He'd thought he could shove this need for her aside, because after all, he hadn't even felt this way about her until five days ago. But he'd found it difficult to concentrate the whole way into Manhattan, sitting in the helicopter beside her, the interior full of her scent. And then in the car on the way to Barneys, not to mention in the store itself, when she'd come out of the fitting room in that gown.

God, she'd looked fucking amazing. He hadn't been kidding when he'd told her he'd wanted to fuck her right there and then. Not the most romantic of feelings, but hey, he wasn't exactly the world's most romantic guy. He was basic, at least his needs were, and right now they were at their most basic. His cock in her pussy. Now.

He shifted on the seat, the pants of his tux tight. Okay, so thinking shit like that was not helpful.

No, he should be thinking about Andrew Elliott and what the hell kind of connection the guy had to the info on that hard drive. And why that hard drive was in his father's safe, for a start.

Sabrina shifted next to him and instantly his awareness zeroed in on her yet again, on the shimmer of the silk that hugged her lovely body, on the way it pulled tight across her small, high breasts.

You can't do this. Remember what happens when you get obsessed.

He was hardly likely to forget. Pippa and her uninhibited sexuality that had so fascinated him at seventeen. She'd been older and the first person to want him for *him* and not because of his family's money or because of his father's social standing. And she didn't need him to be perfect the way his father seemed to. No, all she needed from him was to make her come. So he had made her come. Many, many times.

He'd been so into her. So obsessed. And then she'd gotten pregnant and though he'd been terrified at the prospect of being a father, he'd decided that the right thing to do—the only thing to do—was to marry her.

Until his father had stepped in and told him that she was already married. He'd had no idea—he'd been so fucking clueless—and it had come as a complete shock to him, as had the realization that he'd been lied to. So much so that when his father had told him that he would deal with the mess, Kellan had just . . . let him.

He'd never seen Pippa again after that. Or his child . . .

His jaw ached. Fuck, he really didn't want to be thinking about all that ancient history, but at least it had killed his goddamn hard-on.

Beside him, Sabrina stilled and he realized they were drawing up outside the Met. There was already a sizable crowd of gala attendees moving up the steps, with a few tourists gawking and a scattering of press.

Now it was really time for him to focus.

He leaned forward and gave the driver a few instructions, telling him to wait for Kellan's text before picking them up. Then he pulled open the door and got out, turning to hold his hand out to Sabrina.

Her fingers were cool in his as she took it, easing out of the car, her gown shimmering in the light coming from the stately old building, looking almost iridescent. She gleamed too, her skin luminous, her eyes nearly the same green of her gown.

She looked like a princess and yet the expression on her face was pure Sabrina. Nervous and uncertain, but determined all the same.

A princess and your friend. Who you're bringing into potential danger.

The thought flickered by, making him uneasy. But no, the risk to her was minimal. He would get in, find Elliott, get some answers, then get out again. All Sabrina needed to do was stand there and sip champagne.

No one knew what they were really here for. No one knew their mission. She would be fine.

He gave her a reassuring smile as they turned to join the crowds making their way to the entrance of the building. "This won't take long," he murmured, taking her arm and tucking it against his side. "All you need to do is find yourself a glass of wine, then stand around looking beautiful."

She frowned. "But what about you?"

"I'll go find Elliott, ask him a few questions, then come back and get you."

"By yourself?"

"It'll be easier." He glanced at her. "Plus, it'll keep you away from any trouble."

The crease between her brows deepened. "What kind of trouble?"

No point telling her that he planned to get answers from Elliott whether Elliott wanted to give them to him or not. "It doesn't matter. I just don't want you to be associated with me if any shit goes down, okay?"

She shook her head. "No. This is a team effort. You can't leave me—"

"Bree," he interrupted gently but firmly. "You've done your bit on this mission and you did it exceptionally well. But now it's time for me to do mine. This is what I'm trained for, what I'm good at. So let me do it."

She did *not* like that, her expression becoming set. But all she said was, "Fine. Just . . . be careful."

"Of course." He forced himself to give her a grin. "Careful is my middle name."

Sabrina only snorted.

When they got to the entrance, he had to do a little fast talking because neither of them had invites, but he'd anticipated that and dropping his father's name, plus a few friendly smiles, soon had the security staff letting them in. They weren't even searched, which was a relief, considering the Glock he had concealed.

Inside, the gala was being held in the Great Hall, all the columns and arches in the huge domed space lit up with colored lights. There were stands of flowers everywhere, crowds eddying and flowing as music played and waitstaff circulated with drinks and canapes. There were banners strung around, advertising the charity the gala was in aid of, but Kellan didn't pay much attention to that. He was too busy scanning the crowd for Elliott.

Snagging a couple of glasses of champagne, he handed one to Sabrina before steering her over to one of the columns. "You stay here," he murmured in her ear. "I'll do a quick reconnaissance."

She gave him a nod, but although her expression had that determined set to it, he could see the worry in her eyes. So he bent and brushed his mouth over hers. "I'll be quick, I promise."

And he would be. The watchful, protective part of him didn't want to leave her, not even for a few minutes. Ridiculous when there was no immediate danger.

He wouldn't be gone long anyway.

Kellan stepped away from her and plunged into the crowds. He didn't look back, even though he wanted to, because his concentration should be set on Andrew Elliott, not on his lovely best friend. She would be fine. Absolutely fine.

He moved swiftly through the knots of people, smiling at those he knew—of which there were a few—and stopping briefly to exchange a few friendly words, but then moving on, scanning the crowds.

After a circuit around the entire room, he eventually spotted Elliott over by a spray of enormous orchids. He was the same age as Kellan's father, a distinguished looking older man with black hair shot through with silver and still in relatively good shape physically.

He was talking with a group of people who all looked like they were hanging on his every word. A slight problem when Kellan needed to get him away somewhere private, but not an insurmountable one.

Approaching the group, Kellan waited for a break in the conversation, then he said, "Mr. Elliott, Kellan Blake." He extended his hand. "I'm here on behalf of my father."

Elliott's gaze widened slightly, then he smiled. "Kellan? Boy, it's been a while since I've seen you. I didn't know you were on the guest list."

Kellan gave him his usual charming smile. "Yeah, Dad said you'd be okay with it. He wasn't wrong, was he?"

Elliott smiled back and took Kellan's hand to shake it. "No, of course not. Good to see you, son."

As the other man shook his hand, Kellan took the moment to step up close to him and murmur, "I need to talk to you privately. It concerns Dad."

A look of surprise crossed Elliott's face. Then he frowned. "Now? I'm a little busy—"

"Dad said it couldn't wait." Kellan kept that easy smile on his face, like nothing was wrong. "It's a business matter."

"But I—"

"It'll only take five minutes." He began to move toward one of the doors that led off the hall, subtly urging the other man with him, because keeping him walking and not giving him any time to think was the key to making this work. "I promise. Not even five."

Elliott, drawn irresistibly along by Kellan's urging, let out a breath and turned to the group, holding up his hand, indicating he'd be five, then followed Kellan out the door and into one of the long corridors outside the Great Hall.

It was deserted, which was lucky. Because now he was close to getting some answers, Kellan wasn't about to let this opportunity slip away.

"So." Elliott was smiling as he turned to face Kellan. "What is this all—"

Kellan didn't wait for him to finish, laying a hard forearm across Elliott's chest and shoving him unceremoniously up against the wall.

The older man's eyes widened in shock. "Hey. What the hell—"

"Selling guns to South American drug dealers," Kellan interrupted flatly, leaning in so his face was inches from Elliott's. "Tell me what you know about it. Now."

Elliott blinked, his face still displaying shock. "What? I have no idea what you're talking about. Let me go." He tried to move, but Kellan held him pinned.

"You know exactly what I'm fucking talking about," Kellan snarled, in no mood for games. "Your name has been associated with an illegal arms ring shipping weapons into South America and run by some very powerful men." He shoved his arm harder against the other man's chest, causing Elliott to exhale sharply. "My father has been implicated and I want to know what the fuck is going on."

Bewilderment passed over Elliott's face. "Arms ring? I don't know anything about an arms ring."

Kellan studied the other man's expression, looking deep into his eyes. He'd done a few interrogations over the years. In fact, he'd been the go-to guy in his SEAL team when it came to getting information from people. He was good at reading expressions and body language, plus, he could also persuade reluctant people to talk. He didn't particularly like that aspect of it—especially if it involved having to give people an incentive—but he could do it if the success of a mission was at stake.

Well, the success of this particular mission was at stake right now, and he'd be damned if he let it slip through his fingers. Failure had never been an option for him in the military and it wasn't an option now.

He had to find the truth. He had to know whether he'd been listening to a hypocrite all these years. Whether he'd given up his child on the words of a liar.

Because if he had . . .

It would have been all for nothing. But then you know that already, don't you? You didn't give up your child because of what your father said . . .

No, this was about his father, not himself. His father had been the one who'd told him to do it and because he loved his father, Kellan had believed him. But he'd been lied to before. After all, Pippa had lied to him and he'd never known . . .

"Yeah you do," Kellan said flatly. "Your name was on a set of documents along with a whole lot of South American coordinates. Just your name."

"What documents?" Elliott's cheeks were getting red, anger beginning to flare in his eyes. "Listen, I don't know what the hell you think you're doing, but if you don't let me go right now, I'm calling the police."

Kellan didn't move, merely shifted his forearm higher, so it lay across Elliott's throat. Then he used his free hand to grab his Glock. "You know what I think?" he said casually. "I think you're lying." He lifted the Glock. "And that maybe you could use a little help with remembering the truth."

Elliott's gaze flicked to the gun. "You're crazy. All I have to do is shout and this place will be swarming with security guards. And you'll be in jail." His gaze came back to Kellan's. "Your father won't be happy about that."

Kellan searched the other man's face for the signs, the little tells that gave people away when they were lying. "Yes," he said. "Let's talk more about Dad. Why is your name in that file, Andrew?"

"What file? You're fucking crazy—"

"The file on a hard drive that was in my dad's safe. An encrypted file."

Elliott grimaced, his color climbing higher. "Maybe you should be asking your father these questions."

"And I will, believe me. But now I'm asking you." He brought the Glock a little closer, pressed his forearm a little harder. "So tell me. Why is your name there? And what the fuck does it have to do with my father?"

Elliott began to choke, but Kellan didn't move his arm. The guy clearly wasn't going to tell him anything without an incentive, which meant Kellan would have to provide him with some.

Are you sure he knows anything? Or are you threatening an innocent civilian?

The thought flickered through his brain, unwanted and unwelcome. He'd never hurt a civilian apart from those who'd gotten on the wrong side of the 11th Hour. And those civilians tended to be criminals anyway and had richly deserved what was coming to them. But this guy wasn't a criminal, or at least Kellan had no real proof that he was. So hurting him was not a good thing.

You're not a good man though, are you? You're not a fucking hero.

Kellan bared his teeth, ignoring the way his gut clenched at the thought. Shit, he was only doing what he had to do to get proof of his father's innocence, no more, no less.

And if your father's guilty?

That wasn't a possibility. It simply wasn't.

Then why was that hard drive in the safe? And encrypted?

Kellan shoved the questions from his head, concentrating on the man in front of him. Elliott had gone brick red, his hands rising to grab at Kellan's forearm, scrabbling to pull it away. His mouth opened, a gasp escaping. "Let . . . me . . . *go!*"

"No can do, Andy." Kellan ignored his conscience and let his smile become vicious. "Not until you tell me what I want to know."

A second passed when Kellan thought the guy was going to call his bluff and Kellan would have to choose whether to keep choking the life out of him or whether to let him go, and it was a question that right then, Kellan didn't know the answer to.

But then Elliott forced out hoarsely, "Your father . . . He planted the hard drive . . . It was his idea."

Sabrina leaned against the column next to her and took another sip of her champagne. She tried not to look as awkward as she felt standing by herself, but she knew she wasn't doing a very good job.

She didn't like being in this massive, crowded room by herself and she especially didn't like that she'd just spotted Kellan go off through a door with a guy who had to be Andrew Elliott, and now she couldn't see him. Which meant she had no idea what was going on.

He'd told her to let him handle this and since he'd left her to handle her own area of expertise, she had to do the same for him.

Except . . . it made fear clench sharp claws inside her.

She had no idea what this Elliott guy was going to tell Kellan, and she hoped it would be something innocuous. Or, better, that he wasn't involved with this whole thing in any way.

Of course, that would mean that Kellan would push, and she was afraid of what might happen if Kellan pushed. He didn't like to hear the word *no,* and he was being so protective of his father . . .

Dread joined the fear in her gut. Perhaps she shouldn't have let him go alone. Perhaps she should have insisted on going with him.

She took a sip of her champagne, needing moisture in her suddenly dry mouth.

"I don't want you being associated with any shit that might go down . . ."

His words from outside the gala echoed in her head, making her gulp again at her drink. God, she hoped he wouldn't do anything he'd regret later. He was such a good guy, but there was that dangerous edge to him, the one she'd always found so fascinating. And what if that dangerous edge turned in a direction it shouldn't? How far would he go?

Ah, but she knew the answer to that. When it came to the people he loved, he'd go all the way.

She shivered.

Hell, why was she standing here drinking? She should be going after him, stopping him. She should never have let him go and question Elliott, because he wasn't going to get the answers he wanted, she just knew it.

That proof he was so desperate to find wasn't there. It didn't exist and never had. Sure, a few affairs and a secret child didn't make Phillip Blake an arms dealer, and maybe his treatment of her over the years had made her predisposed to believe the worst of him. But . . . well. From the moment Faith had told her and Kellan about this job, Sabrina had known. And after that seemingly harmless conversation she'd overheard, the uncertainty in her gut had confirmed it.

Phillip was everything Night had accused him of.

She stepped away from the column, beginning to move in the direction of the doorway Kellan had disappeared through. She had no idea what she was going to say to him when she got there, but she was going to have to distract him somehow. Stop him from finding out the truth. Protect him.

Maybe you don't need to say anything. There are ways to distract someone that don't involve talking.

Another shiver whispered through her. Yes, that was true, there were. In fact, she could think of a couple right now.

The crowd eddied and up ahead of her, the door Kellan and Elliott had disappeared through opened, Elliott stepping out. His tux was disheveled and so was his hair, his cheeks a dull red. Sweat gleamed on his brow, a furious expression on his face that was rapidly smoothed over into a look of grim determination as he began heading in the direction of the security staff.

Oh God. What had happened? What had Kellan done? And, more to the point, where was he?

She rushed toward the door out of the hall and pushed it open.

The corridor beyond was empty.

"Kel?" Her voice sounded fragile and echoed, bouncing off the walls. "Kellan? Are you there?" She began to walk down the corridor, the heels of her uncomfortable sandals tapping on the floor, her heartbeat beginning to race. "Kel, we have to go. I don't know what you did to Elliott but he was heading for security." A cold current wound its way through her, the corridor empty and silent. "Kel, please. Where are you? I don't think I—"

Strong fingers wound around her upper arm and she found herself pulled into a side corridor, then pushed up against the wall.

Kellan stood in front of her, filling her vision, the very epitome of movie star handsome in his tux. Tall and broad and blond, like Captain America. Except there was nothing of Steve Rodgers in the look in Kellan's eyes. They were electric blue with rage.

Sabrina's stomach dropped away.

"It was him," Kellan snarled, his voice almost unrecognizable. "It was Dad all along. Elliott told me he planted the drive in the safe and put Elliott's name in it to throw us off the scent. He knew we were investigating him. He knew—" Kellan stopped abruptly, the expression on his face turning fierce, savage, searching hers. "Did you know?"

And she didn't understand what happened then. Maybe she hesitated slightly too long before showing her shock. Or maybe he was simply far too good at reading people and she was far too bad at lying.

Whatever it was, reaction flared deep in his eyes, a blinding flood of it pouring over his face. Shock. Rage. Betrayal. And under all of it, pain.

"Kel," she began, but it was far, *far* too late. The damage was done.

"You did know." He was staring at her like she was a stranger. "You knew all this time."

"No," she said thickly. "Not for certain. I . . . suspected. I overheard a conversation yesterday that—"

"What conversation?" he demanded sharply. "Yesterday? You didn't think to share that with me?"

Her throat closed up and she couldn't speak, tears filling her eyes. She wanted to tell him that all of this had only been because she was trying to protect him, that's all she'd ever wanted to do, but then shouts came from out in the hallway.

Kellan's gaze flickered. Then he grabbed her hand without a word and strode down the side corridor, and she had no choice but to stumble after him. His hold was hard and there was no way she could break it. Not that she wanted to, not when there were clearly security guards on their tail.

Kellan never once broke stride and he never once looked behind him. He simply strode on like he knew where he was going, pulling her with him, turning down other smaller corridors, turning her sense of direction around so she had no idea where they were or where they were headed. Until he shoved open a small door and they were suddenly outside the building, the noise and the lights of the city flooding over them.

They'd come out through a small service exit and she thought they might stop then and try to figure out where they were, but he didn't. He didn't even turn to her, continuing to move fast, tugging her behind him.

They crossed a street and went on down the sidewalk, Sabrina stumbling in her horrible heels, trying to keep up, her throat too tight and sore to speak. His grip was so hard she could feel the anger in it, pressing against the fragile bones of her wrist. It bordered on pain, but she said nothing. She probably deserved it.

Stupid. So stupid. Why wasn't she a better liar? Why wasn't she better at keeping her emotions controlled? Why had she given herself away like that? And, more importantly, what was she going to say now that he knew?

He doesn't know everything.

No, that was true. He didn't know about his father's affair. And he didn't know about the baby. Those things, at least, she could keep from him. God, it was bad enough finding out his father had been running guns, let alone that his father had also had another child.

She didn't know how long they walked, her half running, half walking to keep up with Kellan's long stride as he crossed more streets, turning down different ones until they'd left the Met far behind them.

Then he made another turn, down into a narrow, dark alleyway, pulling her after him, then letting her go so suddenly she nearly fell.

Her heartbeat raged in her ears, thumping so hard, she could barely hear, and her wrist ached. Kellan was a tall, dark figure blocking the entrance to the alley. The streetlights behind him gilded his blond hair, threw his face into shadow, turning that dangerous edge of his lethal.

"Tell me," he said, rage winding through his deep voice. "Tell me how you knew."

Her throat was impossibly dry. A reaction was starting to set in, making her shake. And she realized that she couldn't tell him, because explaining her doubts about Phillip would mean she'd have to tell him about his father's affairs. About the baby. About the money troubles Charlotte had complained tearfully of one night after she'd had too much to drink.

Everything she was supposed to be protecting him from.

Then again, she *could* tell him about the conversation she'd overheard the day before, and hope that he wouldn't ask her how long she'd suspected his father's guilt.

"Yesterday," she began, "before you and he went off to play golf, I was checking out the locks on his study and he came out suddenly. I managed to hide before he saw me but he was talking to someone on the phone. Said something about a 'shipment' that hadn't gone through and how certain people 'wouldn't be happy.'"

Kellan said nothing, but she felt the force of his ice-blue stare.

"I th-thought it sounded . . . sketchy." She'd started to stutter now, hating how uncertain she was sounding under the pressure of that stare. "But there wasn't anything—"

"And you didn't tell me," he said, his tone utterly flat. "You didn't say a fucking word about this."

"Because there was nothing *to* tell you." She swallowed. "It wasn't proof and I didn't want to mention it to you in case—"

"You didn't tell me." he repeated. "You're supposed to tell me, Sabrina."

How could she argue? Yes, she should have told him.

"I . . . didn't want to w-worry you unnecessarily." The excuse sounded lame even to her own ears and worse, it was only going to lead to more questions.

Questions she did *not* want to answer.

So? Distract him. Wasn't that your plan initially?

He was standing there, radiating danger and rage, radiating

betrayal. And she knew talking was only going to make this worse, because there was nothing she could say to him that would make it better. Worse was all she had.

But not quite all.

She wanted to fix this. To apologize. But the only way she knew how to do that was to offer him the only thing she had: herself.

So she walked forward slowly, closing the distance between them, keeping her gaze on his shadowed face. He didn't move and he didn't say a word, only watched her come, until she was standing right in front of him.

He was intimidating like this. She'd never felt the height difference between them so acutely. Never felt so small and fragile and vulnerable. He was a wall in the dark, a tall, broad, hard wall that would never give. Never break.

Her pulse was rocketing out of control and all she wanted to do was run, but she made herself stay there. Made herself look up into his face, the perfect planes and angles of it only dimly recognizable in the darkness.

"There's more," he said, blue eyes all ice, raging. "Isn't there?"

She didn't answer, only stepped even closer, so that she was inches away from his hard, muscular heat. And it took all her courage to put her hands on his granite chest, to rise on her toes and put her mouth over his, but she did it.

He went utterly still, his lips under hers a flat line. But she didn't stop. She ran her tongue along his bottom lip, nipping him gently, coaxing him to open to her. At the same time she spread her fingers on his chest, opening her palms out so they were flat on the white cotton of his shirt, soaking up his warmth.

He didn't move.

She could feel how tight his muscles were, coiled and powerful as if gathering themselves to launch him into an attack.

God, she couldn't blame him if he did. She'd probably feel the same way.

Her throat began to hurt, regret making it ache. Kissing him like this was a mistake. A really, really stupid idea. Why did she keep on being so stupid when she was supposed to be way smarter than this? She should have run instead.

Or maybe you just should have told him everything.

No, it was too late for that. She'd kept those secrets for so long and if he ever found out just how long she'd been keeping them from him . . .

He'll hate you.

Grief clutched at her chest, her courage failing her, and she pulled away, taking a step back.

Or at least she tried to.

Until Kellan's fingers wound around her upper arms and she was being propelled back until her spine hit the rough brick of the alleyway wall behind her.

Her breath caught as she looked up into his eyes. There was a feral glitter in them, his lips pulled back from his teeth in a snarl. "Don't think I don't know what you're doing." His voice was low and very dark. "I know a distraction technique when I see one."

She tried to inhale, but then he stepped in close, keeping her pinned to the wall as he pushed one hard thigh between her legs, his gaze on hers. "Don't get me wrong, Sabrina. I'm not averse to it by any means. But you've got secrets, I can see them in your eyes, and I want to know what they are. Right the fuck now."

Tears made her vision swim. She should tell him, she knew she should. But she'd been keeping those secrets a very long time, and not only that, she'd made promises to Charlotte. And she believed in her promises. She believed in keeping her word.

"I can't tell you," she forced out. "I promised I wouldn't."

His gaze flicked over her face, bright as a searchlight. "You promised who?"

"Kellan, I can't." She twisted in his grip, trying to pull away. "Please, let me go."

He ignored her. "So it looks like my father is running arms to drug dealers, arms that are responsible for the deaths of innocent people, and you knew about it, or at least suspected. And you didn't tell me." His grip on her tightened as he leaned down, his face inches from hers, his eyes burning with rage. "I'm your best friend, Sabrina. Your best fucking friend. And you didn't tell me my father was a traitor."

A flare of unexpected and defensive anger shot up inside her. "I told you that I was trying to protect you," she said thickly. "That's all I ever wanted to do."

He ignored that too, looking deep into her eyes. "There's more to it than that conversation though. Isn't there, Bree?"

The use of her name whispered through her, making her ache. Just like the feel of him against her, so close. His scent so familiar, the heat of his body so seductive. Wrong to be so aware of him now, when she was on the verge of total exposure. When she knew that all she had to do was open her mouth, give him the words he wanted, and their friendship would explode into a million tiny shards, all of them cutting her, tearing her apart.

She couldn't let that happen.

So she did what she should have done the first time. She pressed her hands against the brick behind her and pushed hard away from the wall, tearing his grip from her upper arms. Then she hooked one arm around his neck, holding him close as she kissed him again, biting down hard on his lower lip. At the same time as she brought her other hand down over his fly, cupping the hard length of his cock beneath the wool of his pants, and squeezing. Blatantly.

CHAPTER 13

A bolt of pure electricity shot through Kellan the moment Sabrina's fingers closed over his dick, and somehow it felt like she was touching him skin to skin and not through a layer of wool and cotton.

Her mouth was hot under his, her teeth nipping and biting, sinking into his lip hard as she squeezed him. And the anger inside him shifted and turned, like wildfire coming up against a windstorm, changing direction, burning hotter, faster.

There was so much of that anger.

He'd looked into Andrew Elliott's eyes as all those words had poured out of the guy's mouth, and he'd known then that it was all true. That everything he'd hoped was a lie wasn't.

Maybe there was a part of him that had always known his father was a liar, a secret part that he hadn't wanted to acknowledge. That accepted what Elliott said without even batting an eyelash.

But he'd wanted to be wrong. He'd been *desperate* to be wrong.

Because it meant that all this time, the father he'd looked up to, the man he'd respected and listened to, had been a liar. And he'd believed all the lies. He'd given up his child for those lies.

And to make matters worse, when Sabrina had come to find him, and he'd pulled her aside to tell her the news, she hadn't even looked surprised. There had been no shock at all on her face only . . . regret. Which could only mean one thing. She already knew.

The conversation she'd overheard that she'd only now decided to tell him about explained a little of her suspicion, but given the vagueness of the conversation not all of it. There was more, he was sure of it.

Either way, hearing how she'd decided not to tell him about it made him even more furious than he already was. She was supposed to be his friend. She was supposed to tell him this kind of shit. But she hadn't. It felt like she'd lied to him along with everyone else.

She hasn't told you any lies. She just didn't tell you about her suspicions. And it's not like you've been honest with her. You haven't told her about Pippa or the baby.

Yeah, but that was different. Pippa and the baby didn't concern her. But this . . . Jesus, this was their fucking mission.

He should have pulled away then, just goddamn walked and left her there. Because it felt like he'd been stabbed, twice. Once by his father and again by her.

But her fingers were on his cock and somehow desire had hooked into his rage and made itself a part of the feeling. It was making him get hard, his pulse rate going through the fucking roof.

She was trying to distract him, of course, so she didn't have to tell him her secrets, but if that was the case, then she'd chosen the wrong way to go about it. Because two could play at that game and if that's how she wanted to play, then shit, he'd play. And she'd regret it. He was better at this than she was.

He flexed his hips into her hand, pressing his aching dick

against her palm as he opened his mouth and took charge of the kiss. He swept his tongue into her mouth, tasting champagne and sweetness and that delicious, essential flavor that was all Sabrina. It hit him hard, made him feel savage, that she could taste like his friend and yet be this person he didn't recognize. Who'd kept all this stuff from him and was still keeping things from him.

He wasn't supposed to do this kind of thing, fuck his best friend in an alleyway in the dark. He was supposed to be better than that, a man of honor. A SEAL. A hero. But maybe he wasn't better than that. Maybe all he was, was that fucking clueless seventeen-year-old he'd once been. The one who'd had an affair with a married woman and never realized. Who'd believed the words of a liar and hypocrite and given up his own child.

And you've never thought of that child again, have you? You made sure you never did.

The rage turned inward, burned hotter, and along with it, the desire.

No, he wasn't better. He wasn't any kind of fucking hero. What kind of man gave up his kid without a second's thought? What kind of man concentrated on his military career, on success, on anything else so he would never have to think of that child again? Who'd essentially erased that kid from existence because it hurt too much to think about?

You know what you are. What you've always been. You let your father get rid of your child because you didn't want to deal with it. Because you were only thinking of yourself. Might as well live it.

A growl broke from him and he pushed hard against Sabrina, shoving her against the wall. Then he took her delicate, pointed jaw in his hand and he tipped her head back, kissing her deeper. Harder. Ravaging her mouth as he pressed himself against her, crushing her hand between their two bodies.

She made a soft moaning noise in the back of her throat, a shiver shaking her. The arm she had around his neck tightened, her body melting into his as if he wasn't an animal through and through, as if he wasn't being rough and treating her like shit in a dark alley.

He should stop and he knew it. He should let her go, because she was his friend and he cared about her. But she'd lied to him, and it felt like a knife in the dark, coming from the one direction he'd never expected. Now, he wanted the truth and he'd get it from her any way he could.

She was arching against him, heedless of the rough brick at her back, her fingers squeezing him gently. Then she ran a thumb down his zipper, pressing down, and he felt the reaction go through him like chain lightning, setting off one fire after another along every nerve ending he had.

He wrenched his mouth from hers, trailing it down her neck, closing his teeth around the fragile tendons at the side, her skin salty-sweet on his tongue. "You want this?" he demanded, flexing his hips and pressing his cock harder into her hand. "Then you need to pay for it."

She shivered again, the heat of her slender body seeping through his clothes, sinking right down into his skin. Reminding him of how warm and giving she was, and how honest he'd always thought her.

Until now.

You don't know her at all. Perhaps you never did.

In which case, it wouldn't matter what he did with her, would it? She wasn't his friend anymore. She was a stranger.

He pulled away from her all of a sudden, looking down into her pale, upturned face. The streetlights were shining right into her eyes, the green washed out, leaving nothing but gleaming gold.

He touched her full red mouth, running his thumb along

the cushiony softness of her bottom lip. "Tell me, Sabrina," he murmured. "Tell me, and I'll give you what you want."

Her lashes fell, veiling her gaze. "I can't." Her voice was husky, pain threading through it. "I'm sorry, Kel. I promised."

"Who did you promise?" He pressed down on her lip, testing the give of it. "Who's more important than your goddamn best friend?" Christ, this was all so wrong and he was a prick for doing this to her, especially considering that note of pain. But he wasn't going to stop. She'd lied to him, the one person he'd thought was completely honest with him, and if that meant he had to be the bad guy in order to get that honesty back, then shit, he'd be the bad guy. And fuck if that didn't make him even harder than he already was.

She shook her head. "I can't . . ."

But he wasn't stupid and there weren't many people she could have made promises to. Especially promises about his own father.

"Mom," he said softly, easing his thumb between those soft lips, the heat of her mouth going straight to his cock. "You promised my mom."

She trembled a little and he thought she might pull away. But she didn't. Her lashes rose, her gaze meeting his, and for a second he saw pain burning brightly there. Then it was gone, determination taking its place. That delectable mouth of hers closed tighter around his thumb and she began to suck, and he felt it like she had those lips wrapped directly around his cock instead.

Of course it was his mother, of course. Because it couldn't be his father. She wouldn't have made promises to Phillip like that. Unless he was threatening her, which, God, he wouldn't put anything past Phillip right now.

He should be doing something about it, and yet he found himself staring at how this thumb disappeared into her mouth, the feeling of that delicate suction like the pull of the tide. "Fuck, Bree." His voice was getting ragged and the heat of her palm cupped against his zipper was driving him insane. But he tried to keep himself on track. "What did you promise her? What didn't she want you to tell me?"

Sabrina didn't answer. Instead she let go his thumb and before he could prevent her, she dropped down on her knees in the alleyway, her green gown glimmering around her in the darkness.

Definitely he should be stopping her now, picking her up from the filthy pavement, but her hands were on the fastenings of his pants, undoing the buttons and then pulling down his zipper. And Christ, she was reaching inside his pants for his cock, those beautifully cool fingers slipping over his feverish skin.

A groan escaped him as she drew him out, stroking him softly, gently. And before he had a chance to protest, she was leaning forward and that hot mouth of hers was wrapped around his dick. Her tongue licked him, all around the sensitive head, lapping at the slit at the top, making his fucking legs tremble. Then she was taking him into all that heat, her lips closing around him, and the delicate suction he'd felt around his thumb was now around his cock. Pulling. Dragging.

A low growl tore from his throat and he had to lean one hand on the brick wall in front of him as the pleasure flashed brightly in his head.

Fuck. Why was he letting her do this to him? He should be the one in charge here, not her.

He made a grab for her, twining his fingers in the softness of her hair, pulling loose that little bun, digging his fingers into her curls and closing them tightly in a fist. She gasped as he dragged her head back, the light shining on her face, and he was caught by the sheer eroticism of the moment. Of the sight of his cock sliding into her red mouth and then out again, his hips moving as if they had a mind of their own.

So good. So fucking good.

He flexed his hips again, driving his cock deeper into her mouth, and her hands came up to grip his thighs, holding on. Her eyes were wide, staring up into his, and he couldn't shake the sight of it. Sabrina in her green gown. On her knees in an alley. Sucking him off in public, where anyone could walk up and discover them.

Wrong in every single way there was, and he loved it. He fucking loved it.

He let go her hair and reached down, jerking the material of her gown from her breasts so he could see them. Pale and perfectly round, her nipples tight and hard. He gripped her hair again, keeping her head pulled back so he could watch his cock slide into her mouth and see her bare tits.

So he could watch her face and the golden gleam in her hazel eyes as she sucked him. Fuck, it was the hottest thing he'd ever seen in his entire life.

But like this, she had all the power and he could feel it with every touch of her tongue along his aching dick. With the pull of her mouth and the dig of her fingers into his thighs. He was at her mercy and right now he couldn't deal.

Pulling himself out of her mouth, he ignored her low moan of protest and tugged her up so she was standing, pushing her back against the brick of the alley. The bodice of her dress sagged, giving him glimpses of her pretty tits and he pushed the fabric down so he could see them properly. She made another of those needy sounds as he cupped her breasts, feeling the softness of them, the slight weight pressing into his palms. Her lashes were lying heavy on her flushed cheeks, her mouth open, her breathing loud in the silence of the alley. He watched her as he slowly brushed his thumbs over her hardening nipples, feeling her shiver, listening to her gasp. She arched against the wall, into his touch, as if she didn't care where she was. As if his touch was the only thing that was important to her.

He'd never guessed what a sensual little thing she was. She always seemed so prickly when it came to physical affection that he'd decided she didn't like it. Apparently that was wrong.

Sabrina groaned as he took her nipples between his thumb and forefinger and pinched. Then made another desperate noise when he rolled them, tugging slightly.

He kept his gaze on her face, stroking, then pinching again. "You're going to have to tell me," he whispered, leaning in, nuzzling against the softness of her neck. "You're not going to come until you tell me."

She shook as he tugged on her nipples again, then to increase the sensation, he bent his head and licked one, circling it with his tongue.

"Kellan . . ." His name was a desperate whisper. "Oh . . . Kel . . . God . . ."

He closed his lips around her nipple and sucked. Hard. Her back bowed and she cried out, her fingers twisting in his hair.

"Tell me." He lifted his head, blew air across one damp nipple, before turning his attention to the other. "Or I'll just suck on your tits for hours. Never letting you come."

She whimpered as he sucked her other breast, her body arching again, the softness of her gown pressing against his painfully hard cock.

Fuck, he wasn't sure he could do this. Hold out until she was desperate. Not when he was as desperate as he was. But then he was going to have to. Because this wasn't just an interrogation technique, it was also a punishment.

She should have told him. She should have.

A flare of anger shot down his spine, and he lifted his head. Then grabbed her hips and spun her around so she was facing the wall. Gripping her wrists, he took them above her head and pinned them to the brick. She tried to turn her head, her breathing fast and hard. "W-What are you doing?"

"What you want me to do." He reached and gripped the material of her gown, raising it. "But you can't have all of it until you tell me what you've been hiding from me."

She said nothing, her head half turned against the brick, her lashes lying still on her cheeks, as if she was waiting for something.

He bared his teeth. If she was waiting for him to give her some more incentive, he'd give it to her. He was nothing if not good at giving people incentive.

Yeah, but she's not an informant, is she?

Kellan ignored the thought, his hand delving beneath her voluminous green skirts, finding the soft curve of her ass, sliding beneath the material of her panties and between her thighs.

She jerked as he slid his fingers through the soft folds of her pussy, so slick and hot. Ready for him.

"This is all for me, isn't it?" He slid a finger inside her, pushing in deep, and she moaned. "At least you can't lie about this, can you, Sabrina?"

"I didn't . . . lie." She was panting as he pulled his finger out, then pushed back in again, her slick flesh gripping him. "I just . . . didn't tell you. I can't break a promise . . . I can't . . . Not to her . . ."

He could hear her determination beneath the breathlessness and he was conscious of a spark of awe in her. Because it was easy to underestimate Sabrina. Her awkwardness, fragile self-confidence and painful honesty hid a strong, determined spirit. And so fucking stubborn. She had a backbone of pure steel when it came to giving her word to people, and for her to break that promise . . .

He gritted his teeth. He was just going to have to try harder.

Sliding his fingers out of her, he pulled aside the crotch of her panties and pressed her hard up against the brick, sliding his cock between her thighs, brushing the head of it through her folds.

She quivered, her hips flexing, pulling against his hold on her wrists. Trying to adjust her stance so she could take him inside her. But he didn't let her. He teased her, rubbing the head of his dick through her slick heat, nudging her clit, making her jerk and gasp again.

It was driving him crazy too, his whole body aching with the need to thrust in hard and deep. But he didn't. He kept on slicking through that hot little pussy, teasing her by pushing gently at her entrance and then sliding away. She began to pant, gasping, her hips trying to meet his, low moans escaping her as she pulled at his imprisoning grip.

But this was a punishment, yes it was, and he wasn't going to give her what she wanted, not yet. Instead he pressed her harder to the bricks, beginning to grind against her, the softness of her ass pressed to his groin, his dick slipping and sliding around her pussy.

She whimpered and it was fucking torture for both of them, but he didn't let up.

He bent his head to the nape of her neck and did what he'd been fantasizing about, biting her there, his teeth against her fragile skin.

"Kel . . ." Her voice was ragged. "Please . . . I need . . . you."

"No. Not until you give me what I want." He ground harder against her, his cock sliding along her hot, wet slit, the heat and slickness its own special kind of torture. "You lied to me, Bree. You fucking lied. You think I'll let you get away with that without any comeback? I want you to tell me everything and then, maybe, you'll get what you want."

Fine tremors were shaking her, he could feel it. She was on the edge.

He gritted his teeth, holding on to his control as he shifted his hips slightly, pressing at the entrance to her pussy and easing in slightly. Sabrina gasped, her back arching, her hips lifting, trying to encourage him deeper. But he stayed where he was, just inside her, giving her a taste and no more.

"Tell me," he ordered, low and guttural. "Tell me and I'll make you come. I'll make you come so fucking hard you'll see stars."

Her head fell forward, exposing that soft vulnerable nape, and the long pale length of her spine. He put his free hand on the back of her neck, gripping her hard, then slowly stroking down, relishing the feel of her skin against his. Her pussy twitched around the head of his cock in response and he had to take a deep breath to stop himself from plunging in deep and forget about whatever secrets she had. Forget about everything except her heat and the pleasure she was giving him.

But no, he wanted the goddamn truth. No more fucking lies.

He gripped her harder, slid his cock into her a little more. Enough to drive her crazy, but not enough to make her come. He shifted his hips so she could feel him, pressing forward infinitesimally, then drawing back, small enough movements to drive her insane.

Jesus, to drive him insane too.

He growled against her skin, holding her wrists in a tight grip, concentrating on holding himself back, because he was going to win this one. He needed to teach her a lesson, that she couldn't keep secrets, that she should have told him. He trusted her for fuck's sake.

A low moan escaped her and she shivered and shook, twisting against his grip, trying to push herself back against him so his cock would slide in deep. But he held on to his control, moving in her so slowly, so carefully, giving her small pieces of pleasure but not everything.

"Kellan," she gasped desperately. "*Kellan*, please."

"No." He bit her again, feeling her jerk against him. "It's about Dad, isn't it? What else did he do, Bree? Something bad?" He didn't want to know. Not really. But he had to. He was sick of not knowing. He'd been so fucking ignorant for years already, clueless and stupid, and he couldn't bear the thought of continuing on like that.

He had to know what she was keeping from him. He *had* to.

He slipped his free hand down and slid it around to her stomach, pushing down farther, to the soft damp cluster of curls between her thighs. Then he slicked a finger over her clit as he pressed his cock a little deeper. She groaned and shook. "No . . . oh . . . I can't . . . I promised."

He didn't let up, circling her clit gently, giving her pressure but not enough to tip her over, feeling her wetness all over his fingers, all over his cock.

The pleasure was blinding him, the pull of her insane. But he wasn't giving up. He was a SEAL and this was a no retreat, no surrender situation.

"Bree." He teased her clit lightly, easing his cock into her a bit farther. "I'm your friend. Your best friend. You owe it to me. Our friendship is worth more than your promise to my goddamn mother."

"I promised . . ." she murmured thickly. "I wanted to protect you."

He licked her skin, nipped the side of her neck. "Protect me from what?"

"I can't . . . I can't . . ."

Kellan flexed his hips, pushing, letting himself slide even deeper, feeling her flesh give and take him, then clutch him hard. He closed his eyes, his jaw tight, trying to hold the urge to slam into her at bay, the orgasm he knew was going to break him apart hovering right *there*. "If you care," he murmured in her ear. "If you ever gave even one shit about me, you'd tell me."

He pushed in farther, pressing her hard to the wall, and she gave a choked sob. "Okay, okay . . . I'll tell you. Please . . . just . . . finish this."

He shouldn't. He should make her tell him first. But he

didn't think he could hang on any longer. "Promise me." He nuzzled against her neck. "Give me one of those promises, Bree. The ones you never break."

She inhaled, a ragged sound. "I p-promise."

Kellan didn't wait. He shoved himself all the way inside her, pinning her to the brick, making her gasp aloud. Then he drew his hips back and thrust again, harder. Deeper.

Sabrina turned her face into her arm, muffling her own cries as he began to fuck her against the wall. She pushed back against him, squirming, and he changed the angle, bending his knees to get more thrust, getting in her deeper. She began to sob and then he applied pressure to her clit, she wailed, her whole body stiffening.

She came, her sex convulsing around him, her sobs muffled against her arm. And he let himself go. Hard. Fast. Faster. Until her perfect little pussy was gripping him like a fist, so tightly it nearly blew off the top of his head, and he was coming himself, biting her shoulder hard to stifle his own growls of release.

Afterward, he could only stand there, leaning against the soft warmth of her, his head ringing like a goddamn bell and for once blissfully free of thought.

Then she began to speak, her voice so hoarse he almost couldn't hear her. "I saw your father with a woman one night in the garden outside. She was holding a baby and I saw him give her some money and he told her to never come back here again. Your mother caught me eavesdropping, and told me that the woman was your father's lover and the baby was his." She took a shuddering breath. "She made me promise never to tell anyone and most especially not you, since you idolized Phillip. She told me that you could never know that Phillip had another child because it would ruin the family." Another ragged breath. "So I promised her I'd keep it a secret. I promised I'd never, ever tell you what I saw."

For a second all he could feel was shock, his mind reeling.

His father had had an affair? And had a child from it? And he'd paid the mother off . . .

Then, like a blurry photo suddenly springing into focus, he understood. And his gut lurched. Everything felt unsteady, his nerve endings raw, his whole fucking heart raw.

It wasn't his father's child that Sabrina had seen.

It had been his.

Sabrina kept her eyes closed and stayed where she was, pressed against the wall. She didn't think she could move, her whole body feeling like it was going to collapse at any moment. The aftershocks of the orgasm pulsed through her like small lightning strikes, making her shiver every time they hit.

She couldn't believe she'd let Kellan do what he had to her. Couldn't believe herself either, getting down on her knees to suck him in a dirty alleyway. Letting him fuck her against the wall. Virtually in public.

She'd been trying to show him that she could hold out against him, that she could take whatever he gave her and not break. But, at the end, when he'd been inside her, touching her . . . He'd driven her to screaming point and she knew she couldn't hold out against him.

She'd given him her promise to tell him and then she'd broken the promise she'd made to Charlotte. But it was a mistake. A terrible mistake. He was her friend, the one person she wasn't supposed to hurt and yet she'd ended up hurting him, and badly. She'd made the situation immeasurably worse and now there was nothing she could do to fix it. Nothing she could give him but the truth that would hurt him even more.

You failed. You failed Charlotte. You failed him. You failed yourself.

She should have been more aware. She should have been smarter. But she'd always been stupid when it came to Kellan Blake.

Sabrina swallowed hard, trying to force back the tears that filled her eyes. She didn't want to turn around and see what the truth had done to him, but she wasn't going to be a coward. She needed to face it.

Her wrists hurt, because his grip had been too strong and the brick had rubbed at her skin. But she ignored the pain, lowering her arms and shifting, tugging her gown back up over her breasts before turning around so she was facing him.

He'd taken a step back from her, the streetlights casting shadows over his beautiful face. Her stomach lurched at the pain that was imprinted over his strong features, a grief that tore at her own heart. Charlotte had been right to keep this from him. God, what had she done?

"Kellan . . ." His name sounded so hoarse in her mouth, broken. "I'm sorry. I should have—"

"It wasn't Dad's kid you saw," he said suddenly, his voice strangely emotionless and flat.

Sabrina blinked, not understanding. "What? No, Charlotte told me that it was—"

"Mom didn't know. The kid was mine."

She stared at him, because that didn't make any sense. How could it be his kid? Kellan didn't have any children. "Kel, I don't know what you're—"

"When I was seventeen, I had an affair," he interrupted in that same emotionless voice. "No one knew about it. No one except my dad. She was married and I didn't know, not even when she got pregnant. Then somehow Dad found out and he told me I had to give her and the baby up, that it would cause a terrible scandal if it came out. He said he'd fix it for me, so I . . . let him." His face held no emotion at all. "I didn't know what to do. He told me I had to protect the family, so I did."

Sabrina couldn't process what he was saying. He'd had an affair with a woman when he was seventeen? And he'd gotten her pregnant? But . . . that was impossible. She would have known about it, surely? She tried to remember if she'd seen any signs, but there had been nothing unusual in his behavior. She'd been fifteen and consumed with her crush on him, wishing he would see her as more than a friend, but he hadn't.

Because he'd been seeing someone else.

Cold began to wind through her. "You never told me," she said hoarsely, the first thing she could think of to say. "You had a child and you never told me."

The expression on his face was shut down, icy. The face of a stranger. "Because it had nothing to do with you."

She stared at him, hurt sliding through her along with the cold. A hurt she had no right to feel since he wasn't the only one keeping secrets. She'd kept that secret from him all these years and it turned out . . . She'd been wrong all this time. And so had Charlotte. Clearly Charlotte had thought that Kellan's lover had been Phillip's and that the baby was also her husband's. Her perfect son would never do something so stupid.

Sabrina blinked and she had the impression that both of them were suddenly seeing each other for the first time. And not as friends. As strangers. Complete and utter fucking strangers.

He'd had a child. A child he'd never told her about. A woman he'd been having an affair with . . . And it was . . . it was . . .

He'd never told her. Something so private, so painful and he'd never told her.

You thought you knew him. But you don't.

Her brain couldn't process it, none of it, and abruptly she didn't want to be here anymore. Not in this sordid alleyway where she'd let him fuck her against a wall. She needed to be somewhere else, somewhere away from him, where she could think this through.

But all of a sudden Kellan turned, as if he'd heard something she hadn't, and then there were dark shapes everywhere.

She opened her mouth to shout a warning, but a hand came over it, muffling her, and someone was holding her very tightly.

Fear burst through her and she tried to scream, but nothing came out, and when she tried to struggle, the arms around her only got tighter.

Someone grunted in pain over where Kellan was and she caught a glimpse of his fists rising and falling. She tried to struggle harder against the hands that held her, desperate to reach him, but she wasn't strong enough and there was nothing she could do as whoever it was dragged her from the alley.

CHAPTER 14

He hadn't heard them, not until the very last second. And only then because one of the assholes was a heavy mouth breather and Kellan had heard the harsh scrape of his breath.

Spinning around to face whoever it was, he'd seen nothing in the darkness of the alley but two shapes coming for him, and instantly he'd gone into military mode.

Part of him had felt nothing but relief as they'd fallen on him, an electric kind of energy moving in his blood as adrenaline fired. The sheer relief of not having to think, only to act. To defend himself from attack.

He hadn't had a good fistfight for months—even the last mission he'd been on with Jack hadn't involved more than a brief scuffle with some idiot dealers—and he hadn't realized how much he'd needed something mindlessly physical until the first punch came.

He didn't think about who was attacking him—that could come later—the most important thing was to dodge that punch, then deliver one of his own, at the same time trying to avoid the punches from the other guy.

The fight was brief, intense, and violent.

He managed to punch the first guy in the stomach and while that prick was recovering, he spun to deliver a roundhouse to the gut of the second guy. Number two went down as number one tried to kick his leg out from under him. Kellan dodged, then flicked out a foot to try the same tactic, his heel slamming into the man's shins. The man grunted and toppled over at the same time as Kellan felt an arm come around his neck and jerk back hard. He didn't hesitate, slamming his elbow back into the gut of the man behind him, then pulling on the arm that caught him, jerking it away, then twisting, so that he was now behind the guy and holding the man's arm up behind his back.

The man caught his breath as Kellan pulled it higher, intending to ask him just what the fuck he was doing, but then something hard slammed over the back of his head, making his ears ring.

Shit. Number two must have recovered quicker than he'd thought.

Kellan let go of the arm he was twisting, staggering a second before spinning around again, ready to defend himself, then launch another attack. But the darkness was empty. The two shadowy figures he'd been fighting had disappeared.

For a split second he stared at the alleyway exit, wondering what the fuck was happening, then he took off after them. But as he hurtled out of the alley, coming to a stop on the street and scanning in both directions to check where they'd gotten to, he saw that the street was empty. Whoever they were had gone.

Then awareness came crashing down on top of him. An awareness that in the heat of the struggle, he'd forgotten about.

Sabrina.

Ice crystallized in his veins, but he didn't pause to think about it, turning and sprinting back into the alley, searching the shadows.

But there was no one there.

"Bree!" His voice had gotten hoarse, the ice wrapping around his lungs and constricting, making it hard to breathe. "*Bree!*"

Except he already knew that she wouldn't respond. The alley was completely empty. Sabrina had gone.

He stood there in the dark, his chest feeling like a heavy stone had suddenly been dropped on it, fear for her rising inside him, threatening to drown him.

What the hell had he been thinking? He'd been so caught up in all those fucking revelations, about how she'd thought she was protecting him all this time and the betrayal he'd felt that she'd kept secrets from him. And then there was the fact that she'd said she'd seen Pippa with his child.

Pippa whom he'd thought had moved away with her husband and hadn't ever come back.

But according to Sabrina she had come back, with his baby, and apparently his father had given her money—

No, shit, he couldn't think about that. Not now. Not when Sabrina had vanished.

He took a breath, trying to shove the cold feeling in his chest to the side, to think like the fucking SEAL he used to be and not some frantic, panicking civilian.

Okay, they'd been ambushed pure and simple, and he'd bet anything on the fact that the men who'd attacked them had also taken her. And considering they'd run off before doing anything to him, he was sure the whole reason they'd been attacked in the first place was so they could take Sabrina.

The question, though, was who had taken her? And why?

You really need to ask yourself that question? You already know . . .

Kellan's jaw ached, tension crawling through him, drawing all his muscles tight. Yeah, he knew.

There was only one reason Sabrina had been kidnapped and

it had to be because of their current mission. Because they were getting close to finding out who was behind this gun running bullshit.

And given what Elliott told you, you can guess who might have had reason to take Sabrina.

His muscles drew even tighter and he had to inhale deep and slow, because even now, even when all the evidence was piling up, he didn't want to believe that his father might have something to do with this.

But Elliott had told him the truth back at the Met, Kellan had seen it in his eyes. Phillip had known, somehow, what Kellan and Sabrina were after, and he'd planted that hard drive for them to find. And somehow, he'd also known what they were doing here in Manhattan. Maybe he'd had them followed, or maybe Elliott had told him how Kellan had threatened him, not that the hows or whys mattered much right now.

The only thing that did was that Sabrina was gone and he had to find her. And if it ended up being true that it had been Phillip who'd taken her . . .

What then?

He had no fucking idea. He could barely get his head around the fact that his father appeared to be as guilty as Night had told Kellan he was, let alone that Phillip had no qualms about kidnapping the woman who'd been considered part of his own family.

Except . . . she never had been, had she? At least not by his own parents.

And you never noticed.

The anger that had been burning inside him since he'd confronted Elliott at the Met leapt high. Anger at himself and his own failings, and there was no doubt about it, he *had* failed.

He'd failed Sabrina.

Just like you failed your child.

Something yawned wide inside him, a rush of fierce and savage rage filling the void, and he wanted to hit something so badly that he turned to the blank alley wall and launched his fist at it, his knuckles smacking into the brick.

Pain was a bright light exploding in his head, but he made no sound, gritting his teeth against it instead.

Christ, he shouldn't be standing here pummeling a goddamn wall like a kid having a tantrum. That wouldn't help anyone. Sure, he'd failed his kid all those years ago, giving him or her up without a second's hesitation, then never thinking of them again. And there was no chance to rectify that mistake, that decision had been made years ago and he couldn't change it.

But he couldn't let himself fail Sabrina. He flatly refused.

She was his best friend and the secrets that she'd kept from him had turned out to be his own secrets come back to bite him. His own secrets come back to threaten her too.

This was all his fault and he knew it, and if anyone hurt her because of him . . .

A low growl escaped his throat. Whoever it was who'd hurt her would pay. They'd fucking pay dearly. Even if it was his goddamn father.

His phone buzzed. Automatically he took it out of his pocket and glanced down at the screen. It was a text from an unknown number. *This is a warning. She's safe, but only if you stop looking into what doesn't concern you.*

Kellan went very still. There could be no doubt as to who "she" was. He stared down at the message for a long moment, a thousand different responses going through his head, anger burning like a bonfire in his gut.

Instinctively he wanted to tell whoever it was that it was too late, he already knew his father was behind this. But did Phillip know that he knew? Elliott might not have told him that he'd opened his big mouth and let slip what he shouldn't have done to Kellan. That would be a huge failing.

Whatever. The first order of business was to get Sabrina back and unharmed ASAP.

Kellan stared down at the text glowing on the screen, thought for a moment, then typed a reply that gave away nothing: *What do you want?*

There was a brief pause and then a response came back. *Go to your friends and give them the information on that hard drive. Tell them nothing else. Once that's been done, she'll be returned unharmed.*

So the information on the hard drive must be fake in some way. It had to be if Phillip had planted it deliberately for them to find.

Kellan bared his teeth at the screen. He wanted to push, but since that might put Sabrina at risk, it would be a stupid thing to do. Instead he typed in, *Before I do anything, I want proof she's ok.*

After another pause, longer this time, a photo came through on his screen. It was dark, but seemed to show the interior of a van. The photo was focused on the pale face of a woman illuminated by the glare of a flash, her freckles stark against her pale skin, her eyes wide and frightened.

Sabrina.

The rage inside him turned cold, icy.

And all of a sudden he knew what he had to do.

Without responding to the photo, he scrolled through his contacts and found the one he needed and pressed the call button.

"What do you want?" Jack's deep voice answered on the second ring.

"I need a cell traced. Can you do it?"

There was a moment's silence.

"I thought Sabrina was with you." Jack said. "Doesn't she normally do that kind of shit?"

"She can't right now. I need you to do it." Kellan took a

silent breath. "And I need you to not tell Faith. This is just between us." He couldn't let the rest of them in on what had happened, couldn't let them see how badly he'd screwed this up in his insistence that his father was innocent.

Your fault. All this is your fault.

Yeah. Which meant it was up to him to fix it.

Jack said nothing and Kellan listened to the silence, hoping like fuck he'd been right. That Jack had been the one to call since he'd done everything he could to save the woman he loved.

The way you love Sabrina.

The though insinuated itself in his head, but he pushed it away before it could take root. He couldn't be thinking about emotional crap now. He needed to be hard and cold and focused the way he'd learned to be in the military.

"You want to tell me what's going on?" Jack asked eventually.

"No, I fucking don't."

"Fair enough." There was no expression in Jack's voice. "I'll see if I can run the trace and I won't tell Faith. But only on one condition."

Kellan's fist was beginning to ache from where he'd slammed it against the brick. "What?" he growled, flexing his fingers to make sure he hadn't broken them. What a dumb fuck if he'd broken them.

"If you need help, you fucking ask me."

Kellan blinked, not expecting that. He'd gotten to know Jack a little over the past couple of months and military-wise the guy was definitely *the* man to have along on a mission. Personality-wise, he was incredibly reticent and not overly friendly, but he did have a certain dark humor and no-bullshit approach that Kellan very much appreciated.

Apparently he also had your back when it was needed.

Kellan let out a breath. "Why?"

"Because you and Sabrina helped me get Callie away from her prick of a father. So if you need the favor returned, let me know."

For a second Kellan was tempted to let him. But this mission was already such a goddamn mess and he didn't want to make it any messier by including more people.

Apart from anything else, he didn't trust anyone to get Sabrina back but himself.

So all he said was, "Thanks, man. I'll let you know. Text me when you've traced that cell." Then without another word, he disconnected the call.

Sabrina woke up with a terrible headache and a mouth as dry as Death Valley. Opening her eyes involved light stabbing at her and making her headache worse, so she kept them closed and simply lay there for a couple of minutes, listening and trying to get some sense of where she was.

She was lying on something soft that felt like a bed, and she couldn't hear anything, which had to mean she wasn't in the back of that van with a phone shoved in her face and a flash going off in her eyes. And . . . no, her hands didn't seem to be tied and neither were her feet, which was good since those fucking assholes who'd taken her had had to tie her up after she'd kicked them quite a few times.

Except her head hurt. Why did her head hurt?

A flash of memory came back. Of her struggling like a madwoman against the cable ties around her wrists and legs, barely conscious of anything but the need to get back to Kellan. And then one of the men, who'd caught one of her feet in his thigh, had gotten up suddenly and raised his hand. There had been the gleam of metal in his hand—a gun—and she'd had the thought that this was it, this was the end. They were going to kill her and she'd never even told Kellan how much she loved him. Then the hand had come down and stars had exploded everywhere, and then she'd been pulled under into the darkness.

Though she hadn't been shot. She'd only been hit over the head, judging from the way it was aching.

Great.

Gathering herself, Sabrina cracked open an eye. There was a second's agony as the light hit her, but she kept it open and soon the pain subsided from a shrill scream into a dull roar.

She appeared to be in a bedroom, lying on a big bed covered in a white quilt. The room had a bookcase along the wall opposite the bed and big windows along another. The windows looked out over a whole lot of skyscrapers, all lit up for the night.

So was this a hotel room? An apartment? There were no personal effects anywhere and it had the smell of a place that hadn't been lived in, so it could have definitely been a hotel room.

Slowly, carefully, Sabrina levered herself upright on the bed, dizziness making her have to sit there and breathe deeply through a sudden bout of nausea.

She found herself staring down at the green silk gown she was still wearing, the hem of it stained with the dirt from that alleyway. It reminded her of Kellan, of what he'd told her before those men had come for them.

He'd had a child with someone. A child he'd had to give up. A child she'd then seen thinking it was his father's . . .

A shudder went through her and she pushed the thoughts away. She could think about that and all the implications later. Right now, finding out where she was, was more important, not to mention discovering who'd kidnapped her and why.

Fear was a small, hard stone in her gut, but she ignored it in favor of looking around the room again, searching for any clue as to what the hell was going on. But there was nothing. Unsurprisingly, the little purse that had her phone in it was gone, so sadly she couldn't call for help or use it to pinpoint where she was.

Dammit. Was she going to have to sit here and wait until whoever had kidnapped her came to get her? And when they did, what would they do with her?

The little stone grew a layer of ice around it, freezing her.

Shit, she couldn't think of that either, or else she'd end up panicking and that wouldn't help. No, she had to figure this out somehow. She was supposed to be a genius, right?

Pushing herself off the bed—slowly because of her aching head—she then moved over to the window and looked out. Still in Manhattan obviously, which was something. She turned back, pacing over to the bed and then to the bookcase, using the movement to help her think.

Okay, so it was likely that the guys who'd attacked them had something to do with the arms ring she and Kellan were investigating.

Which meant . . .

She stopped dead in her tracks, staring at the wall. Oh hell. Was this Phillip? He'd been the one who'd planted the hard drive for them to find, sending them off to question Elliott. Why had he done that? Perhaps he'd expected Elliott not to say anything and that Kellan, having reached a dead end, would give up. God, if so, he didn't know his son.

Whatever, clearly he'd found out that Elliott had talked and the attack in the alley was his response. He had to stop Kellan and herself from getting to the truth somehow and the easiest way to do that was to threaten one of them.

The dull hurt of betrayal sat just behind her breastbone, though why she had no idea since she'd always known what kind of man Phillip was. It should be no surprise that he hadn't hesitated to use her against Kellan. He'd never welcomed her into the family the way Charlotte had and shit, if he was the kind of man who'd pay to get rid of his own grandson, then he was definitely the kind of man who'd use her as a tool to get Kellan to do what he wanted.

Anger joined the ache in her chest. Goddamned Blakes. All she'd ever been was a tool for them. An ear for Charlotte to pour all her troubles into and now Phillip using her as a means to manipulate Kellan. And Kellan . . . had she only ever been a tool for him too? A friend to make him feel good about himself?

You know that's not true.

Sabrina swallowed, but held on to the anger. It was better than the betrayal and the sick, anxiousness that clutched at her whenever she thought of Kellan in that alley. Surely if those men had been Phillip's, he wouldn't have hurt his own son?

But thinking of that was a bad idea. What she needed to do now was to concentrate on figuring a way out of her situation, because she'd be damned if she let the stupid Blakes continue to use her.

She was her own woman, with her own life, but she'd been dancing to the Blakes' tune for far too long. It was time to make that tune her own, play her own fucking song.

Determination settled inside her. Moving purposefully over to the door, she tugged hard on the handle. It was locked, which didn't exactly shock her, but beside the door was a keypad which seemed to indicate that the lock was electronic.

How lucky.

Sabrina turned and did a quick look through the room, trying to find something she could use to somehow lever up the pad so she could access the electronics inside the lock. There was a low chest of drawers near the bed, but sadly nothing inside she could use. In fact, the only thing that seemed like it could do the job was a heavy china vase.

She picked the vase up, then carried it over to the door and without waiting, slammed the base of it hard into the keypad. Then she did it again and again, with force, until the keypad crunched, the plastic denting, then cracking.

The risk was screwing the lock completely and then she'd never get out, but she didn't have a lot of choice. She had to try. She didn't want to wait here passively until Phillip—if it was indeed Phillip who'd kidnapped her—decided what to do with her. She didn't want to be used and, apart from anything else, she *had* to find out what had happened to Kellan.

The decision gave her even more impetus and she slammed the vase into the keypad until there was a crack and the whole thing bowed inward, sparks flying as the electronics failed.

Sabrina ignored that, tossing aside the vase and pulling away the cracked plastic until she could access the wires. She'd done research into electronic locks while she'd been with the 11th Hour, and she suspected that if she could get at the wires, she might be able to open the door manually.

After a couple of minutes of fiddling, she finally found the wires she was looking for, then tugged hard, ripping at the ones she wanted so that one end came free of the mechanism. Then with a quick, practiced movement, she tore off the insulation around each wire so that the ends were bare and, her heart beating hard in her chest, touched the pair of wires together.

More sparks flew.

Either she'd unlocked the door or killed the lock completely.

Letting go the wires, Sabrina reached out for the door handle, her mouth dry. And turned it.

The door opened with a click.

Relief flooded through her, so strong she had to pause and take a couple of deep breaths before she went through it.

She had to be careful here. There was no knowing who was waiting for her outside and although she'd made Jack give her a few self-defense lessons—just for preparedness sake—she was under no illusion that she could take on anyone serious in a fight.

Cautiously, her heart drumming loudly in her ears, Sabrina pulled the door open wider and peered around it.

Outside was an empty carpeted hallway. There were a couple of pictures on the white walls, the lighting subtle. Definitely wasn't a hotel hallway, so it looked like she was in some kind of apartment.

They hadn't expected her to get out of the room either since there wasn't anyone guarding her door.

Okay. So far, so good.

Sabrina moved silently down the hallway to the end where there was an entranceway, holding her dress up to prevent the rustle of fabric. Beyond it lay another larger hallway, dimly lit, with a hardwood floor and expensive Persian rugs covering it. Small recesses revealed exquisite and expensive-looking pieces of art, while again, on the walls were more pictures.

The whole area gave off an aura of subtle wealth, which only cemented her suspicions.

And then she heard a familiar voice, confirming it.

Phillip.

Her head was hurting, fear like the ache of hunger in her gut, and she knew she should run down the hallway, find the entrance to this place, and get away. Not stay and let herself be used.

But something inside her wouldn't let her.

It *was* Phillip who'd taken her. Phillip, who was as guilty as she'd thought.

Phillip, who'd made Kellan give up his own child.

Anger flooded through her, drowning her fear and the ache in her head, propelling her down the hallway in the direction of that voice. To another entranceway opposite that gave onto a living area.

Huge windows framed the glittering lights of Manhattan outside, low couches and chairs in dark leather surrounding a tall man who stood facing the view, his back to Sabrina. He had a phone held to his ear and he was talking in a low voice, one hand thrust casually in his pocket.

His hair was graying, but there was no doubting his height

or the broad width of his shoulders, the way he held himself. Kellan had inherited those things for a reason.

You need to go. Get out. Find Kellan.

She should. But there was no fighting the rage that filled her.

Sabrina stood in the entranceway instead, the fingers of one hand clutching tightly to the skirts of her gown, the other in a fist, and she said in a shaking voice, "You prick. I knew it was you."

Phillip turned sharply, his blue eyes—so like his son's—meeting hers. For a second they widened in surprise. "I've got to go," he murmured to whoever it was he was talking to, then disconnected the call.

There was a moment's shocked silence as they stared at one another. Then he demanded, "How the hell did you get out?"

Sabrina ignored that, taking a couple of steps toward him. "I knew you didn't like me. But I never thought you'd use me against your own damn son!"

An expression of irritation crossed Phillip's face. "I'll do what I have to do to protect him and Charlotte, and if that means using you, then so be it." He glanced at someone over Sabrina's shoulder. "Get her out of here, Collins, for Christ's sake. And this time makes sure she stays put."

"What do you mean, protect him and Charlotte?" she demanded, ignoring the hand that closed around her arm, taking her in a hard grip. "Protect them from who?"

But Phillip wasn't looking at her. His attention was still over her shoulder, the expression in his eyes flaring in recognition.

Then someone said quietly, "I wouldn't do that if I were you."

Sabrina went still, all the breath leaving her body. She'd know that voice anywhere. Anywhere at all.

Kellan.

The hand around her arm was jerked away so suddenly she stumbled.

"Touch her again and I'll fucking kill you," Kellan said, his voice utterly cold.

Sabrina spun around.

Kellan was standing behind her still dressed in his tux, though the jacket was open and the shirt was half torn, partially revealing the smooth golden skin of his chest. He was pointing a gun at the man who'd been holding her, a bruise darkening his perfect jaw, blood staining the knuckles of the hand that held the gun. He was radiating a lethal kind of danger that made all the hairs on the back of her neck lift in reaction and a deep shudder, half fear, half excitement go through her.

The easygoing friend she knew was gone. In his place was the warrior.

He looked at her, silver-blue eyes electric. "Get behind me and stay there," he ordered in a tone that brooked no argument.

"But I—" she began, not even sure why she was talking, but he was already moving toward her, the ferocity of his stare making everything inside her shake.

"Get. Behind. Me. *Now.*"

Sabrina shut her mouth and did as she was told, and there was a certain relief to stand at his broad back, to have him between her and Phillip. To know he was here, because now he was, surely everything would be okay.

But it wasn't.

Kellan kept his gun aimed at Phillip's henchman, but his attention was squarely on his father, and Sabrina didn't need to see his face to know what his mood was.

He was absolutely furious.

"So, Dad," Kellan said conversationally. "What the fuck do you think you're doing?"

Phillip didn't reply, simply staring at his son. Then he glanced at his henchman, the man acting on the unspoken order by backing away completely.

"You found out, I see," he said eventually. "How did you know to come here?"

"It wasn't hard. I have a few friends who can do a cell phone trace and get access to security cameras."

"Ah." Phillip's tone was utterly neutral. "Well, to answer your question, I thought it was obvious what I'm doing. You need to drop this investigation or whatever the hell else it is."

"By threatening Sabrina?" There was a rough undercurrent in Kellan's voice, his anger clearly bleeding through. "By using her against me?"

Phillip's expression didn't even flicker. "Like I said to her, I'll do what I need to do to protect you and your mother."

"Me and Mom?" Kellan spat. "What the fuck has threatening Sabrina got to do with protecting us?"

"If you think it's just me behind this thing, you can think again," Phillip replied flatly. "There are powerful people involved. People who will do anything to keep their involvement secret." A muscle flicked in his jaw. "I thought sending you to Elliott would put you off the scent, but then he talked. So I had to take action."

"Right." Kellan's voice was suddenly coated in ice. "But see, I'm not really interested in Elliott, Dad. I want to know about Pippa and the visit she paid you. With my child."

CHAPTER 15

Kellan watched the puzzlement spread over his father's face. He didn't blame Phillip for being taken off guard by his statement. It probably wasn't the first thing the old man was expecting him to say.

But that was too bad. He'd let the past stay buried for too long. And now his immediate concern for Sabrina had been dealt with—seeing her standing there whole and unharmed had been a massive relief—he could turn his attention to the only other thing that mattered to him right in this moment: his child and what had happened with Pippa.

What Sabrina had told him, about seeing Pippa and the baby, had stayed with him, and even though he'd pushed it aside so he could focus on finding his father and Sabrina, he couldn't get it out of his head.

As it turned out, finding his father had been easy once Jack had traced the cell phone call. The building it had come from had soon been located and after Jack had gotten a contact of his to do a bit of Sabrina-level hacking with the security cameras, Kellan had even narrowed down the floor the call had come from.

Taking down the guys guarding the door had been simple, and he couldn't deny there had been a relief to that simplicity. To letting go of his control and simply being the warrior he was, doing what needed to be done to protect the people who mattered.

But now that was handled, now Sabrina was okay, and Kellan wanted the truth from the man who'd lied to him for so many years and he wanted it now.

"Visit?" Phillip echoed, frowning. "What visit?"

Kellan didn't look behind him to where Sabrina stood, but he could feel her warmth at his back. It made him uneasy for reasons he couldn't quite pinpoint.

"Sabrina told me she saw you one night with Pippa." He tried to ignore the woman standing behind him, keeping his gaze on his father's. "And a baby. You gave them money."

Phillip blinked, his frown deepening. "She might have. I'm not sure I—"

"No more fucking lies, Dad," Kellan interrupted harshly. "Just no more fucking lies."

There was a moment's silence as his father stared at him, his expression absolutely impenetrable.

Kellan met him stare for stare. He would have this from Phillip, he fucking would.

"Yes," Phillip said finally. "Pippa did come to me after the baby was born. Turned out the money I'd already paid her to keep quiet wasn't enough. She wanted more."

Sabrina had already told him what she'd seen and yet hearing the confirmation from his father felt like a blow.

"You didn't tell me." His voice was hoarse, but he didn't give a shit. "She came with my baby and you didn't tell me."

Anger flickered over Phillip's face. "No, of course I didn't. I wanted to protect you, don't you see? You'd made your decision and moved on, and nothing good would have come of seeing her again."

Yes, he had made a decision and it was one that despite all his attempts not to think about, he regretted. Regretted bitterly.

"But the baby." It was all he could think about, all he could focus on. "She brought the baby with her, didn't she?"

"Yes, she did. But I don't see what—"

"What was it?"

Another flicker across his father's granite features, almost like irritation. "What does that matter? It was years ago—"

"Boy or girl, Dad." Kellan's heart was beating so fast, so hard. "I want to fucking *know.*"

His father's jawline hardened. "A boy."

Kellan's gut lurched. A son. He had a son.

Behind him, Sabrina made a soft, shocked sound, and he wished she wasn't there. So she didn't have to hear about all the things he didn't know about his own kid. All the things he'd refused to think about.

What kind of man doesn't think about their own child? Not even once?

No fucking man he'd be proud of being, that was for sure.

He swallowed, acutely conscious of the gun in his hand, of the adrenaline coursing through him. Of the intense burning ache in his heart.

He shouldn't be asking these questions. He should be dealing with the issue at hand—his father's gun running activities. And yet . . .

"You saw him?" he demanded, before he could stop himself. "You saw my son?"

"Yes, I saw him." More irritation moved over Phillip's face. "I don't understand why you're—"

"Do you know where he is?" Fuck, he shouldn't be fixating on this, but the ache was getting stronger, deeper, a pull he couldn't ignore.

You don't have the right to ask these questions. You don't have the right to know, not when you ignored the fact you even had a child for fifteen years.

He didn't have the right. But he couldn't seem to stop himself from wanting to know all the same.

Phillip eyed him. "Just what the hell do you think you're going to do?"

"Answer the goddamn question," Kellan snapped, his patience running thin. "Like I already asked you, do you know where he is?"

A muscle leapt in his father's jaw. "Yes."

And something hot flared up inside Kellan, a burst of intense possessiveness. He could find his boy. He could see him.

No. You gave him up and with him, the right to be a father years ago.

It was true, all true. Yet the words came as if he had no control over what he was saying, no control at all.

"Tell me." Kellan ordered. "Tell me where the fuck he is."

Phillip was silent again, his expression like stone. Then he seemed to draw himself up, his shoulders becoming set, and Kellan's heart came to a shuddering halt. Because he recognized the signs; his father was about to tell him something he wasn't going to like.

"Stop investigating this arms ring, Kellan," Phillip said, steel glittering in his eyes and threading through his voice. "Walk away. And then I'll tell you."

Kellan stared back, feeling like the older man had somehow taken his Glock from his hands and shot him with it. Or like he was back in the hospital, lying in bed after the helo accident, where everything hurt, the very air moving over his burned skin an agony.

"You'd do that?" He couldn't keep the fierce shock and anger from his voice. "You'd use your own grandson to protect yourself?"

Phillip's expression twisted and he took what looked like an involuntary step forward. "It's not me I'm protecting, you fool. Didn't you listen to anything I said? I'm protecting you. This is *all* about protecting you."

"From what, Dad?" Kellan shot back, fury filling him. "A bunch of assholes with too much money and too much power? In case you hadn't noticed, I'm a motherfucking SEAL with a paramilitary organization at my back. I think I can handle them."

"You don't understand—"

"No." Kellan took a couple of steps so he was right in front of his father, only inches away. Looking into a pair of blue eyes the same color as his own. "You're the one who doesn't understand. I don't give a fuck about who might come after me. I don't even give a fuck about what kind of bullshit you've involved yourself in, though civilians have died because of what you've done." His voice was rising but he made no attempt to stop it. "All that matters right now is knowing where my goddamned son is. You made me give him up, Dad. So you can tell me where to find him again."

Phillip didn't move and his expression didn't flicker. "Drop the investigation and I will."

"*No.*" Another voice, light and feminine but no less fierce. "Just no."

Then silk rustled as Sabrina came up beside him and moved past him, putting herself between him and Phillip.

"How dare you!" She didn't pay any attention to Kellan or the gun he was holding, all her focus on Phillip. "How dare you use a kid like that. Against your own son!" Her whole body was quivering with outrage, her voice shaking with it. "I can understand you using me, but not Kellan's child!"

Automatically Kellan reached out and put a hand on her shoulder, gently pulling her back because he didn't want her to be part of this. It wasn't her fight and he didn't want her to get hurt. He didn't want her to put herself in his father's line of fire.

"Bree," he said quietly. "This is my battle, not yours."

She didn't turn, her furious attention still on Phillip. "If it's yours, then it's mine too." Her tone was flat and utterly certain.

She's fighting for you. She's protecting you.

Because that's what she did. That's what she'd always done. And he . . . didn't like it. Not here, not now. Not when they were discussing the son he'd given up.

Not when he sure as hell didn't deserve it.

"This has got nothing to do with you, Sabrina," Phillip was saying coldly. "This is a family matter."

And Kellan didn't miss the slight flinch that Sabrina couldn't quite hide. Another casual reminder that she wasn't family and never would be.

Another hurt she had to bear for being here, defending him.

You don't deserve her. You don't deserve her friendship.

The thought hit him like yet another bullet, exploding inside him, causing yet another wound. Because that was true too. He'd deliberately not seen how his parents had treated her in the same way as he'd deliberately not thought about the kid he'd given up.

He hadn't wanted to see. Because it might have meant Sabrina leaving, and the thought of her leaving, of not being his friend . . .

Selfish asshole.

Yeah, maybe he was. And maybe that needed to stop.

Kellan slid his gun away—it wasn't needed now—then he put his hands on Sabrina's waist and turned her to face him. Her eyes widened, furious green staring up into his.

"This is my fight now, baby," he said very calmly. "So let me fight it, understand?"

"But I don't want—"

"You're the best friend I ever had," he interrupted. "The

most loyal, the most caring. And I couldn't have done without you. But this is mine to deal with." He paused. "And I don't want to see you hurt. Not ever again."

She blinked, staring up into his face. But he was already moving, pushing her behind him with gentle hands. "I know you're there, Bree," he said as he returned his attention to his father. "You've got my back, right?"

She didn't say anything and he wondered if she was going to protest. But then she put her hand between his shoulder blades, a wordless show of support.

Christ, he didn't deserve her. He really didn't.

"This has got nothing to do with her," his father said again. "She's already made a—"

"Don't you talk about her," Kellan cut him off coldly, his rage turning protective. "Don't you even mention her goddamn name. If you hurt her again, I'll hurt you, father or not, understand?"

Phillip scowled. "Are you threatening me?"

"It's not a threat, Dad. It's a fucking promise." He took a step forward, getting right up in his father's face. "Now, give me a reason you think you can use Sabrina and my son against me, and you'd better make it good."

"I already told you," Phillip said, implacable. "I'm trying to protect you from people who'd do worse than a bit of kidnapping or blackmail. And if you think you can handle it when they come after you, you can think again."

"That's not a good enough reason."

"I don't care. I'll do what I have to do to keep you safe. So if you want to ever see your son, Kellan, you'll walk away from this investigation and you'll do it now."

There was nothing but determination in his father's eyes, the same determination Kellan felt burning inside himself, and he knew Phillip wasn't going to back down.

Which meant he had a choice. He either walked away from

Night's mission and got his father to tell him where his son was or . . .

Or he gave up his son for the good of someone else.

Again.

Oh come on, what are you really giving up? You never thought about him before now. You never even knew "he" was a he. Acting like you give a shit now is a bit disingenuous, don't you think?

It was. Yet he couldn't get rid of the ache in his heart, the pull that he'd been denying for so many years. The need to see the son he'd created.

The son you don't deserve.

That was true too, wasn't it? So why was this even a choice? He knew what the right thing to do was. The only thing to do.

Agony whispered through him, a pain far more sharp and subtle than those fucking burns, his brain stumbling ahead, thinking and thinking.

How old would his boy be now? Christ, he'd be a teenager. Had Pippa ever told him who his father was? Did he blame Kellan for leaving him? For never looking for him? Did he want to know who Kellan was?

What if he does? What will you tell him? That you're the kind of man who gave up his child and never thought about him . . .

The kind of man who'd keep a friend close despite how it hurt her, simply because he didn't want to give her up.

The kind of man who'd give up a mission and everyone depending on him purely to satisfy his own selfish needs.

There was a slight pressure against his spine: Sabrina's hand pressing down, reminding him that she was there. That she had his back.

Another reason—as if he needed it—of what the right thing to do was.

Kellan had given Night his word he'd bring back the evidence of his father's guilt if Phillip had turned out to be guilty, which he had. Night himself didn't mean much to Kellan, but giving his word did, as did not wanting to let down the rest of the 11th Hour team.

But more than anything else, he didn't want to let down Sabrina. She'd put herself at risk for this, both physically and emotionally, and he couldn't let that mean nothing. He wouldn't.

She matters more to you than your own child?

Something shifted inside him. Something that had always been there, but he'd never seen or looked at too closely, because it had always looked like friendship to him.

Except it didn't look like friendship anymore. It looked more complicated than that. Multifaceted, deeper, bigger.

Yes, sex had changed things between them, added something that hadn't been there before, a possibility he hadn't considered. But he was considering it now, oh yes, he was.

His chest tightened, his heart beating hard and fast.

Give up the son he'd never met or disappoint the woman who was beginning to mean more to him than merely a friend?

It wasn't really a choice.

Yes, he wanted to see his son more than he wanted his next breath, but that was what *he* wanted. Was that the right choice for the boy? Kellan couldn't simply walk back into his life after years of not even thinking about him. And what would he say to his son anyway? If he asked Kellan why he hadn't come for him sooner?

No, his son didn't need him and probably didn't want him either.

But Sabrina did. She might not need him, but she definitely wanted him.

Christ, and apart from anything else, what his father was doing was illegal and how could he let that go on a selfish whim? How could he even contemplate it?

People were dying because the guns his father was importing were getting into the wrong hands. Innocent people. Their lives were way more important than finding his son.

You'll never see him. Dad'll make sure of it.

Pain fractured somewhere inside him, a grief he hadn't known was there. Grief for the loss of a hope he hadn't realized he'd been nurturing and a future he hadn't understood that he'd wanted.

But there was no other choice.

He was a guy who did the right thing and the right thing now was to complete the mission.

Sure, the consequences of turning his father over to the likes of Jacob Night wouldn't make things easy for his mother, but Kellan could handle that. He'd have to.

Sabrina's palm pressed a little harder against him, the warmth of her touch reminding him again that she was the one constant in his life. Still loyal and unwavering, even now she must know how far short of the hero mark he fell.

Somehow that touch made the words he didn't want to say easier to force out. "Then I guess I'll have to settle for not seeing my son."

Anger flared, blue and hot in Phillip's eyes. "Don't be ridiculous. You'd really give up your boy to keep pursuing this?"

"You're running guns, Dad," Kellan pointed out, pushing away the grief that clutched at him, because he had no time for it. His decision was made. "They're causing the deaths of innocent people. Innocent civilians. And I have no fucking idea why you thought that would be a good idea, but right at this moment, I don't give a shit why you did it. What it is, is wrong on just about every level, especially if it ends up involving threats to the people I care about. And I only have one response to that."

Phillip made a disgusted sound. "The deaths of those people have got nothing to do with me, or you for that matter. Besides, you have no idea what these people will do. I'm doing this for your protection—"

"No, you're not. You're doing it for yourself. Because if it was for me, you'd never have kidnapped Sabrina. Never used my son as a bargaining chip. Never threatened the people I love."

All at once his father's expression went cold. "What do you know about love, son? You've got no goddamned idea."

But Kellan was done. He didn't want to listen, not anymore. Once he'd cared about what this man said, but now? Now, he didn't give a shit. Not when the ache inside him was still raw, the grief that was going to hurt worse than the pain of his burns once he let it in. But he wasn't going to let it in. Later, when he'd gotten Sabrina away from his father, he'd have plenty of time, but not now. Not here.

He turned away from his father and grabbed Sabrina's cold fingers, and without another word, he strode out of the living area, pulling her along with him.

"You should have listened to me, Kellan," his father called after him. "You'll never find out where he is. I'll make sure of it."

Kellan kept on walking.

"I can't let you do this, son. I can't let you leave."

But no one stopped them as they walked out the front door of the apartment. No one at all.

Sabrina's heartbeat was thundering in her ears as she found herself being pulled along by Kellan for the second time that evening.

He strode down the hallway outside the apartment where she'd been held captive, stopping only when they got to the elevator. He punched the button, then turned to glance up the hallway once more, obviously checking out to see if they'd been followed. He'd taken that lethal-looking gun out again and had half raised it, keeping it at the ready.

The elevator chimed, the doors opening, and she found herself pushed quickly into the elevator car with him following hard on her heels.

"You okay?" he asked brusquely. He kept the gun raised as he hit the button for the first floor, his attention on the numbers above the door as the elevator began to move downward.

Her throat felt thick, the pulsing ache at the back of her head making her temples throb. "Yes." Her voice was thick too, her legs shaky.

She couldn't get the sound of his voice out of her head, the grief that had laced it as he'd demanded his father tell him where his son was.

His son. *Kellan's* son . . .

Listening to all of that, to him, had hurt and at first she'd thought it was simply because if he was in pain, then she felt it too. But gradually, as his father had held the fate of his grandson over his own son's head, she realized it wasn't simply sympathy she felt.

It was more.

She'd gotten it wrong. All these years she'd thought it was Phillip's baby and that she'd been protecting Kellan from a terrible truth. But it hadn't been Phillip's baby. It had been Kellan's, which meant she'd been protecting him from precisely nothing. And, worse, she'd been keeping something from him. Something that was clearly important to him, as that confrontation with Phillip had shown.

He cared about his child. And giving up that child had hurt him.

God, if she'd only told him what she'd seen, maybe he would have been able to do something about it, gone after his lover . . . But she hadn't. She'd kept it a secret the way Charlotte had wanted her to. Yet Charlotte had gotten it wrong too.

She should have said something more to Phillip when he'd threatened not to tell Kellan where his son was, but Kellan hadn't wanted her to. It was his battle, he'd said, and he was right. But standing behind him while he'd faced his father had made her feel . . . wrong in some way. Like she wasn't being a good friend and protecting him.

At least until he'd said those words to his father, the words that had resonated oddly inside herself too.

"*You're only doing this for yourself . . .*"

She didn't understand why she couldn't stop thinking about those words. Or why she kept asking herself if she'd been doing the same thing. Thinking she was protecting him by keeping all these secrets, and yet, in the end, only protecting herself.

You had to have a reason to be needed by him.

Cold wound through her bloodstream. No, that wasn't it, was it? Charlotte had made her promise not to tell him and so she hadn't, because she didn't want to hurt him.

But he was hurt anyway and now the secret is out. Now you have nothing to protect him from anymore. So what use are you to him?

The cold deepened.

"Bree."

She blinked and looked at him.

His eyes were very blue and there was something burning in them, a determination she'd never seen before. It made her shiver.

Then he moved toward her, one hand coming to cup the side of her face, his thumb brushing along her cheekbone. "Did he hurt you?"

Her throat got even tighter, because the touch of his hand was so light, tender almost. "No." A lie when the back of her head ached, but that pain was minor in comparison to the ache in her heart. "Kel . . ." She began, then stopped, because she had no idea what the hell she wanted to say. She didn't even know where to start.

He said nothing for a long moment, but there were shadows

in his blue eyes. "I didn't think I wanted to know," he said eventually. "All these years I've been telling myself that it was in the past, that it didn't matter anymore. But it did matter, Bree. It mattered a lot."

She didn't need to ask what he was talking about. She knew. "You could have let Phillip go. You could have found your son again."

But Kellan shook his head. "No. I couldn't. I gave my word to Night that if Dad was guilty, I'd get him the information he wanted. Plus, people are dying because of those guns. Not to mention you putting yourself on the line coming here with me . . . Christ, I couldn't have let you down or the team, simply because Dad may or may not have told me where my son was."

Her heart tightened even further. "But . . . your son, Kellan."

His winter-blue eyes flashed silver a second, pain stark in them. "I know. But I gave up all my rights to him years ago. He doesn't know me anyway, and I can't just rock up into his life and say 'hey, son, I'm here. Got a hug for Daddy?' He may not even know I'm his father anyway." His thumb moved against her cheekbone, softly stroking. "Besides, finding him is what *I* want. And that may not be the best thing for him."

Everything inside her hurt for him, for the grief she saw in his face. But what could she say? Kellan had always been the guy who did the right thing and it was clear what the right thing was in this case. "We can find him," she said. "Your father might think to keep him secret or whatever, but I bet I can find him."

Oddly, the ghost of a smile turned Kellan's beautiful mouth. "If anyone could find him, it would be you. But maybe it's better to leave things as they are. He'd be a teenager now and being a teenager is shitty enough without your long-lost father turning up out of the blue."

"Kel—"

"Let's deal with the mission first," Kellan interrupted, stroking her again, the touch softening his firm tone. "Dad might have let us get away, but I doubt he'll wait long before he starts protecting himself." Steel gleamed in his eyes for a second. "I'm going to get in contact with Night straight away so he can move on this, because I'll be fucked if I sacrifice seeing my kid for nothing."

She wanted to tell him that he didn't have to sacrifice anything. Because she could find his kid, she knew she could. But what he'd said about not wanting to disrupt the child's life . . . well, she could see that would be an issue also.

There you go, wanting to be useful to him again, and he's not having any of it.

She swallowed, that strange, cold feeling tightening its grip on her, the doubts in her head suddenly looming large. But if she wasn't there protecting him or helping him find his child, what else could she give him? Sex maybe? He'd liked that. But then how long would that last? Eventually the passion would fade and he'd move on . . .

Besides, you think he'd really want you after everything you've kept from him?

Oh God. And he'd been so angry with her out there in the alley, after she'd told him.

"I'm sorry," she blurted out hoarsely. "I'm sorry I didn't tell you about Phillip and the b-baby. I just . . . promised Charlotte and I didn't know . . ."

"Hey, it's okay." His thumb moved gently on her skin, his voice full of an understanding she didn't deserve. "You did what you thought was right at the time."

No, you didn't. That was an excuse. You know who you were really protecting.

Her eyes prickled. "You forgive me? Just like that?"

"What's done is done. Besides, I wasn't exactly open with you about the existence of the baby in the first place." He paused. "I'm sorry I didn't tell you. Pippa was married and I was ashamed of what I'd done. I didn't want you to think less of me."

As if she would.

"Kel," she began, wanting to tell him that, but at that moment the elevator chimed.

His attention flicked to the door, his hand dropping away. "Come on, let's get out of here."

He was right, what was done was done. But the cold feeling lingered as they got out of the elevator and made their way to the entrance of the building and the sidewalk outside.

It was dark and late, and yet there seemed to be lots of people around. Kellan didn't pause, drawing her along with him as he began to walk with purpose along the sidewalk. He'd put away his gun before they'd left the building, and now he tugged out his phone, punching a few buttons, obviously sending off a few messages before raising it to his ear.

He began speaking to Faith, relaying what had happened with his father. There was no hesitation, his voice deep and sure as he answered questions. If he'd had any lingering uncertainty about his father before, it was obvious he had none now.

They kept on walking, she mostly pulled along by the grip he had on her hand, listening to him give Faith the address of the building his father had been in, then a complete rundown of its security and the number of men who'd been guarding it.

"I would move now," Kellan said. "He'll start protecting himself and once he does that, the opportunity for surprise will be gone . . . Yes. Good plan. I'll leave it up to Night to secure him then." There was a pause, him obviously listening to what Faith was saying. "Yes, okay. I need to get back to Southampton to deal with my mother. She had nothing to do with this—or at least she probably didn't." Another pause. "Sabrina's okay, but I'd prefer her to be back safely in San Diego."

Sabrina stiffened, but he went on. "Yeah, I've already sent

for the car to take her to the airport. She can get the jet from there."

He really doesn't need you.

The thought whispered in her head, making those cold doubts settle further down inside her. So he had it all under control now, did he? He was handling it. Her usefulness to the mission was now at an end.

Your usefulness to him too.

She caught her breath. What did that mean for them both? If he handled things here, sending her back to San Diego, what was going to happen when he was done? He'd told her he hadn't finished with her, but surely, now that he knew everything she'd kept from him . . .

He won't want you.

Sabrina's steps slowed and she tried to pull her hand from his, suddenly finding the contact unbearable.

Kellan stopped and turned around, still talking to Faith, one fair brow rising in a silent question.

She tugged at his grip again. "Let me go."

He frowned. "Call you back in five," he said to Faith, then punched a button on the screen, disconnecting the call. But he didn't let go of Sabrina's hand, merely pinning her with that blue gaze of his. "What's up?"

People moved past them, late-night diners, early club goers, bar hoppers, and tourists wanting to take in the Big Apple at night.

Sabrina ignored them. All she was conscious of was Kellan's fingers around hers and the warmth of his touch, a touch she wanted with every breath in her. A touch she wanted forever.

But it was never going to be forever, was it? She'd kept things from him, using those secrets and the lies she'd told herself to ensure she stayed useful to him, and now . . .

Now she had nothing else to offer him.

The thought left her breathless and panicky.

"Why are you sending me back to San Diego?" she demanded, trying to distract herself, jerking her hand away again and this time succeeding

He made no move to grab her, but the frown on his face deepened. "Because shit's going to hit the fan once Night moves on Dad, and if Dad's right, and those powerful people come after me, they'll come for you too. And I don't want you anywhere in the vicinity."

He was protecting her, because that's what he always did and she loved that he did. But she didn't deserve it, not after all the secrets she'd kept from him. And she had nothing to give him in return. She didn't have the physical skills to help guard his back. She couldn't help him deal with Charlotte and Night would be handling whatever was going to happen with Phillip.

Her usefulness was at an end.

"I . . . want to stay with you," she said, unable to stop herself.

His expression softened, his blue gaze searching hers, and she had the terrible feeling that everything she felt was written all over her face and that he could read every last word. "Don't worry, baby. I'll be okay. And hey, the rest of it we'll deal with once this bullshit with Dad has been handled." He took a step toward her. "There's some things we need to talk about, I think."

Things to talk about . . .

She swallowed, the panicky feeling getting more intense. "What things?"

His smile was slow and sweet and it made her go hot all over. "You know what things, Bree. Things like you and me."

You and me . . .

Her breathing got faster, her heartbeat accelerating, and not in a fun way. He wanted her, she knew he did, and even a couple of hours earlier, that had been enough for her. But now things had changed. The secrets she'd kept from him were out in the open and she had nothing left to protect him from. Nothing left to offer him but herself and her friendship, and she hadn't even been that good of a friend.

So what was left?

Your love.

No. She couldn't give him that, not when she had no idea whether he'd want it or not. After all, no one else had, so why would he?

But what if he did?

For some reason that thought, the one where she got everything she wanted, made her even more panicky. It was easier to tell herself that he didn't want what she had to offer than to accept that perhaps, he might. Not when she didn't deserve it.

"Yeah," she said shakily, "About that."

His frown was back. "What do you mean 'about that'?"

Her throat was dry and she couldn't seem to get a breath. "I don't know if it's such a good idea after all." Her hands twisted unconsciously in the skirts of her green gown. "I mean, you've got to handle your mom and there's bound to be some stuff you'll have to deal with if these guys come after you . . ."

"So? All of that has nothing to do with us." His blue eyes glittered all of a sudden and he was moving toward her, so fast she had no time to move, and then he was there right in front of her, his hands reaching to cup her face between his large warm palms. "Why are you scared, Bree? And don't try to deny it, I can see it in your eyes."

She trembled. He was so close, his hard, hot body brushing her skirts, the heat of his hands seeping right down through her. Making her ache. Making her burn. Making the panic settle right down into her bones. "I just don't think this is a good idea," she babbled inanely. "You and me, I mean. The timing is really bad and I—"

Kellan bent his head and abruptly his mouth was on hers, stopping the flow of words, the taste of him flaring through her, bright and intense. And for a second all she wanted was to open up and let him in, kiss him back, show him how hungry and desperate she was for him.

But the fear wouldn't go away and with it, the knowledge that if she let him take what he wanted now, she'd never have the strength to push him away again. And she had to.

The full realization of the secrets she'd kept from him, and their consequences, would eventually hit him and she knew what would happen then. He wouldn't want her anymore, because who would? After the kind of shitty friend she'd been? He would leave and it would break her heart. People never stayed. People never *really* wanted her. And her heart had been broken so many times before, she didn't think she'd survive it breaking again, and definitely not if Kellan was the one doing the breaking.

Actually, if it was Kellan doing the breaking, he wouldn't simply break it. He'd pulverize it completely.

Sabrina wrenched her head away and tried to take a couple of stumbling steps back, but his arm only tightened around her, holding her against him.

"What is it?" he demanded, his laser focus zeroing in on her. "I thought this was what you wanted."

She pushed at him, desperate for some distance. "Let me go, Kel."

But his hold was unbreakable. "Not until you tell me what the fuck is going on."

Sabrina jerked her head up. "I don't want this after all, okay? Like I said, you and me is a bad idea."

"What?" Something glittered in his eyes. "Since when?"

"Since now."

"Why?" He was searching her face, holding her like he never wanted to let her go. And she hated that and loved it too. "What changed, Bree? What did I do? Was it me giving up my kid? Did you expect me to just let everyone down and—"

"No," she interrupted, cutting him off because she couldn't bear to let him think it was him. Not when the trouble was hers. "God, no. It's got nothing to do with that. It's . . . me. I don't think I'm ready for a relationship with you, I mean if that's what you're after." It wasn't quite the truth but it was all the truth she was capable of.

"Of course that's what I'm after. You really think I'm a fuck and run kind of guy?"

She began to shake. "Well, isn't that what you've been doing up until now?"

Okay, sure, it was a low blow, but shit, she was desperate.

"Yeah, but not with anyone who was after more." Anger gleamed hot and blue in his gaze. "Come on, Bree, you should know me better than that. And anyway, I'd never do that with you. Christ, you're my best friend."

Of course he wouldn't do that. He was basically perfect, her handsome prince. Another reason why it would never work between them. Not when she was so imperfect.

She shoved at him again. "Let me the hell go, Kellan."

But he didn't. Instead his hand came up, cupping her face the way he had in the elevator, warm and gentle and tender, making her want to cry. "Tell me what you're afraid of," he murmured. "Don't push me away like this."

She shuddered. "You." Her voice came out croaky, the truth sounding harsh. "I'm afraid of you."

Shock replaced the anger in his expression. "Why?" he demanded. "What the hell have I done to make you afraid of me?"

Her throat was tight and her head ached and she knew she wasn't making any sense. "You won't let me go," she said thickly. "And I need you to, Kellan. I need you to let me go in all senses of the word."

CHAPTER 16

Sabrina was warm in his arms, but he could feel her shaking, could see the fear in her lovely hazel eyes.

He also had no idea what the hell she was talking about.

Let her go? Seriously?

Yet there was no denying that fear, so he slowly released his arm from around her waist and stepped back. Everything in him was screaming at him to ignore what she'd said and keep her close, but he'd done nothing but fuck up this entire mission and now that he was on the path to fixing things, he didn't want to fuck up any further.

Letting her go was the right thing to do, so that's what he did.

His own heart was beating like a drum and he couldn't kick the feeling that she was slipping away from him. That the distance between them was widening with each passing second, and all he wanted to do was reach out and pull her back.

He almost did, but she'd taken a few steps away from him, putting her out of arm's reach. Her face was pale in the night, her freckles standing out, her eyes darkened into deep green.

She looked so fragile, standing there while the foot traffic moved by on either side of her. So alone.

"Bree." He struggled to keep his voice even. "What are you talking about? Let you go? What do you mean 'in all senses of the word'?"

Her chest rose as she took a deep breath, like she was bracing herself for something. "It means I can't do this, not with you. I can't sleep with you and be your friend. It doesn't work for me."

"Then don't be my friend." He stared at her, every inch of him desperate to reach out to grab her, only his iron control holding him back. "Be my lover instead."

"I can't." She shook her head slowly and as she did, he could see something gleaming on her cheekbone. A tear.

His chest went tight and he took a helpless step toward her, but she backed away, trembling as if she was on the point of bolting entirely. He stopped, trying to hold himself in check. "Why not?" There was a hoarse edge to his voice that he couldn't quite hide. "I know you want me. I know you do. So what's stopping you? I'm here for you. I told you I would be and I am."

"I know you are." She blinked, then looked away. "But . . . if it doesn't work out between us, I don't think I could stand it."

He could understand that. It was a big step they were taking. They were changing things between them and no, that wasn't easy. But hell, they'd crossed the line physically anyway and there was no coming back from that. Fuck, he didn't want to come back from it.

Getting physical with her had felt like the final piece of a jigsaw fitting into place. A piece he hadn't even realized was missing, and now it was back, it revealed the whole picture. A friendship he'd always counted on, becoming deeper, richer. Different and yet so much more.

He wanted that. He wanted to explore that. He'd always

loved her as a friend, and now, staring at her as she stood alone in the crowd, so lovely in her green dress, so lost, he loved her as something more than a friend. And it didn't feel like a shock or a surprise. It felt like something he'd always felt but hadn't recognized.

A feeling he did *not* want to lose.

"Then we'll make it work," he said hoarsely. "*I'll* make it work."

"Why?" She looked at him like he'd spoken in Greek. "Why on earth would you want that?"

He almost laughed, the question was so ridiculous. Did she really not know what she meant to him? "Because you matter to me." The words came out without any hesitation at all, true and right and absolutely certain. "Because I love you."

A stricken look crossed her face, as if he'd said the worst thing in the entire world. "Oh no," she whispered. "You can't."

"I can. I do." Abruptly he was sick of the distance, sick of doing the right thing. She was crying, she was in pain, and she was scared, and he refused to let that stand.

He began to move toward her, but she flung up a hand. "*No,*" she cried, the desperate note in her voice stopping him in his tracks. "You can't love me."

He stared at her, not understanding, because that just didn't make any sense. "Why not? Why shouldn't I love you? Give me one good fucking reason."

But there was a fierce light in her eyes, burning away the tears, and he recognized it. Her goddamn determination. "Because I don't want it, okay? I don't need it. I don't need you. I'm not some pathetic little orphan and I'm not some stupid abandoned stray. I'm not your pet project that you have to protect either."

What the fuck? He'd never seen her like that or treated her in that way. Never.

Are you sure? You liked being the only one to make her smile. To make her laugh. You liked her doing things for you, giving you all her attention. But it wasn't about her. You liked the way it made you *feel.*

Regret and a kind of shame swept through him. Yes, he *had* liked the way she'd made him feel. And maybe he'd been greedy with her attention and her friendship. Hadn't tackled the way his parents had treated her, because he hadn't wanted anything to change. After what had happened with Pippa, he'd needed Sabrina's unwavering support like he'd needed air to breathe.

So he'd let it go on, let himself be her go-to guy. The person she relied on, because she didn't have anyone else.

You took her for granted, you selfish asshole.

Maybe he had back then. But he wasn't now. Things were different now and so was he.

He held her angry green gaze. "Yeah, I made some mistakes and maybe you're right. Maybe I did treat you like that. But that's not how it is now. Not this time, Sabrina."

Something shifted in her eyes, shock or surprise, he couldn't tell, but then the anger was back. Even more fierce this time. "I don't care what it's like now. Two weeks ago I was still your best friend, barely even a woman, and yet suddenly you're in love with me? Suddenly you're expecting me to fall into your arms because it's what *you* want?" Her chin lifted. "What about what *I* want? Have you even asked me what that is?"

There was a heaviness in his chest, a weight that began to press down, making breathing difficult.

She was right. This *was* all about him and what he wanted. Shit, had he *ever* asked her what it was that she wanted? About anything? He couldn't remember and he had a horrible feeling that he hadn't. He'd always assumed that she wanted what he wanted, because she always had.

Say it again with me: selfish asshole.

The heaviness was like a Chinook had landed directly on his chest, the skids settling down onto his breastbone, the entire weight of the helo resting on him.

"What do you want then?" he asked, because he had to, even though he already knew what she was going to say.

She stared at him, pale and lost in the night, tears shining on her cheeks. "I want to be free, Kellan," she whispered, but he heard, oh yeah, he did. "I want to be free. Of you."

Weird how words like that—a few simple goddamn words—could feel as if they were flaying him alive. Cutting into him like the scalpel had cut away his burned and ruined skin.

Except this kind of cut didn't help him heal like the scalpel had. This cut felt like it was killing him instead.

Free of him. She wanted to be free of him.

Which means if you don't want to continue being a selfish asshole, you have to give her what she wants.

But . . . he'd already given up something that he'd cared deeply about. Did he really have to give up another?

Why are you even asking that question? You know what you have to do.

The right thing. He had to do the right thing, even if his whole soul rebelled against it. And after all his selfishness, the right thing was to give Sabrina what she wanted.

The right thing was to set her free.

"Fine." He had to force the word out, the weight on his chest crushing, making it feel like it was full of broken glass. "If you want to be free, then you're free."

Anguish moved over her face, as if the words had hurt her as much as they'd hurt him, but then it was gone. Green glittered in her eyes, no gold there at all now. "Don't come after me. Don't try and contact me. Just . . . leave me alone."

"Okay." Every word in his mouth tasted wrong, but he made himself go on. "I won't come after you or contact. I'll leave you alone."

She gave a little shiver, her shoulders hitching as she drew in a shaky sounding breath. "I don't know if I can be friends again. I'm sorry . . ."

"It's fine," he repeated, even though it wasn't fine and it never would be again. "If you can't, you can't."

She looked down at where her hands were twisted in front of her, and for a moment he wavered, almost obeying the voice that was screaming at him to ignore whatever it was that she wanted and close the distance between them, grab hold of her, and never let her go.

But he was in control now, not that voice and certainly not his stupid fucking heart, which had always been wrong in the past. And he remained where he was as the friendship he thought would always be there fractured and broke into a million pieces right in front of him.

Mercifully, at that point a car he recognized pulled up to the curb—Sabrina's ride to the airport.

"Time to go." He couldn't bear to say her name, so he didn't, moving over to the car instead, pulling open the back door and holding it for her. "This'll take you to the airport. The jet will be all ready to go."

Her gaze met his and he thought he saw denial there, with longing and fear and anger all mixed in together. And he braced himself, as if waiting for her to say something, anything.

But she didn't. She only nodded, then tore her gaze away, moving toward the car, her expression full of nothing but determination now.

"A goodbye would be nice," he said, as she paused before car door, preparing to get in.

Color stained her pale cheeks, but she didn't look at him, not this time. "Goodbye."

He wanted to call her on it then, tell her that destroying their friendship after so many years wasn't the answer, and that what she was doing was being a coward.

But that was his own pain talking, not hers, and besides, it wouldn't help matters.

So he said nothing as she got into the car without another

word, and he shut the door behind her. Then he watched the car move away until the taillights disappeared into the late night traffic, feeling like he'd been shot and was watching the blood run out of his body and into the dirt. And there was nothing he could do to save himself.

"I don't need you," she'd told him.

But he had a horrible feeling he needed her. Because he didn't know what his life was going to look like without her in it.

He was afraid that it wouldn't be much of a life at all.

Sabrina let herself cry all the way to the private airfield and then sob a little more as she got onto the jet that would take her back to San Diego.

It was the longest, most depressing flight she'd ever been on, and even though she thought the tears would help her sleep on it, they didn't.

She sat there, looking out the window at the darkness outside and felt that darkness crawl inside her, filling every part of her.

She'd told him that what she wanted was to be free of him, and that was true. She did want to be free of him. Free of the years of helpless longing, helpless desire. Free of the fear that she would never be to him what he was to her. Free of the endless hope that no matter how hard she tried to crush kept springing back up again.

Hope that one day he would fall as deeply in love with her as she was with him.

But he did. And you pushed him away.

She swallowed, staring out at the night beyond the jet's narrow windows, her eyes gritty and painful from crying, her throat sore.

The moment he'd told her he loved her, everything she'd ever wanted was suddenly right there in front of her, ready for her take. Yet what had she done? She'd panicked and run from it instead.

Coward. You're a coward.

The knowledge sat inside her like a Trojan virus inside a computer, eating away at her, deleting data and corrupting it. Making her feel like shit.

Yes, she was a coward. And why not? She was only protecting herself from his eventual realization that it wasn't love that he felt for her. Because he would realize that. Her father was supposed to have loved her and yet he'd walked away, leaving her completely alone. Her mother was supposed to have loved her and yet she'd left too, dying in the river along with Sabrina's brothers.

Love didn't keep people from leaving you.

How could he suddenly think he was in love with her anyway? After so many years of not even noticing her? They'd had sex twice and a few deep conversations, but that didn't mean love.

Maybe Kellan had gotten confused with friendship. Maybe he thought the friendship he felt for her was something more based on the sex they'd had. Whatever it was, she couldn't trust it, not when he'd simply let her go. She'd asked to be free and so he'd freed her. Without even an argument.

Come on, that's not fair. You told him what you wanted and he gave it to you.

He had. And it *was* what she'd wanted, wasn't it?

The stewardess had brought her a tumbler of bourbon just after takeoff, and Sabrina had drained that, then asked for another. She picked up the second glass now and drained that one too.

Perhaps getting drunk was a good idea. It would certainly help the flight go quicker, not to mention block out the memory of Kellan's face as she'd told him all she'd wanted was to be free of him.

There had been shock there and a blue flicker of pain. Yes, it had hurt him and part of her had been savagely glad that the boot was on the other foot for a change.

But another part of her had hated that she'd hurt him. And

hated herself for doing that to him. Yet how else was she supposed to push him away? How else could she protect herself?

God, she was a mess.

Picking up the empty tumbler, she stared at it, debating whether or not to have a third bourbon. This damn flight was interminable and her chest ached and she felt like she'd been hit by a bus, and all she wanted right now was to feel better.

But she wouldn't. In fact, she had a feeling that getting free of Kellan Blake was going to be worse than going cold turkey from some horrible drug. Cutting off her supply was the easy part. Surviving the addiction was another thing entirely.

You said you didn't need him.

And she didn't. She really didn't. Maybe if she kept telling herself that, some part of her would actually believe it.

She got a third glass of bourbon in the end, which did a good job of making her forget, but a shit job of making her feel better, the rest of the flight passing with agonizing slowness.

The jet landed hours later as morning painted bright streaks across the sky, and she stumbled down the steps still in her green gown, feeling like death warmed over and served slightly tepid, to find Faith and a car waiting for her.

Faith's sharp blue gaze moved over her as Sabrina approached, a crease appearing between her straight dark brows. "You look like you've had an adventure," she observed. "Nice dress."

Sabrina ignored the comment, coming to a stop in front of the car. "If you want a debrief, you're going to have to have it now." She took a deep breath. "Before I resign."

One of Faith's brows rose skyward. "Resign? Are you serious?"

Maybe it was the remains of the bourbon talking. Or maybe it was simply lack of sleep and heartache. But all at once, Sabrina couldn't think of anything worse than being in the 11th Hour HQ every day and seeing Kellan. Having to speak to him, work with him. Having him there all the time . . .

God, no, she couldn't do it.

If she wanted to be free of him, she needed to be physically free of him. Which meant going somewhere he wasn't. Resigning was a big step, and not one she took lightly since she really enjoyed her work with the 11th Hour, but it wasn't as if she could ask him to leave. Not when the issue was with her.

No, she would have to be the one to go. In fact, she'd probably have to leave San Diego, period. Yeah, that was the best idea. Leave the city, make a clean break, and start a new life somewhere else far away from him.

Hell, she could go back to Silicon Valley. She knew of several firms who'd be glad to snap her up, it wouldn't be difficult finding another job.

"Yes, I'm serious," she said, meeting Faith's gaze head-on.

"Ah." Faith paused. "Can I ask why?"

"No."

The other woman was silent, studying her.

Sabrina glared back, in no mood to explain herself.

"Okay," Faith said at last. "Why don't you get into the car and come back to HQ? Kellan already gave me and Night a full rundown while you were on the plane, plus, he sent through the contents of the hard drive you downloaded Blake's computer onto. Night thinks there may be information on it that could be of interest."

Instantly Sabrina felt irritated. "How does he know? Did he get someone to examine it for him? I could have done that if I'd had the—"

"He does have other people to call on," Faith interrupted smoothly. "And considering you're resigning, it's probably a good thing."

Sabrina shut her mouth with a snap. Yes, it *was* a good thing. And getting territorial about a job she didn't want anymore was stupid.

Faith turned to the car and opened the door. "Shall we?

You look like you could do with a shower and several hours of sleep."

And Kellan. You could do with Kellan.

But he wasn't an option anymore. She would have to learn how to do without him.

Sadness tugged at her, but she forced it away, gritting her teeth as she got into the car.

The drive from the airport back into the city felt like it took an age, but at least Faith didn't try to talk to her about her decision to resign, or try to convince her to stay. In fact, the other woman spent most of the time on the phone, leaving Sabrina to sit there and marinate in her own misery.

By the time they'd gotten back to the 11th Hour building Sabrina was sick of herself and the thoughts revolving around and around in her head. As she stalked down the hallway that led to her room, she could hear chords from Callie's guitar drifting in from HQ proper, and the rare sound of Jack's laughter following them.

It made her heart feel tight and her throat ache. They were happy, those two. They'd found each other. Yet another reason that staying was going to be unbearable.

Hey, you could have had that. But you walked away from it, remember?

Sabrina strode into her bedroom and slammed the door hard behind her. Shutting out the happy sounds of Callie and Jack, and the insidious thought that maybe, just maybe, walking away from Kellan had been the wrong thing to do.

But no, it was too late now. She'd made her decision and she couldn't come back from it.

She and Kellan were over. Lovers, friends, it was *all* over.

Sabrina crossed to the bed and flung herself down onto it.

And cried.

CHAPTER 17

Dealing with his mother and having to tell her the whole story, first about his father and his involvement in illegal activities, then about the existence of his son, was every bit as bad as Kellan thought it would be.

Charlotte was by turns shocked, devastated, and then—quite unlike her—she burst into tears, which meant Kellan had to take her in his arms to comfort her.

After watching Sabrina leave, he didn't have a lot of fucks left to give, but he managed to pull some together for his mother, who once the initial shock had passed, became very, very angry at her husband.

In his debrief with Night, the guy had given him some assurance that Phillip's activities would be kept on the down-low as much as possible so that Charlotte was protected. Not that anything was going to happen publically in the immediate future since Night was in the middle of running his own private operation that required the arms dealing to remain hidden for the moment.

In the meantime, Night had told Kellan that Phillip would

be told in no uncertain terms to cease all his involvement in the illegal arms trade, or else risk having his name splashed through every available news outlet and his reputation absolutely ruined once Night's operation was over.

Since Kellan had learned more about the reality of his father's behavior—affairs, financial issues, emotional abuse—from his mother, he decided that he no longer gave a shit what his father did, and so had left the whole issue to Night to handle. That included protection from the "powerful men" his father had insisted he was protecting Kellan from also, not that Kellan was particularly worried about that.

Not when the only thing he could think about was Sabrina.

About how she was gone and how he'd let her walk away.

Charlotte didn't mention Sabrina or the engagement, though maybe that wasn't surprising given all the shocks Kellan had delivered to her. All her focus was bent on the grandson she hadn't known about and who apparently Phillip knew the whereabouts of.

She'd tried to convince Kellan that she could talk Phillip into revealing where her grandson was, but Kellan told her in no uncertain terms that she wasn't to do so. If he didn't want to disrupt the boy's life with his own presence, he certainly didn't want his mother doing the same thing. Charlotte hadn't liked that one bit, but just before he caught the jet back to San Diego a day later, he'd extracted a promise from her *not* to find the kid. He hoped she'd stick to it.

On the flight back, he spent the time focusing on a report for Night, not to mention drinking copious amounts of scotch. All the while resolutely not thinking about Sabrina or the relentless ache in his chest, situated in about the same region as his heart.

He'd made his decision to give her the freedom she'd wanted and he wasn't going back on it.

It was the right thing to do.

San Diego was hot and bright when he finally touched down and he decided he hated the place. There was a car waiting for him to take him back to HQ and he hated that too, wanting to go straight back to his apartment and drink himself into insensibility instead.

But he had responsibilities and so he pulled open the car door, pasting a smile on his face as he prepared to get in, because no doubt Faith would be waiting inside for him with yet more orders.

It wasn't Faith who was waiting inside.

It was a man Kellan had never seen before.

He was built like a brick shithouse, his tall, powerful form taking up most of the back seat. He had a boxer's face, with a nose that looked like it had been broken more than once, scarred cheeks, and the blackest eyes Kellan had ever seen, deeply set beneath a heavy brow.

He looked like a prizefighter or a mercenary, and Kellan would have laid money on the fact that he'd once been both.

He was also oddly familiar.

It was Jacob Night, of course. The shadow he'd seen in the alley.

"Mr. Blake," Night said in his deep, rough voice, as Kellan shut the door behind him. "Glad to see you back safe and sound."

Kellan eyed him. "So I get a personal visit? I'm honored."

The other man smiled, his teeth white against his dark olive skin. "The mission was a difficult one, I appreciate that. And I appreciate that you and Ms. Leighton got me the information I wanted, despite the personal connection."

The mention of Sabrina shivered through him, and his brain automatically started thinking about how he needed to talk to her, tell her what had happened with his mother, get her thoughts about how he was going to deal with his broken family in the future.

Then he remembered that he couldn't do that. Not when he'd promised to set her free from him.

Pain curled inside his chest, like something had been cut away from him.

"You don't seem surprised," Night murmured.

Kellan shoved away the hurt and went for his usual smile. "Surprised about what?"

"That I was able to get the information I wanted."

His brain flailed a second and then he remembered. He'd emailed the contents of Sabrina's little hard drive to Night on the off chance there would be something in that the guy could use.

"Uh, right," he said, pulling his focus back to the immediate present. "So there was something on that drive?"

"Yes. I was going to get someone else to find it for me, but Ms. Leighton was adamant she do it." Night's gaze was oddly sharp. "Her last task before she left."

Kellan went still, a cold shock moving through him. What the fuck? Sabrina was leaving? "What do you mean 'before she left'?"

The other man tilted his head to the side, studying him intently. "She handed in her resignation yesterday."

The shock deepened, widened.

This was his fault, wasn't it? She was leaving because of him. Because she wanted to be free of him entirely.

"I hope Faith didn't take it," Kellan said, conscious that his voice had gotten rough. "She's not leaving because she wants to."

"That's her decision. I have other people who can take her place."

"No," he said before he could stop himself. "Don't accept it. I'll resign. I'm more easily replaceable than she is."

Night said nothing for a long moment, his black eyes glittering as he stared at Kellan. "Understand me, Mr. Blake, I would rather not have to replace either of you. I'm at a delicate stage with another operation and looking for alternatives right now is going to be a pain in my ass. So may I suggest that you resolve your differences and not disrupt the team with whatever bullshit is going down between the two of you?"

Everything tightened inside him. "I can't resolve them. One of us will have to leave and it might as well be me."

Night continued to stare at him, his dark gaze far too perceptive. "Ah," he murmured. "So it's like that."

Denying it felt wrong, so Kellan didn't bother. "Yeah," he said. "It's exactly like that."

The other man frowned. "I fail to see the problem then."

It was weird to be talking to Jacob Night about the mess he'd made of his friendship with Sabrina, especially when the guy was virtually a stranger. And he had no idea why he felt the need to justify himself, but he found himself doing so all the same.

"Sabrina would prefer us not to see each other again," he said flatly. "So that's what we're doing."

"But you don't want that?"

"What I want doesn't matter. It's the right thing to do for her."

The other man laughed, a deep, cynical sound. "The right thing to do . . ." Night echoed, as if that was the stupidest thing he'd ever heard. "Right for who? Her or you?"

"Her, of course." Kellan bristled. "She wanted to be free so I let her go."

Night's eyes gleamed. "Why?"

"I told you. Because she asked."

"And you just let her go?"

Anger coiled inside him, hot and heavy. "That's none of your fucking business."

"It's my fucking business since it concerns two of my most valued employees," Night snapped. "I don't care how you fix it, Mr. Blake, but you need to fix it. I need both of you and so does the team."

"It can't be fixed," Kellan growled. "And what Sabrina needs is more important than what you need, asshole."

There was a silence.

Night sat back against the seat, his gaze direct, and Kellan had the disturbing impression that the bastard could see the entire contents of his soul. "Who, exactly, are you trying to be a hero for, Mr. Blake? Because if it's for Ms. Leighton, I can pretty much guarantee that's not what she needs."

Fury licked up inside him. "How the hell would you know what Sabrina needs?"

"I don't. But you do." Night's smile was a hair short of feral. "Take what you want, Mr. Blake, and fuck what anyone else thinks. That's my advice."

Longing rose inside him, dark and desperate, but he forced it back. "That's not what she wants."

"Fuck what she wants too." Night's smile sharpened. "I've never met a woman who wanted a hero. Deep down, they always want the man."

And you're not a hero. So why are you even bothering with the pretense?

Everything in him tightened. She might not need him, but he needed her. Fuck, he *needed* her.

Take what you want . . .

Why shouldn't he? Why should he always be the one giving up what mattered to him? What was important? Why should he be the one always making sacrifices?

She'd told him she wanted to be free, but he didn't want that. He never wanted to be free, not of her. He wanted her tangled together with him, bound so tightly she would never get away.

Christ, he'd given up his own damn kid. Why should he have to give her up too?

You weren't going to screw things up by being a selfish asshole anymore.

No, he wasn't. But fuck that too. Why was he the one who always had to do the right thing? And anyway, things with Sabrina were already screwed to hell. How could he make it any worse?

Night had asked him who he was trying to be a hero for and in that moment, he couldn't honestly think. Two weeks ago he would have said his father, but his father had turned out to be a liar, so where did that leave him?

He was trying to be a hero for Sabrina, that was where it left him, and Sabrina didn't want him to be a hero. Sabrina didn't want him at all.

You know that's not true.

Something went very still inside him.

No, it wasn't true. She did want him. He knew it. He'd seen it in her eyes, felt it in her touch, heard it in her voice every time she'd cried out his name. Shit, she'd fucking told him how long she'd wanted him for.

So why had she pushed him away? Was that truly what she'd wanted? She'd been scared that night on the street in Manhattan, he'd seen that in her eyes too, especially when he'd told her he loved her.

She's lost everyone who was supposed to love her, her mom to the river and her father to grief. Everyone she loved has either let her go or left her. Is it really such a mystery that she's scared?

And he'd let her go too.

It hit him like a shock, like a blow to the head.

She'd told him she wanted to be free and so he'd freed her, without hesitation, without argument. Letting her go so very easily. As if she didn't matter to him . . .

The shock began to fade, a deep, intense determination taking its place.

Fuck doing the right thing. Fuck trying to be unselfish.

He wanted her. He needed her.

She was his friend. She was his lover. She was the most important thing in his entire fucking universe, and he wasn't going to let her go without a fight.

Because Sabrina Leighton was worth fighting for.

And if that made him a selfish asshole, then he was a selfish asshole. He'd own it. Hell, if it convinced her to change her mind, then he'd fucking glory in it.

"You look like you've made a decision," Night said into the silence of the car.

"Yeah." Kellan glanced at him. "I've decided that heroes are overrated."

Night smiled. "Good decision, Mr. Blake."

Sabrina was sitting on the bed in her room, folding up a couple of T-shirts to put in the suitcase she had open at her feet. Her hands were shaking and the material wouldn't fold properly, so she ended up balling up the T-shirts and throwing them in instead.

She was going to have to leave and leave now, because Kellan would be returning to HQ at any moment and she didn't want to be here when he arrived.

Coward. You're a coward.

Yeah, well, she already knew that. He'd promised her he wouldn't come after her and she believed him, but it was herself she didn't trust.

She'd hear him arrive, probably, and his voice would drift down the hallway, deep and so achingly familiar. And it would take everything she had not to fling open the door and go to him, tell him that she hadn't meant what she'd said in New York, that she did need him. She needed him desperately and if he still loved her, she'd take it.

She'd take any crumb he wanted to give her.

But no. She couldn't do that. She couldn't risk it. The only way to keep herself absolutely safe was to leave before he got here, remove herself from temptation's way entirely.

Pushing herself off the narrow bed, she went over to the dresser in the corner and pulled open the bottom drawer, rifling through the jeans that were folded there. Grabbing some at random, she moved back to the suitcase and chucked the jeans in. Then she closed the case, locked it, gripped the handle, and moved toward the door.

She had no damn idea where she was going to go—some crappy hotel—and she was still cursing herself that she'd gone and fiddled with the contents of that hard drive for Night, searching for what she'd missed earlier. That she'd found what he was looking for, heavily encrypted and almost undetectable, paled in comparison with the time it had taken to find it. Because if she hadn't taken that time, she would have been long gone from the 11th Hour HQ and safely removed from Kellan's arrival.

Now though, she wasn't sure she'd be able to even get out before he got there, not when she'd overheard Jack telling Isiah only minutes before that Kellan was en route from the airport.

She put her hand on the doorknob only to feel it twist beneath her fingers, and then her door was opening, and she was stumbling back, her heart beating so fast she thought it was going to come out of her chest.

And Kellan was in the doorway, those extraordinary sky-blue eyes slamming into hers, pinning her in place.

He was dressed in a white T-shirt and his usual beaten-up jeans, the white of the cotton making his golden skin gleam and his eyes look even bluer. There was stubble on his jaw and his blond hair was spiked as if he'd run his hand through it too many times, and there was a wildness to him she'd never seen before.

A certainty that made her want to run from the room.

Except she couldn't run because he was standing in the doorway.

The suitcase fell from her nerveless fingers, and Kellan glanced at it a second, before looking back at her. "Running away?"

Sabrina swallowed, her heartbeat deafening in her ears. "You promised. You promised you'd let me go."

"Yeah, well." He smiled at her, a sudden, savage kind of smile. "I fucking lied."

"Kellan," she began, backing away. "I don't think you know what—"

But the words died in her throat because he was coming, slamming the door behind him as he strode into the room, heading straight for her. She stumbled as she backed away more quickly, trying to get some distance between them, but then her shoulders hit the wall and she knew it was too late.

"No," she said pathetically as his hands slammed into the wall on either side of her head, caging her. And then one hard thigh was shoving between hers as he pinned her there with his body.

She gasped and tried pulling back, but there was nowhere to go. No more room to run. He was right there in front of her, blocking her, lowering his head until they were nose to nose, and his blue eyes were all she could see.

They were blazing, full of heat, full of certainty. "Oh no, baby," he said in a low, fierce voice. "You don't get to push me away, not again. I'm not going to let you."

Sabrina began to tell him to stop, only to have his mouth come down on hers, silencing her completely.

A hard, hot, desperate kiss. Full of need, full of desire.

Tears started in her eyes, because she wasn't going to be able to hold out against him, not against this. The taste of him exploded through her as he pushed his tongue into her mouth, deepening the kiss, blinding her with heat.

She began to shake, her hands lifting to the hard plane of his chest, pushing at him, trying to shove him away, but she might as well have been trying to shove at a mountain. He didn't move and he didn't stop, kissing her deeply, hard, ravaging her mouth as if it was his to do whatever he wanted with it.

His fingers shoved into her hair, pulling her head back to make the kiss even deeper, and at the same time, he pressed his thigh hard against the seam of her jeans, the pressure against her clit striking sparks through every nerve ending she had.

She shuddered, the familiar scent and feel of him making the tears impossible to hold back, so she let them fall, tasting salt as they mixed with the heat of his wicked, wicked mouth.

He must have tasted them too, because he broke the kiss and lifted his head, staring down at her, intention in every line of his body. "I have to tell you something, Sabrina," he said very softly, very clearly. "When I let you go in New York, I made a mistake."

Her heart ached, everything ached. "You bastard. I wanted you to leave me alone!"

"I tried. I can't."

"This is not just about *you.*"

"Yes, this *is* about me, and I don't fucking care." One hand tightened in her hair, while the other drifted to her cheek, touching her cheekbone with aching gentleness, then drifting down to her neck, stroking the side of it in another light touch. "I have to show you, Bree. I have to show you how much I fucking want you. How much I fucking *need* you. And I don't care if that's selfish or wrong, that's what I feel." His hand moved lower, to the material of her T-shirt, taking hold of it and jerking it up to reveal the plain cotton of her serviceable bra. "I've been doing the right thing, not being selfish for so long, and I'm not doing it anymore." He pulled aside the fabric covering her breast and then his hand was there against her bare skin, cupping her, his thumb finding her hardened nipple and brushing over it, his blue gaze blinding as he stared down into her eyes. "You're too important to me to let go without a fight."

The sheer electricity of his touch was almost unbearable. It made her shake, made the tears fall faster, because she couldn't hold out against his intensity, she never could. "And what about me?" she forced out. "What about what I want?"

"I think you want me." He pinched her nipple, the silver in his eyes vanished, leaving them a deep, glowing sapphire. "I think you need me as much as I need you."

"N-No. It's not true." Her voice was cracking under the weight of his touch and the heat of his body, the way he was rolling her nipple between his fingers, sending more shudders through her. "I don't need you. I don't want you. Don't you understand? I can't do this, Kellan. I can't do this with you anymore."

"Yeah, I heard." He bent his head, brushed his mouth against her neck, his breath warm. "But you're wrong. You need to trust me, Bree. Why don't you fucking trust me?" He nipped her then, his teeth against her skin, biting the sensitive place where her neck met her shoulder, making a low moan break from her.

"I do t-trust you," she tried to say, unable to stop herself from arching helplessly into his hand as he kept on teasing her nipple.

"No, you don't." He pinched her again, harder, and she whimpered. "If you did, you'd never have pushed me away. You'd have believed me when I told you that I loved you."

Those words again. Those terrible, beautiful words.

Fear wound its way through her, cutting through the pleasure.

"Don't say it." She turned her head away, denying him. "Don't say those fucking words."

But he wouldn't let her. He released her breast, his hand coming up to grip her chin, turning her back to face him. "Why not?" he demanded. "Did you think I didn't mean them?" There was no escaping that intense blue stare or the heat in it. No denying that the fire in his eyes was burning hot and all for her. "Tell me why they scare you. Tell me why they're so terrible."

She desperately wanted to pull away, desperately wanted to run from him and the things he was telling her. Things she'd dreamed and fantasized about but had always told herself she could never have, because he didn't feel that way about her.

The lie that she protected herself from pain with.

"You don't mean them," she said hoarsely, still lying, still afraid. "You don't. How can you? You've been my friend for so long and we had sex twice and now suddenly you're in love with me . . . It doesn't happen like that."

"Yeah and what if it *does* happen like that?" His fingers pressed against the side of her jaw as he shifted that long, muscled body of his, pressing his hips to hers, making her so very aware of the hard length of his cock nudging against her zipper.

Her breath caught, sparks of electricity scattering through her, and she wanted to shut her eyes because she didn't want him to see. Didn't want him to know what he was doing to her or how badly she was failing at resisting him.

But she had to resist. The alternative was giving herself totally to him, letting herself have everything . . .

Fear came like a wave, swamping her and then she did shut her eyes, blocking him out. What would happen if she lost it? If she lost *him?* If he let her go the way her mother had or walked away like her father? What did she have to keep him with?

Nothing. You have nothing.

"Look at me," he murmured, that low, deep voice of his winding around her, hypnotizing her. "Look at me when I'm talking to you."

But she shook her head violently, denying him.

Then his mouth came down over hers again in another kiss, feverish and desperate, and his hips flexed, grinding the hard ridge of his cock against her zipper.

She groaned and arched, helpless against the pleasure that

was filling her with every move he made. "Don't do this, Kel," she whispered brokenly against his mouth. "Don't do this to me. Let me go."

"No." He rocked his hips against hers, deepening the friction, the pleasure dirty and raw. "Everyone else let you go, Sabrina. But I'm not going to."

She gave a little sob, keeping her eyes closed, so deeply afraid. "I . . . don't believe you."

His hips circled in a slow grind, making her thighs tremble. And she felt his mouth brush against her lips, a featherlight touch. "I don't care whether you believe it or not. It's a fact. I gave up my kid, Bree. But not you, never you." Then his tongue was running along the seam of her lips, coaxing her to open, pushing inside again in another soul-destroying kiss.

She sobbed again, her whole body tensing with denial, trying to resist the push of his hips and the heat of his mouth. The feel of his muscular body covering hers and the pleasure that was slowly making it harder and harder to understand why she should be resisting in the first place.

Your heart, remember? He'll destroy you.

"Feel me." He reached for one of her hands and drew it down between them, holding her palm over the huge ridge behind the zipper of his jeans. "Feel how I want you." His voice had gotten rough. "Feel how I need you. No one else makes me feel this way, Sabrina." He pressed her hand down harder. "No one but you."

"So you're hard for me," she said thickly, clinging to her resistance for all she was worth. "Big deal. It's just sex, Kellan. You'll get over that soon enough."

His fingers clenched around hers, leaving her no choice but to feel the rock-hard length of him against her palm. "If it was all about sex, do you think I would have come back? Do you think I would have said 'fuck you' to those promises I made you?" His voice was shaking now, his blue eyes blazing down into hers. "No, Sabrina. No, this is about more than just sex. This is about *you.*"

She wanted to protest that, wanted to tell him he was wrong, but then his hands were at the fastening of her jeans, pulling at the button, then the zipper tab, tugging it down. He pushed his fingers between her thighs, beneath the cotton of her panties to the slick flesh beneath, sliding through her folds, stroking.

She should have stopped him. Should have told him no and pulled away. But she didn't. Instead, she groaned as he kissed her again, her hips bucking, the thrust of his tongue in her mouth mirroring the stroke of his fingers in her pussy. It felt so good, *he* felt so good.

Why resist? When you can have this?

She didn't know. She'd come to the end of her strength anyway.

He was everywhere and he was relentless, overwhelming. Implacable. He'd decided she was his castle for storming and the attack he'd mounted wasn't something she was strong enough to fight.

She could feel her will breaking down with every touch of his fingers, with every stroke of his tongue, and when she began to cry, his touch gentled. Became slower, softer. Maddening.

He slid two fingers inside her, pushing in deep as his thumb stroked over her clit and just like that she was shuddering, on the verge of climax, tears running down her cheeks.

But he didn't push her over. Instead he moved again, and she heard the sound of his zipper being pulled down and then his sure grip catching her behind the knee, lifting her leg up around his lean hips, opening her up.

She groaned as she felt the head of his cock push against the slick folds of her sex, the pleasure of it unbearable.

"Look at me, baby," he murmured softly. "Look at me, now."

She did, like she was his to command, finding that burning blue gaze hot on hers. And she couldn't look away as he began to slide inside her, the intense pleasure laid bare in his eyes. Something more too, something deeper, hotter.

She was shaking as he slid all the way into her, her body bracing for the force of his thrust. But he didn't move, staying buried deep inside her. "You have to trust me." His gaze was intense, absolute. "I would never lie to you and I would never tell you things I don't mean." His hips drew back, long and slow, before pushing back in again. "I need you in my life and in my bed, Sabrina." And again. "I need you there forever."

It was too much. The feel of him, the intense pleasure he was giving her, the burning look in his eyes and the words he was saying. All too much. She couldn't resist anymore. She was broken. She was gone.

The tears wouldn't stop falling and she didn't try to brush them away. "I have loved for you for so long," she whispered hoarsely. "So, so long. And I didn't think . . . I didn't think you would ever love me back. Not the way I wanted you to." She shuddered. "And I'm scared you'll leave me. I'm scared I'm not enough to keep you."

Kellan stared down into Sabrina's lovely eyes, feeling the jolt of those words go through him like lightning through a lightning rod.

I have loved you for so long . . .

She had loved him. She had fucking *loved* him.

Something inside him caught fire, blazing, and all he was conscious of was a deep, primitive possessiveness filling him, swamping what was left of his doubt and sweeping it away entirely.

Yes. *Fuck,* yes.

She loved him and he was never letting her go.

Ever.

He dropped his hands, sliding them down her back to the waistband of her jeans, then pushing beneath the denim and down farther, over the curve of her delicious ass. Then he gripped her tight, holding her in place, his cock buried deep inside her.

She shuddered, the gold in her eyes flaring. Yet he could see fear in them too, heard it in the way her husky voice had cracked. Which was wrong, so fucking wrong.

"Not enough to keep me?" He stared down at her, letting her see how certain and sure he was. "Baby, I have no idea where you got that idea from, but it's just not true." He squeezed her tender flesh in his hands. "This beautiful ass is enough to keep me. And here . . ." He shifted his hands, pulling them out of her jeans and cupping her breasts in his palm. "These pretty tits are enough to keep me."

She gasped as he rubbed his thumbs gently over her nipples, then gasped again as he flexed his hips, never taking his gaze from hers. "And this hot little pussy I'm deep inside right now is more than enough to keep me."

"Kellan . . ." she croaked, a tear sliding down her cheek.

He bent, kissing it away, tasting salt. "But you're right, those are all about sex and it's more than that, Bree," he whispered against her skin. "You're more than that." He kissed away another tear. "I love your determination and your honesty. Your strength. Your protectiveness and your loyalty." He moved lower, brushing his mouth over hers, tasting more salt and the sweet, heady flavor that was all her. "The way you fight for me, the way you always have my back. There's so much to you, Sabrina, so fucking much. Didn't I tell you that night when you had your nightmare? How you made my life better? And, God, I haven't explored even the half of you yet. You're enough, baby girl. You're enough to keep me forever."

She shuddered, staring at him as if he was going to disappear at any second. "Mom let me go." Her voice was thick with tears. "Dad walked out. And after I kept all those things from you . . . I didn't think . . . I didn't think there was anything about me that you'd want after that."

His heart went tight in his chest and his whole body ached. For her. For her pain. For how little she thought of herself when there was so much to her.

"Then I guess I'm going to spend the rest of my life showing you exactly what there is to want about you," he said quietly and with great certainty. "Aren't I?"

She stared at him for one long, aching second, and then her hands were on him, on his chest, gripping his T-shirt in her hands and holding on. And she was kissing him back, hungrily and desperately, her mouth so hot and so sweet.

Such relief. Such fucking relief to have her in his arms. To be inside her, so close to her. To have her say those words to him, to have her love him.

Yeah, he'd been selfish to come here, to pin her against the wall and use seduction to show her what she meant to him, but he couldn't bring himself to regret it. No, not for one damn minute.

Not when all this time, she'd simply been scared.

Scared that she wasn't enough for him.

Silly girl.

He gripped her hips again, pinning her to the wall at her back, beginning to move a little faster, a little harder. Feeling her tremble and gasp, tasting her desire as her kisses became wild, her body trying to move to keep up with his.

He wanted to go slow, give her as much pleasure as he could for as long as she could stand it, but all too soon she was gasping against his mouth, her pussy convulsing around his cock. And it was all he could do to hold himself back and not give into the urge to drive himself inside her until he came too.

But no, not yet. He wasn't done.

Withdrawing from her, he gathered her close before moving

over to the bed and gently laying her down on it. Stripping the rest of her clothes off, he did the same for himself, then pushed her back and pinned her beneath him. Settling his hips between her thighs, he eased himself back inside her, relishing the tight squeeze and the slick glide of her flesh against his. The shudder she gave and the long, low moan that escaped her.

She stared up at him as if she'd never seen him before, her eyes wide, the hazel fading into brilliant gold. "You weren't supposed to come back," she murmured. "Why did you?"

"I already told you." He ran a hand down her side, stroking her skin, smooth and pale and scattered with pretty freckles. "I couldn't give you up. Night told me you'd handed in your resignation and that I had to fix it because he didn't want to lose either of us. And I realized that I couldn't lose you either." Kellan settled his hand on her hip, then gave a slow, lazy thrust, watching the gold leap higher in her eyes. "I know it's selfish and I know it's wrong. And I know the right thing to do is to let you go the way you wanted. But fuck, I don't care." He stared down at her, unable to resist the urge to challenge her, now, while she was pinned beneath him. "I'm not a hero, Bree, and I'm tired of trying to be one. And if that makes me a bad guy, then fuck it, if it means I get you in my life, then I'm a bad guy."

The gold in her eyes deepened. She raised a hand and cupped his cheek, her touch reaching inside him, making him shiver. "You're not a bad guy, Kellan. You never have been. And even if you were, I wouldn't care. I don't want a hero. I just want you."

He grinned at her, a fierce joy bursting inside him. "That's what Night said."

She blinked and her mouth curved. "Night said he wanted you?"

Christ, was she teasing him?

He gave another lazy thrust, angling his hips to push against her clit, relishing the sound of her sharply indrawn breath. "Are you flirting with me, baby? Because if so, I like it."

Sabrina gave a little moan, arching her back. "Can we not talk about Night right now?"

He thrust again, deeper, slower, loving the way she caught her lower lip between her teeth. "Are you sure?"

"Yes . . ." Sabrina lifted both hands to his shoulders, stroking him, then sliding them down his back as she arched up into him. "Oh God, yes. . . ."

He bent, nuzzling her neck, loving the feel of her slender body against his and the heat of her pussy wrapped around his aching cock. "I showed you how much I need you, Bree. Why don't you show me how you need me."

She sighed. "I thought you'd never ask."

And she showed him.

CHAPTER 18

Three weeks later, Sabrina woke up in her customary position, curled up tight against Kellan's side in his apartment. It was still early in the morning but she felt wide-awake, which meant she probably wasn't going to get back to sleep again.

Easing aside the heavy arm of the man sleeping next to her, she slipped from the bed and pulled on some clothes, then moved soundlessly out of the bedroom.

Through the windows in the living area, she could see dawn touching the horizon, and she suddenly felt the need to get out and breathe some fresh salt air. She hadn't done a morning walk on the beach for a long time and right now, she could use one.

The past couple of weeks had been the happiest she'd ever known. She'd moved in with Kellan, both of them cautiously exploring the new relationship they found themselves in.

It was better than anything she'd imagined or even fantasized about, and she still couldn't believe it was hers. Not that there weren't problems.

She'd taken back her resignation and while working on a

new 11th Hour mission, she'd been doing a bit of investigating on the side: searching for the location of Kellan's son.

It hadn't been all that difficult, and she'd soon discovered where the kid was. The issue now was whether to tell Kellan or not. He'd been adamant that he didn't want to intrude on the boy, but Sabrina knew how much it had taken from him to give the kid up, to not be involved in his life. And she suspected that not knowing where the child was, was Kellan's way of keeping himself from temptation.

Yet it wasn't only Kellan's choice. What if his son wanted to know his father? If she'd been in that position, she sure as hell would, and it seemed wrong to deny both man and boy the choice. Then again, she didn't want to give Kellan the information if it was going to hurt him . . .

God, choices, choices.

Seemed like a good head-clearing walk was in order.

Grabbing her keys, she got into the car and drove herself out to Coronado and the long white beach, empty in the early morning light.

The sand was cool beneath her bare feet—she always took her shoes off—the sound of the traffic stirring and the wash of the waves the only sound.

She walked slowly, letting her mind rest, smiling as a bunch of Navy SEALs in training jogged past. They were shirtless and she ogled them shamelessly, thinking about the golden-skinned man she'd left sleeping that morning. Yeah, these guys were cut, but nothing beat Kellan Blake naked.

As she watched them jog away from her, she saw in the distance one guy trailing the pack. Then she realized that in fact, he wasn't trailing the pack. He was someone else entirely, walking slowly toward her, the early morning light striking gold from his hair.

There was no mistaking that height or the breadth of those shoulders or the easy grace with which he moved.

Kellan.

Sabrina caught her breath, staring at him. What the hell was he doing here? She'd thought she'd left him lying asleep in bed.

He said nothing as he approached, simply holding her gaze as he came closer and closer, until he was standing right in front of her, towering over her. Blond and beautiful and perfect.

And all hers.

"What are you doing here?" Her voice had gone all breathy, the way it inevitably did whenever he was near. "I thought you were asleep." Then she frowned. "And actually, how did you know where I'd be?"

His sexy, sensual mouth curved. "I tracked your phone."

"Not creepy at all, Kel."

"That's me. Not creepy." He was looking at her very intently, searching her face.

"And you looking at me like that isn't creepy, either." She frowned. "What?"

His smile deepened, as if he knew a secret she didn't. Then he dropped to his knees in the sand in front of her.

Sabrina blinked. What the hell was he doing?

But he was already reaching into the pocket of his jeans and as she watched, her heartbeat starting to race, he brought out a small box. Then he opened it to reveal a ring glowing in the middle of it.

A ring with a sapphire the exact blue of his eyes.

Her heart slowed to a stop in her chest, clenching tight, and she couldn't speak. Because the ring was familiar. It was the ring she'd chosen that night in his father's study.

With calm, assured movements, Kellan took the ring out, put the box in his pocket, reached for her hand, and held it gently as he looked up into her eyes. "Sabrina Leighton," he said quietly. "Would you do me the honor of becoming my wife?"

On the beach, she'd told him when he'd asked how they'd

gotten engaged, that fake story for his parents' benefit. On her early morning walk on the beach.

He'd remembered.

Her eyes filled with ridiculous tears. "Oh . . . Kel . . ."

"I told you I wasn't letting you go," he said steadily. "Never, ever. You'll never be free, Bree, so you may as well give in now."

Her heart swelled up, making her chest constrict. "I already did, you idiot," she managed to force out. "Back when I was ten years old."

His smile was fierce and bright and all for her. "Then make it legal, baby. Have me for real. Have me forever."

"Yes," she said, because there was no other answer she could give him. "I will be your wife." And she let him slide the ring on, and when he got to his feet and kissed her, she kissed him back twice as hard.

A minute or two later, the pair of them breathing hard, Sabrina put a hand on his chest and kept it there, meeting his gaze. "I found him, Kel."

Kellan's eyes flared. He didn't ask who she was talking about, he didn't need to. He knew. And for a second he looked away, as if, even now, he couldn't bear her to see what was in his heart.

But she lifted a hand to his face, stroking along his sharp jaw, letting him know it was okay. That she knew the contents of his heart anyway. "He should have the choice," she said quietly. "It's hard, I know. But he should know you're there."

Kellan lifted a hand and gripped her wrist, holding her palm against his skin. And this time he didn't hide the trepidation in his eyes when he looked at her. "What if he doesn't want to see me?"

The hoarse note in his voice made her throat close, but she didn't look away. "Then we'll take it from there. I'm here for you, whatever happens."

His blue gaze searched hers. "I gave him up, Bree. I don't have the right to make claim on him. Shit, I don't deserve the right."

But she wasn't having any of that. "You deserve it. And your son deserves it too. He deserves the right to know who his father is."

"I'm not—"

"A hero?" she finished for him. "A good man? A decent man?" She stared up at him, into his beautiful face, willing him to see what she saw. "You're all of those, Kellan Blake. You're all of those and more. And I'll fight to the death anyone who tells you any different."

He was silent a long time, looking at her. And then, just when she thought he wouldn't, he smiled, warm and tender, the smile he kept only for her. "My dad used to be my hero, once. But I think I've got a new one now."

"Oh? And who's that?"

His smile became even warmer, even more tender. He took her hand from his jaw and bent, pressing a kiss to her palm. And when he met her gaze again, his eyes were bluer than the sea. Bluer than the sky.

Bluer than the sapphire on her finger.

"It's you, Bree."

EPILOGUE

Jacob Night had never been anyone's hero and he was fine with that. More than fine.

In fact, he far preferred being the villain of the piece.

Villains got far more respect than heroes any day of the week and they didn't have to work within certain parameters.

Jacob hated parameters. Especially ones he didn't set.

"I don't know," Phillip Blake said, his voice hard and clipped. "I told you that already."

Jacob sat on the white couch in the Blake's elegant sitting room, considering the societal parameters he was dealing with now and how fucking annoying it was that he couldn't simply get up and use a bit of friendly violence to get the guy to tell him what he needed to know.

He couldn't, of course. The last thing he needed was the law getting all up in his business.

Then again, the law didn't have to know.

"I suggest you think harder," Jacob said pleasantly. "You might find it easy to betray your son, Mr. Blake, but I'm a very different sort of man." He smiled, to prove his point. "For example, I'm not averse to providing you with a little incentive, should you need it."

Blake's features tightened. "If you touch my wife—"

"I have no interest in your wife," Jacob interrupted. "She's not here anyway and I want the information now."

"My son then. If you—"

"Mr. Blake Junior is a valued member of my team, even if you don't seem to value him as highly as you should." Jacob smiled wider. "But that's not my problem." His patience at an end, he pushed himself off the couch. "I've given you a couple of weeks to withdraw from the syndicate, and you've done so. Which counts in your favor. However . . ." He took a step toward the other man who was standing in the middle of the room, a look of trepidation on his face. "You're remarkably forgetful about certain things, which does not."

A look of alarm crossed Blake's face and he took a step back.

Too late.

Jacob grabbed a handful of the other man's shirt in his fist and hauled him forward. Then he pulled the photo from the back pocket of his jeans and shoved it in the guy's face.

The photo he always carried with him. The photo of Faith Beasley.

"Tell me what you know about this woman, Blake," Jacob hissed. "Tell me everything."

Acknowledgments

To all the usual suspects. You know who you are. Thanks.